Praise for
VIRGINIA HAMILTON'S
Arilla Sun Down:

OINT·SIGNATURE

VIRGINIA HAMILTON

Arilla Sun Down

SCHOLASTIC INC.

New York Toronto London Auckland Sydney

No part of this publication may be reproduced in whole or in part, or stored in a retrieval system, or transmitted in any form or by any means, electronic, mechanical, photocopying, recording, or otherwise, without written permission of the publisher. For information regarding permission, write to Scholastic Inc., Attention: Permissions Department, 555 Broadway, New York, NY 10012.

ISBN 0-590-22223-6

15 14 13 12 11 10 9   2 3/0

Printed in the U.S.A.   01

Author photo by Jimmy Byrge

For Leigh who taught me Number Base Five
For Arnold, Jaime, and Jan
And for all who remember twelve

1

Late in the big night and snow has no end. Taking me a long kind of time going to the hill. Would be afraid if not for the moon and knowing Sun-Stone Father is sledding. Way off, hear him go, "Whoop-eeeee!" Real thin sound, go, "Whoop-eeeee!"

If Mother could see me, she would say, *What you doing up? Get back under the covers. Catching your death.* But Mama sleeping on. I can slip on out to the moondust snow. She not seeing everything I do, like she say.

Now hurry to follow all of the tracks going deep in the snow. Knowing there is some big hill where all tracks of children go. Downhill is deep in a moonshade and ends at a cliff. Only Stone Father can stop a sled in time. I can't stop it. Jack Sun Run wouldn't care to try. I am smallest, knowing nothing for sure. But I think my brother, Jack, is a horse.

Jack Sun Run still sleeping. He is bigger. But I'm who slipping away.

Sun Run nearly always high above me. Legs stamping. Up he is with the sun in a sky behind his head. Can't seeing his face, brown shade. No eyes, nose and no mouth. Brother mine can be running whinnying or throwing rope circle of his. Up so high, flinging his mane and stamping. Never go so near him when he sleeps. For fear his long nose snorting.

Going a long time in a moonlight dark. Calling out — "Father! Sun-Stone Father!"

I answer back all around the moonlight. Scares me so. But I go on and find the hill so long kind of time. There he is! Him just climbing back up and with a sled coming up behind him.

"Father!"

"What — you! Out of bed and not even a hat — !" Staring eyes don't send me away. Sun Father always so glad to see me.

"Heard you," I tell him. "Coming to ride with you."

"You sled out here and your mother will make it worse for me."

"She is under the pillow. Jack-Run is sleeping, too."

"Little one, aren't you cold?" he says.

I do not feel my ears as his hands cover them. "They have fallen off," I tell him. "I will pick them up on a way back after we ride." Knowing probably they have not fallen off.

2

Father laughs, eyes in the moonlight. "Well, just once, since you've come so far. But you have to be quiet. And you have to go home right after."

"Twice," I tell him.

"What?"

"Twice to be riding down a hill," I say, "or I will tell Mother and Jack-Run, too."

"Arilla, you are too hard on me. But all right. You must not yell, you hear?"

"I hear you. But *you* yelling," I tell him.

He laughs again. "I can't help it. It just comes over me. Now. I'll try to be still," he says. "And you try not to be scared. And don't ever tell Mother."

"I'm not scared with you, and I won't tell Mother. I won't tell Jack-Run."

"Sun Run always wakes up early, anyway, before I'm through," Father says.

Brother is nothing but a horse.

"Arilla, now hear me," Stone Father says. "If the creeps come over you, don't let loose, or I'll never catch you in the present time."

"Knowing that for sure," I saying. Downhill ends at a cliff. Over the cliff is another time. Having seen no one go over or coming back. They say three people have gone. Two boys and an uncle, so they say.

Once Mother saying to Father, *Why in heaven's name won't they make it safe for children! Don't they know there ought to be a fence at the bottom of that hill?*

She to Sun Run, *Arilla is not to go to the hill by herself.*

Jack Sun Run saying back, *Only fools go there. Arilla should never go there.*

Now. Father sits him easy on a sled. Gets him all ready with feet to push steering. Looking to me. "Ready," he says. "You get on in back."

Once Mother saying to Sun Run, *Arilla will follow the other children. She will slip away.*

Then tie her to the sumac, Jack Sun saying back.

Is she your pony to be tied up? Mother. *You are to watch her.*

My business is the pony. Sun Run. *Not somebody's baby.*

Now. I get on a sled behind Stone Father. Easy. And so careful.

Once Mother to Sun Run, *Not somebody's baby! She's your sister — you know she can slip away. You know what happened last time.*

Sun Run saying back, *I got my own business to care for. You watch her. You wanted her.*

Now. Hold tight to Stone Father, hugging his jacket. Never watch us pushing off. Runners go skud-skud and long skuuuuuuuuuuuuud. Looking around just once to see a town way back there sinking behind a hill. And closing eyes tight.

We sled on down the moonlight. Turned to the front again with a jerk. Feeling we go fast enough to take the air. We will fly away!

"Be-utiful!" Stone Father shouting. "Whoop-eeeee!"

Bumping, we slide sideways. Father's back straining to put us straight. He will hold us safe in the present time. We straighten. We fly on down the moonlight.

Never thought to be here sledding. Jack Sun Run has never done it.

Now Stone Father getting us ready. Coming to the end of a present time. Break and turn a sled somehow. The way I have heard him and James False Face talk about doing it.

"Arilla, hold tight!"

Father is best of anyone. Better than a brother, Run.

We must stop at a flat place. Downhill, we must stop at the end of a present time. Father jerking a sled sideways. We do not slow. He sticking his legs out to brake. Big snow feet pushing against the blue powder. I find me peeking through eyelashes. The ground is in a hurry.

"Hold on! Arilla, hold tight!"

"We will be safe."

"Arilla—!"

Sled tipping over. We falling on a side and sliding along the bumps. Father catching hold on my ankle. Slide. Stopping and hurting my side.

My arm stretched out. Hand catches nothing. Out there, seeing the great darkness. The moon going away over another time. They say there is a way of walking down a cliff. You walk down, there is not another time, so they say.

Wind comes downhill, cold and burning. Father lifts me on my feet. Brushing me off from snow. And hurry us up the hill. Taking us some kind of time going up. We keep sliding and falling. His feet crunching loud. I can walking right on top of snow when I can stand up. Toes of mine are feeling numb.

Hilltop, we stand with wind at our backs. Stone Father's arm around my shoulder. Trembling, nothing he has but skin under his jacket. Holding me to his side maybe thinking I will slip away. He holding sled, leaning it on his other side.

"Sledding is faster than a horse," I tell him. He saying nothing.

Father's cap pulled flap-down over his ears. His breath steaming around his face. Hair blowing long fur, thick and black. Eyes gaze far out to the moon. They go off-on, red-dark, off-on, red-dark. I see fading moonlight in them. Stone Father is a black wolf with fading moonshine in his eyes.

So James False Face has said it. *You, Father Sun, are a great wolf, hungered and wounded too many seasons.*

What great wolf there was has long since fled these sorry bones, Father said.

Sound not so down in front of the child, said James False Face, looking sad.

I am the child. James-Face always speaking good things to me. I am with him most often. Father is with Jack Sun Run most often. Father

6

likes horses. James-Face likes me and teaches me. He is old and holds many stories.

One day you will keep my stories, he tells me, *and you will truly be the name I have given you.*

They say I do not speak like a child of today. I speak like an old one, like James False Face, so they say. Mother says we have got to get away from here.

Now. Father turning me and a sled toward the town. We see that there is faint light behind a town, where the sun will come up. I pulling back. He begins walking away from the hill.

I tell him, "That was only once on a sled. We have to sled again."

"It is too cold," Father says. "The wind has made ice."

"I don't mind the ice."

"The ice is a danger," he says. "The sled cannot grip it."

"A promise is a promise," I tell him, walking back to the starting place.

He says, "For one so little, you know many words."

"That is who I am," I say, "The One With Many Words." But that is not it. Even to him I never say the name old James has given for me alone.

"You are too cold," Father is saying. "You are about to freeze, and I have to get you home." But he comes up to stand beside me. The moon is there above another time.

I tell Father what James False Face says: "A promise is a moss agate too large to slip through fingers."

Father sighs. "Take my hat, then," he says. "Maybe if we do it fast and get it over with — "

He takes off his hat. Now wind blows his hair around his ears. Stone Father has hair so black like James-Face but not so straight. He smiles all a sudden, happy to sled again I know.

I smile as he ties the hat strap around my neck. Hat so warm still from his head. I do not tell him about my hands. I put them in my pockets and cannot feel them there.

Father says, "I think you will sit in front this time. I think that way my weight will slow us down."

Father sits first at the back of the sled and holding the sled cord in a hand. The cord part of Mother's clothesline cut to fit just so. Ends of cord knotted through holes of steering on each side of a sled in front. Stone Father holds the cord like a reins at his waist. His feet press against the steering. He can work a sled with his feet or with the reins, or both.

I climbing on a sled between his feet. Scooting back until I am snug. Father holding me tight around a middle with free arm of his. All this done fast, wind to our backs.

We coast so quickly, it takes my breath. The wind pushing, pushing us. We sail. We sail faster than my thinking. No time to close my eyes.

Father does not holler. We bump hard and we fly. I jolt forward on the sled. Arm of Father pulls me back and pulls back hard on the reins in another hand. We are not sledding. We are sliding this way and that way on the ice. We take a long skuuuuuuud when Stone Father says in a sound of far-off humming:

"Oh-my-god, my-god, oh-god."

To the flat place at the end of the present time we have come. My mouth stretched open full of air. Screaming and screaming I hear. Sled leaping forward. I see the moon. The moon is coming back. Nothing to feel under us. Stone Father howls the wolf sharp and lonely. I see into another time where fear of mine is screaming.

A great circle of pain. Growing tighter, it binds my chest. Father and I are bound together in a great pain. The sled hangs in the air. The pain pulls tight arms and takes my breath. We are pulled. We are pulled back. One long moment, Father's legs kick the darkness away. We hit the cliff edge. The sled hits us. On our sides we scrape along the edge. Pain cuts into my shoulders. I cannot. I cannot. Breathe. Scream. We are scraping along inch by inch in the present time. We are saved.

What has saved us? The pain. I cannot. Think. Breathe. Until Stone Father forces his arm between me and the pain. His both hands slip under the pain. I see he still clutches the sled cord.

We inch on up the icing. Lying on a my side.

Stone Father is to my back. We are both lying down, running with our legs.

Sun-Stone Father does not howl. There is quiet. There is Father's hard breath and straining. My shoulder pain makes me weak. Sleepy me, I want my bed. Legs cease to kick. Father hammering his heels into the icing. Pushing heels, helping pain back up the hill.

I hear stamping. I hear a snorting. Slowly, head lifting, I see toward the sleepy hilltop.

There it is, the light of sun coming behind the hill. There he is, pressed against the light. Brother. Run. Jack Sun Run has his line out all the way to us. Sun Run pulling on the line, reeling us in hand over hand. He bucks and pulls back, head down, feet stamping. My brother Sun such a horse.

Hand over hand, Father inches up the line. The line is shortened. I am so sleepy. Are we fishes? Sun Run reeling and howling, not to the moon, not to Father. Howling to wake the town, I think. I am numbing up. The pain where he has roped us does not hurt much now. No longer thinking of sleep. I see. I see.

There he is, almost running. Old James False Face coming to save me. He moving around the horse my brother until he has a rope line and begins to pull. Watch out for Jack-Run's hooves.

Here they come, men from a town and other men, shouting and running. Stone Father and I are halfway up the hill. We move so slowly up to the men, who cannot stand on the icing. They fall and the long line is slacking. We slide back down. Father hands hold tight the line. Father hands turning the line red, and dotted red drops on the bluing ice.

Now James-Face speaks in the old way. Men slipping and sliding do not understand. I understand. He says: "Try crouching. Feet inward. Feet inward."

The men do not understand. They come to crouching anyway. And soon we move on up the hill. Soon to be over.

There she is. There's my pretty mother. Holding on to Father's robe over a long puffy nightgown. She with one black boot and one brown boot same size, that Sun Run find in a rummaging shop. One minute there are only men. Next minute she pretty is there. Leaning back, bending forward, holding tight the robe of Father. Hands knotted. She yelling something higher than men's voices: "My god, she's frozen — how could you, you-crazy-fool!"

We had a good time, my Stone Father and me. Mother, I'm not frozen or feeling anything. We go down the hill twice and seeing how dark and alone place is another time.

Here we are. At the top of the hill so many people leaning around. Jack Sun Run loosens a rope. He never was a horse. I think I knew that. A horse will stand still by the tall tree. I think I have seen that.

"Arilla," Run says, and everyone is quiet. I listen. Jack-Run's voice like a summer rustling in a tall grass. "Arilla, do you hear me?"

I hear you.

"Don't waste time. She may be hurt. We get her inside," James-Face says in the old way, but they don't understand. "Take her up," he says so that Run can understand. He leaps for the big horse of Jack-Run. I see long hair of his tied down his neck. He has leaped as if he were not old James, and Sun Run lifts me up.

"Give her to me — What do you think you're doing!" Mother spits a words. "Let me *go!*" Someone holding her off. It is Stone Father.

Sun Run lifting me in his arms, but I feel no arms. It is like riding on the air. Then he has me in one arm.

"Treat her like a sack of coal?" Mother yelling at him. Sun Run is up high with me in front of him. Holding me tight with one hand, just the way Stone Father did it. He holds the reins with the other hand, just like sledding. I have never been on a horse — have I? Now I have been on a horse and a sled all in one night.

"Wait," Sun-Father says.

"No time," James False Face says. But Father barely understands.

Sun Run waits. Father comes up. He takes off his jacket and covers me with it. His skin is brown and glistens in the sun-up. "To the Doc, in town," Father says. "Take her."

Run wraps his arm across the jacket, holding me inside it. Father is standing in his skin and sun-up to the waist. I want to say, Father, Father, you will catch your death. Mother is crying.

"Hurry with her!" Mother tells Run.

"Hur'm up, Strider!" Jack-Run says.

Horse's ears flicking up. Horse a-walking. We move. Me and Jack and James-Face up in back of my brother.

"Hur'm up, Strider!" Softly Run. Run making a squeaking with his mouth. Strider rushing into the wind. The town I see come quickly. Town spilling along crease of hills like scattering rocks. James-Face saying something as hooves pounding fast. We soon slow down and do not go into a town. Edge of crease, I see our house. Sun-up has not reached it. House always in shade. Is dark, as if we do not live there. Darkly hides among tall trees. Is James-Face a tall tree the first time I'm seeing him? Now I see our sumac as we pass into the yard. I see old tire swing swaying and sweeping in a wind. I see a pony corral, clean and empty with just a trough and icing. I see a meadow and a sluice coming down from hills. I see trampled and dirty snow all covered with icing.

We slide off the horse. James-Face flies into the house with me in arms. Swiftly takes me through the house. Kitchen, there he holds me in front of fat cookstove. I see red of coals through the stove eye. I feel no heat. Old James False Face speaks to Run so that my brother will understand. Sun Run taken a tub and fills it water from a pump. Water comes cold as ice from a pump. Place it on a stove to make it steam for washing. Sun Run does not do this. He fills a tub and swings it to the floor, spilling some of it. He pulls up a chair to the tub. James False Face sits on a chair with me on his knee. I watch him like always. He does not speak a story. I look from him to Run and down at a tub of water. I see spilled water has darkened the moccasins of old James. James False Face makes three pair of moccasins at once and no one else knows how to do that. I have seen him do it. "Shoe-making," he has said, "is the same as spear-fishing. One must know how to begin."

Run takes my boots and my coat. He takes my father's hat. He throws boots to the floor. My coat stands up stiff green ice and snow on a floor. Hat is a ball of snow.

Now they lift me into a tub. I have seen James-Face wash fish in such a tub. I am to be made a fish? They stick my legs into the tub. I see my knees like red knots in a water. They pull my hands and arms in, too. I feel weight of water, but I do not feel what must be cold water. I feel something not quite warm and then a feeling is gone.

Old James holds me up in the water. I watching his face, seeking a sign through dark glasses he always wears. He speaks to Run, and Run hur-

14

ries. Taking a pot and spoon, and with a spoon Run digs in the clean-grease jar. Lumps heaps of grease in a pot. He throws wood and coal into a stove. He sets a pot on the stove eye. Soon Run is back from a stove with the pot and James False Face tells him how to do.

They work fast. Jack Sun Run brings two old towels. James lifts me from a water. Holding me, dries with one towel my hands and arms, feet and legs. Jack Sun hands another towel and James tears it into strips. Run puts his hands in a pot and cups his hands full of melted grease. Spreads grease over one of my hands and my arms. And James-Face wraps all up my arms with the strips of towel.

"Can you feel the warmth, little moonflower?" so saying James False Face.

"Quickly now," he says to Run when I cannot answer. They have my hands and my arms wrapped and finished. I am feeling needle pricks all up and down my arms when I hear voices and sounds rushing. So sleepy am I now, trying to stay wide awake to see who is coming. Jack Sun spreading grease over my feet, rubbing. Rubbing it into the toes, when Mother bursts open the door. The door bangs a wall. Father comes in. Lines and wrinkles stiffen cold in a face very sad. Closing the door, my great Stone Father.

"Why did you bring her here?" Mother says.

No one else speaks a word. Quickly, old James helps my brother with the grease and wrappings.

Looking at Mother only once, old James. I think I see his eyes running behind his glasses. Never has he stayed in a room with my mother. Wait to see him make a sign and leave. He does not do either. He rubs my foot in strong hands and wraps it up.

"Oh, no," Mother says.

"Jack," she says. "I thought at least you would have more sense."

She comes to kneel before me.

"Baby," she says. Patting wrappings. "Arilla, does it hurt?"

"Mother," I say. Hearing my own voice this time. All at once, everything begins to hurt me. I cry and cry.

"Give her to me!" Mother pushing James aside. Taking me.

"Pain is good," old James says to Father. "Means life."

Mother holds my face to her neck. She carries me to a rocking chair and we rock. And we rock. Crying, I have oh so many shivers. Jack-Run brings a blanket. I feel him place it about me. I have never known my brother to bring me anything.

Father builds up the kitchen fire. James False Face is standing the way he will lean above a stream watching fish. Shoulders hunch high. Arms at his sides are still. So close to me I smell the woods and dinner fires burning.

"James False Face," I say.

"I hear you," old James says.

Rememory. Fish baked in soil of clay, tasting so sweet.

Closing my eyes, I say, "Tell a story." Mother rocks and will not send old James away. Jack Sun Run is being quiet. Great Sun, Stone Father, is over there.

James-Face leans above me. He talks a telling in the old way. He has taught me how to see pictures in bunches of his words. Rememory. Bunches he calls children: *little moonflower, children are bright blue today and wish to play with you.*

Now I listen to his telling as in a sleep, and I see:

"came one long time The People were the only ones. they looked the same and spoke the same when they needed to speak. where they were, the forever forest was one immense silence. The People were mostly quiet, knowing how to speak with their hands to one another. the land of the forest was sacred to The People, never to be abandoned by them and never to be sold. thus, The People lived where their spirit was one spirit and the unseen power which filled the forest. all of the forest had the unseen power; and through great effort they made contact with each animal and each tree.

"came another long time of terrible change when the forever forest and the immense silence was broken. the Irinakoiw came walking with his anger in a pouch, followed by the white man,

17

who carried an ax and war in a basket on his back. they walked closely on the same path. one season the Irinakoiw would lead; the next season the white man would lead. Never could they decide who would lead forever, and so they hated one another. the white man took his ax and felled a tree. the Irinakoiw tripped over it as the white man had hoped. but the white man was also a clumsy man and he in turn tripped and fell over the Irinakoiw. there they lay, with anger in a pouch and war in a basket spilling out over the sacred land of the forest. The people fought anger and war, which spread around them. but it was no use, for there is no winning over anger and war.

"in a final time one of The People went walking. he searched for a place to stay and for peace. he found no pipe of peace to smoke and he found no home. but he did find a field with one last flower untouched by anger or war. he was comforted and lay down by the flower. the moon brought a blanket to cover him, and he fell into a weary sleep. sleeping, he breathed upon the flower the goodness of his kind. dreaming, he made signs, and the flower watched and understood.

"at the end, the one who went walking found rest at last. as he ceased to dream, he ceased to breathe. the little flower had become strong so near to one of The People and shielded by the moon's blanket. grown from soil untouched by anger or war, the flower understood the land. she knew the way of The People and she held on to her seeds for a better time."

All still. James-Face leans above me. Finished telling in an old way.

"Moonflower," he saying softly.

"Hear you, too," saying so sleepy.

"Have your dreams now and hold on tight."

Hearing the door close softly. Soon as he's gone, Mother saying: "The doctor not a mile away and he covers her with grease."

Jack Sun Run says: "It worked and we didn't have to pay."

Mother says: "But what if it hadn't, what about that?"

Jack-Run says: "James-Face is never mistaken."

Father says: "It's my fault. She heard me sledding. I take the blame."

Mother says: "It's your fault for acting the fool every winter night."

Run says: "It's not his fault, it's your fault. You take the blame."

Father says: "Run, that's enough."

Run says: "Mother, you wanted a baby. We were just fine the way we were. It's your fault."

Father say: "Enough, Sun Run."

Mother says: "I know one thing, Jack. If you are ever cruel to her, you'll answer to me. I know that."

Run says: "I'm never cruel to her. I'm never one way or another."

19

Father says: "He is just acting strong. He is just the young warrior. Did you see how he saved us, how he roped us in?"

Mother says: "Why the need for saving? It should never have happened."

Run says: "I am never cruel. I don't care one way or the other."

Mother says: "We have got to get away from here."

2

For sure, my Birthday would be a disaster. I mean, worse than the time they tell about when that Learjet piloted by some rock-and-roll star-boys crash-landed in Wilson Onderdock's Black-Angus pasture a mile outside of town. Knowing something about Black Angus and Onderdocks gives a clue to what kind of engagement went on in that cow pasture for half the night. Even if one of the star-boys was bleeding all over the place, Wilson Onderdock said *nobody* was getting any blood transfusion and an ambulance ride until his prize bull hanging in little chunks on the fence was paid for.

My Birthday was shaping up to be the same kind of for-real bust. I would be surprised if there wasn't a little blood and guts somewhere in it, too. Because any event that had me at the edge of it when I was supposed to be dead center, and had Jack Sun Run at the center when he shouldn't've been there at all, was doomed any sixteen ways you wanted to look at it. It was just that with my brother being the Sun, if the day didn't naturally revolve around him, then it couldn't happen. It hadn't even been formed yet. Or it was a piece of clay; and no matter how I might want to mold it, my brother, Sun Run, would come along and have to flatten it. He'd smack at it, beat it and work it over into whatever kind of shape suited him. That was his power.

By the time school was out, I was one wreck trying to figure out just how Jack Sun would manage to destroy anything. Having to sit through Chorus, which I hate, and then Math, which I despise, and Assembly in I have to admit a pretty neat dress and in shoes which have always hurt my poor feet, I'm sure would have caused any other kid I know to pull a stomach upset.

Why is it girls always get the lousy jobs? I mean, someone ought to complain to the Student Council. Because somebody made all the Seventh Grade girls divide into two groups. This one group had to collect money from the boys and buy flowers; and the other group had to bake cookies — I mean, *had* to, and right in school. Then the flowers and cookies had to be taken over to Mercy Medical Clinic, where Patricia purple-prissy Reynolds was recovering from being knocked off her ten-speed rip-off by Logan's Cleaners' panel truck. I mean, there is this whole *crew* of purple-prissies in school who shouldn't even be allowed tricycles, let alone ten-speeds out of control all over town.

The less said about Patricia Reynolds is probably the better. I don't get wise with her on account of her dad's some kind of big deal in the State House of Representatives. Some kids do. But I dislike her pure and simple because she is a stuck-up, gross-out idiot. Maybe next time she'll plow into a freight train. Still, I figure her father deserves whatever pleasure he can get from being a Representative, whatever that is. At least he does if he works as hard as my own Stone Dad.

I said to my own dad after Patricia got knocked senseless by the cleaners' truck: "Did you go and vote for Lou Boyd Reynolds?"

And my dad said, "I'd a sooner vote for a honey-dipper with advanced leprosy before I'd vote for that clown."

"What in the foggy world is a honey-dipper?" I asked him.

And my dad leaned back and said in that soft way of his, "You mean you've forgotten old James False Face?"

Now, that took me back. I felt real queer a minute and I got sort of confused all in my mind. "Well, I don't know," I said, which is my way of giving myself time to think, or not telling the truth, or not wanting to talk, depending on the scene. In this situation I was truly trying to think back. "I know James was old," I said finally. "But his hair wasn't ever so much gray, but black. I remember he was an Indian."

Dad's face kind of looked unhappy when I said that. "James-Face never much took to the name Indian, so don't use it," Dad said. "Use Cherokee or Santee, depending on which people you are talking about. Or you can say The People, which is what old James used to say most of the time."

I stayed quiet to see where Dad was going with it. For some reason, I didn't want him to go too far. Pretty soon, though, he was back in a good mood, like always.

Dad said, "James False Face became the honey-dipper back in Cliffville, where we lived. Oh, he could do marvelous work. He knew how to make all kinds of things from the old time, too. But a honey-dipper was a man who went to the trouble for little reward to clean and whitewash out-houses once or twice a year. That's why they called James the honey-dipper."

"No kidding?"

"Truth," Dad said.

James False Face. I get the feeling I was always with him. A cleaner of johnnies-on-the-outside. 'S what my brother liked to call them. I don't remember ever seeing old James at work, either. But thinking back always makes me feel like I'm coming down with something incurable.

Anyway, I don't know a soul who ever thought much of the Reynoldses, mainly Patricia, even if her mother was in the school every day as the school psychologist. She and Mr. Representative Reynolds were divorced. And lucky I wasn't one of the three girls that had to go with one of the aides into that smelly clinic and bring Patricia the flowers and cookies and have to talk to her. But two of those girls were coming to my Birthday.

I can hear her now: "You'll have to stand, you can't sit on my bed." Just as selfish and stuck up as ever. "Mommy says I can't take any pain at all. Every time I close my eyes, I can see that truck running me down." Running her down! Ten speeds for a pea-brain. She was showing off for Joey Montgomery and ran smack into that truck.

Thank goodness I don't have to worry about not inviting her to my party. Not that I'd ever invite her as much as a block away from where I happened to be. Not that Patricia would come, either. She's a regular at one of my mom's dance classes, Advanced, and then pretends she doesn't know me in school.

My mom. She always will say, "Arilla, I have to admit that one of my great disappointments is the fact that you refuse to learn The Dance."

I always answer her right back: "Dear Mother, my biggest sorrow since we moved here is the fact that my mom has to be the dance teacher for the biggest snobs in town."

We talk that way to one another sometimes. It is like joking and not daring to laugh. I can't explain it, exactly. My mom's the one who wanted me to have a Birthday. She and Jack Sun Run. I didn't care one single bit.

"Think of all the presents you'll get," Mom told me.

"Makes no difference to me," I told her, "so long as you and Dad get me something nice."

"And your brother?" she said.

"Probably give me a rusty horseshoe wrapped in manure."

"Arilla!"

So now I have to wait for these girls we picked for my Birthday to come out of school. They mess around so much flirting and take so long. I was the first one out of Assembly, beat it to my locker and was outside with my books before the buzzer stopped, almost. There's no reason to hurry, except that I'm so nervous. I never had a party before. Of the six girls we invited, two of them left for the clinic before Assembly and barely got back in time. Now they have to make an oral to the Teacher-Counselor. And I heard they have to clean up the dishes they used for baking cookies. I mean, that's the way they treat B students while pea-brains get served in bed!

So I wait, sitting on one of these concrete slabs which are scattered around. Supposed to be some kind of indestructible, modern seating arrangement for us kids in front of our modern, indestructible, windowless, one-room open school. I don't hate the school here; but if I want to be cool, I can't say that out loud. I really like it. The only time I ever get scared is in cyclone season when we are like sitting ducks in a box. No inner walls, no basement to hide in. I like to sit here, though, watching the kids flow out, running for buses.

One girl for my party straggles out and then another. They look real nice, too. We say hello. I try not to look at the presents they are hiding against them on top of their books when they sit down near me at the other end of the concrete. They are older-looking, being in the Eighth Grade. Mom says all the girls out here are over-grown, corn-fed. Not a one of them refused to come to my party and I can't think of anything to call over to them. It's okay, though, with so many kids flowing out and yelling, and some sitting around, waiting for parents to drive them home. We are all pretty worn right after school, anyway, although I always do pick up a little after four o'clock. It looks like it'll be four before we get out of here.

This place is a campus, with the middle school and then the high school across the road and the parking lot from the middle school. Another girl comes out. She gives me a smile and a nod and sits over with the other two. They are glancing over their shoulders toward the high school. I'm doing it, too, before I realize it, before I figure we are not just anxious about my Birthday but about my brother, Sun Run, over at the high school. Then I get kind of mad and start arranging my books and looking up assignments like I wasn't thinking about Sun at all.

It's a peculiar position I hold with these girls. Everybody looks on my family as this peculiar bunch. I don't suppose anybody'd notice me at all if it weren't for Mom and Jack and my dad. Mom grew up in this town of ten thousand. When we came back to live here, right away Mom opened her dance studio on Wheeler Avenue, and from the start she did real well. She could coax any brat of any age into one of her classes, stopping their moms on the street or calling up their homes. She seems to know everybody in town, from the mayor to the garbage collector.

One time Mom explained to me how things were. "My family has lived here for at least a century. Of course, my parents both passed away — Arilla, I'm sorry you never knew them, they were so good to me — and others have left and come back and left again, great-aunts and cousins. Some few do still remain. We were never close, but we are still relatives. I have *credit* in this town. . . ."

I never ask why we never came back to visit because I guess I know she, and the rest of us, never quite fitted in.

Mom said, "A town full of generations of your kin owes you something — I don't know why in the world I waited so long to come home."

She had credit, all right. She'd go through the phone book, letting her fingers do the walking down the names until she came to the ones she knew. She'd call up a number and, like, say, "Mrs. Hamrand? This is Lillian Adams. You may remember me as Lilly Perry over in the west town? Yes! Yes! That was my father! Well, for heaven — " And off she'd go talking for a half-hour, ending up making two lines in her dance-class book for the Hamrand girls.

Besides the fact that she had credit, Mom was what my dad called "a beautiful woman." It's true, too, you don't see many people out here with that kind of stage beauty she has. Mom never goes even to the supermarket without her face made to look glowing and with the eylashes, not too long, but full and soft. Tall, with a dancer's lean strength; and hair, kind of kinky-long down her back, or pulled up in a full, crinkly pony tail like a question mark on her neck. She has the longest, slimmest legs I have ever seen on any-body's mom.

Last Fourth of July we all four — Mom and Dad and Jack Sun Run and me — went over to the Spangler Park for the celebration, and to sit on the hill to watch the fireworks as soon as it got dark. Everybody in town seemed to be there, and we walked in to the field all dressed up like everybody else. It was one of the few big occa-sions since Lilly Adams moved back to town. She was already some famous for her classes, and the local *News* and the *Fairmont Gazette* had already done stories on her. How she had her own group down in Cincinnati when she was so young and had even taken it to New York. How she toured the whole country after that. And how she quit for a while after she'd married. I guess I was proud she was my mom, but I did get disgusted the way all the kids, from the littlest girl to the biggest boy, kept running up to her at the Fourth of July: "Hi, Miss Lilly! Miss Lilly, I'm all ready for tomorrow. I practiced real good, Miss Lilly!" Enough to make you barf.

"Arilla, you are a disappointment," Mom always did say. "Every girl in town who's anybody, and the ones who want to be somebody. And you won't even do the warm-up."

Probably I would've joined The Dance if it hadn't been for the fact that kids who dance are always so slew-footed and like they are swayback. Besides, leotards cause my legs to itch something awful. I know I wouldn't be able to concentrate on what Mom was teaching for scratching. It'd be awful for her to have me so short and stubby next to her. I'd just be an embarrassment, and I'll never be tall, even if my legs are long.

Anyway, we came to the Fourth celebration with Mom dressed in the nicest green chiffon dress anybody ever saw. She was holding on to Dad's arm and he was walking slow and careful, the way he always will. Dad has his airs, too, but they are nice airs. Mom is five-foot-eight and Dad is just under five-eleven, and he walks like he is walking on cotton, kind of creeping. Or sometimes like he will be careful not to snap some twigs underfoot. His shoulders are strong and thick. His arms never swing, his hands being most of the time deep in his pockets. His hair is black and sleek down to his shoulders, which some kids say is too long for somebody's father, but I like it. Just combed back like a mane of a lion, when a lion's mane is black and bouncy. He had on this white suit Mom bought him. He didn't much like any suit, but he wore this one like he dressed so fine every day. People might say Dad looked just like Cochise playing the part of a movie star. Dad was even more handsome than usual because he was feeling good about having this job as supervisor of the food-service crews in the dining halls of the town's technical college. Of course, we didn't know how long he would last. Dad is what Mom calls erratic.

It's true, tomorrow Dad might take it in his head to walk off the job and keep walking until he is back in Cliffville where we used to live. He did that every once in a while for no reason I knew of. Sun Run would have to catch a ride and bring him on back home. Each time Dad left, he'd've squandered some pay and Mom would be good and depressed for a month. Otherwise, I loved him a lot, though I did worry some that he might go and not come back.

All the time I'm thinking, I'm sitting on the concrete slab waiting for my Birthday girls to gather. When all at once they are there and I don't recall the rest of them coming out of school, although I guess I must've spoken to them. I feel so downhearted today, I can't tell why. So I stand up, looking around. Being twelve isn't like I thought it would be. When I was eleven, I thought being twelve was really big, like these girls. But yesterday is the same as my Birthday. It's not being big or little, it's like dangling at the end of a rope and not being able to let go.

These girls are so peculiar. They think I'm waiting for something when I'm not. They think I'm waiting for Sun Run.

"We'd better get going. It's time," I tell them. Should've taken a bus, but the buses all have gone. They give a glance to one another and shake out their hair. It's fun to pretend I don't know very much who they are. The truth is I know all about them. I'm acting cool because I want them to think I have everything together. But I didn't know Sun wasn't coming. I was sure he'd come and take over, parading the girls through town.

We start out, walking the long way over to Mom's studio, which is now called the Beaux Arts, and which she moved to Ryder Ripple Road off South Ekker Avenue. The party girls and I just sort of fill up the sidewalk in no kind of order. I walk out on the edge near the curb so they won't think some of them have to be with me. I'll feel better away from school. School has all these banks of glass doors in front tinted bronze. You can see out, but you can't see in. Even when you wait outside, you know people are watching you. *It* watches you. School has a mind of its own. It watches me and everyone, and puts me and everyone into a slot that is never-changing.

The Birthday girls are talking in little bursts, not to one another, but like lines going side by side and never touching or crossing. We walk by the Spangler Park, which, in this late fall going into winter, is full of soccer players. The girls slow down to look at boys. I wonder if any of them is thinking about that Fourth of July when Mom and Dad, Sun and me were all together and feeling fine in that park?

That is, Mom and Dad and Jack Sun were feeling swell. I was feeling self-conscious, as usual. We came into the Spangler Park with people on every side and with the hillsides — that huge green standpipe is at the top of the hill — already covered with folks and kids. Blankets with beer hidden under them. And Coke and other soft drinks, and food to help everybody, even the babies, enjoy the fireworks as soon as it was dark.

We walked in and, I swear, every head on the hillside turned to look at us. I guess we were a sight. I *know* we were, what with Jack-Run prancing on his show horse in the lead and with me holding back, bringing up the rear. I was so jumpy that day, I could have covered my head with sixteen pillows and it still wouldn't've been enough. Because Jack Sun will always try to put folks on. By this time everybody in town had at least heard of him. They thought he was crazy-wild, but smart and put-on wild. Yet, if anybody could get away with a prancing show horse on a hot Fourth after folks had spent hours washing and polishing their "hogs" out of respect for the celebration, Jack Sun Run Adams could. Maybe.

Folks had filled up the parking areas with their polished hogs, even when some of them lived only a block away from the park. They'd dressed themselves up, too, casual but trying to look expensive in light-weight jackets and wash-'n'-wear slacks. And here is my brother, Sun, wearing nothing above the waist; wearing cowhide leggings and Wellington boots, with his bare arms, shoulders and back shining like antique gold from his sweat. You might say Sun Run had polished himself. And wearing one thin band of black leather around his head to match his boots, with one eagle feather sticking out of the headband in the back.

When the kids on the hillside see him, they started in doing what they thought was some Indian war whoop. Like that really high and shrill yell made from their hands hitting their open mouths. I was about embarrassed to death. But my brother wasn't. He didn't pay them any mind at all because he knew all about them. He knew if he showed their noise bothered him, well, they wouldn't think he was for real.

I'm not sure Sun is serious about being an Indian. I mean whether he for certain believes what he pretends. I know I don't believe it, but I don't really know what he is, either. If he's an Indian (I mean Native American — he usually will call himself an Amerind), then what am I supposed to be? I don't much look like Mom and I surely don't look like my dad. I just have Mom's coloring. I'm a throwback to someone else, I guess. Or secretly adopted.

Sun Run says I probably came from the moon, and laughs. He says Mom came from the moon, too. Says she's a light-skin, like people will say red-skin, and laughs again. He says that's what people around here probably call her behind her back — light-skinned. And that it's because even now they can't bring themselves to say black out loud, since they already spent so much time hating the word and what it stood for. Sun Run says this town never got itself beyond the 1940's; and that here you can't even tell the 1960's ever happened. Maybe he's pretty right, too. But this town is still a pretty relaxed place to kind of pass the time. It may have its Saturday-night rip-offs and a drug bust about once a year. But there's nothing here you could call some organized, for-real and bad-scene crime. Even if the only fame it has is its technical college, Dad says it's still a good college.

The town kids waiting for something to happen to them will copy the college kids down to the blue jeans, beer and long hair. But none of them, including the college ones, can look as out-of-sight cool as Jack Sun Run. Mom says Sun has an "aura" about him. It's true, because about every sidewalk sale they have in the spring, when they close off the streets downtown, folks will stop what they are doing to watch Sun parading Jeremiah. Sitting so still in his skins, like he is taking a long ride through a painted desert — it will seem like the day is holding its breath until he is finished showing off. Anytime something seems to be missing, or some event is going to turn into a real bore, all of a sudden here comes Jack Sun Run and the day just sucks its breath, then breezes in place around him.

So here we come into the Spangler Park with every head turned to look at us and then the war whoops; finally comes a large silence growing as thick and worrisome as flies. Sun stops Jeremiah's prancing and lets him show-walk, his black mane sort of trailing in the hot breeze. Telling you true, a girl never had a more exciting brother to watch, nor a worse enemy to contend with, either, than Jack Sun Run Adams.

Sun had already passed by these three men standing on the grass just beyond the parking lot into the park. Mom and Dad had barely passed them. They didn't even notice me coming by. Nobody ever does. But just then one of them turned to the other two and said, to my complete surprise, "Lilly Perry always was the best-looking light-skinned woman in town. You can take the breed or leave him, they say he ain't that bad. But that kid of theirs is about the nastiest son-of-a-snake this side of Geronimo." Then he laughed, rocking back on his heels, with the other two joining in.

Well, that man had to say it. Didn't he know, with the kind of keen sense Sun and Dad have, they'd have to hear him? I could've died. I wished I was dead so I wouldn't've had to witness what I knew was going to come down.

Mom and Dad, strolling along looking swell, with Run parading Jeremiah right in front of them. When all of a sudden Dad turned around, walking the way we had come. And Sun wheeling Jeremiah so that he was moving the same as Dad. Just the two of them, mind-readers. Dad moving fast but in that creeping, cat-cautious way he can do. In a second he is standing in front of the three men. Sun Run and Jeremiah are right with him, with Jeremiah's nose snorting and giving whinnies over Dad's right shoulder. They were so still, with Sun and the horse and Dad not moving a muscle, you could tell the "aura" had curled itself around the three of them.

So that the man who had talked about Lilly Perry kind of touched his Adam's apple and commenced grinning like a maniac. "Hello, there!" he shouted to Dad, as silly as he could sound.

Dad spoke so soft and polite: "Mrs. Lillian Adams is the best-looking woman's name," he says.

"My son's name is Jack Adams. Meet Jack Sun Run Adams. Say hello to him, mister."

Then Sun Run had to raise Jeremiah up on two legs. That big, gorgeous stallion with his hooves tapping air above my dad's head. The man's mouth flew open in disbelief. Shaping the word *hello* or *oh*, it was awful hard to tell. I mean, that horse was a terrifying sight almost even to me, with those dangerous hooves about to kick out Dad's brains. Yet Dad didn't move a muscle. Sun Run didn't either, it looked like. He, Jeremiah and Dad kind of made this tableau, Mom said later, with the three men scared to move an inch and all the people on the hill watching.

The scene only lasted a moment. And it would've been the end of the whole thing — Dad with Sun on his show horse scaring three dudes to death. Only, Sun Run didn't know when to let go. He never did know when something was finished. He always had to go too far.

Dad just turned on his heel. People on the hill could tell words had passed and maybe a little something extra, but that was all there was to it. They weren't laughing at Dad, just kind of snickering at the men for looking so scared of a horse. Mom had been sort of rushing back and forth in a small space of grass. And now she rushed around Sun and Jeremiah and took Dad's arm.

"Please," she whispered. "Don't make a scene."

That was a laugh. What'd she think he'd been doing? She took hold of Dad's arm again and they started on toward the hill and all the folks up there watching pleasant, not unhappy to have Lilly Perry back in her hometown, when they noticed her at all.

When Jack-Run had to go too far.

Sun rode Jeremiah with a good roping saddle, although there never was much rough riding in our part of the country. It was hand-tooled leather with a full leaf design. He kept it oiled, rubbed and polished, and the dally horn could hold two ropes, although Sun never used more than one. Its cantle was a Cheyenne roll with a three-inch rise so Sun could mount and dismount as quick as he wanted. What with its full-size skirts and fenders, it was maybe too much saddle, a cowboy might say — too much of a put-on. But Sun loved it. It cost him more than three hundred dollars on the layaway plan. He paid it off in about eight months working for my dad. Sun is about the best waiter in town, and being so polite to the students and out-of-town customers, half of the price of the saddle he made in tips.

Just when everyone on the hill was about to settle down to their own private eating and drinking, Sun takes his rope from the saddle horn. That rope was about a forty-five-foot nylon lariat and waxed to make handling with it easy. He commenced to twirl a running noose of the rope until he had a full circle above his head.

The three dudes Dad had talked to had already

turned away and were sauntering off. One of them must have sensed something, for he stopped in mid-stride. Maybe he heard the sound as Sun let the lasso go. It whirled through the air with a low whizzing, like a giant band spun out of the sky. No sooner did the rope start dropping down over the three dudes than Sun took his end and looped it around the pommel and wheeled Jeremiah in the opposite direction. By the time that lasso was at the level of the dudes' shoulders, Sun had played out most of the length of it. That circle tightened around the dudes so fast, they didn't have a chance to duck out of it. They were stone caught, squeezed facing one another so that they looked like they were preparing to kiss.

Oh, it was a sight, for sure. A shout went up in the crowd on the hill; and a whoop and a holler from high-school kids at the base of the standpipe. Every one of them up there got to their feet to get a better view. That was all my brother needed. He had a look in his eyes like I'd only heard about. It was a combination of murdering anger and killing righteousness, like the time Mom says when I was six and he was ten. We were in Cliffville and Sun had let a sick mother rat have her babies on the kitchen floor right next to the stove. When Mom saw what it was, she gave Sun a backhand that spun him clear out of the house. And she threw the rat and babies in the stove to burn to a crisp before she thought. They say the smell was awful. And Sun stood outside with that look in his eyes. Shaking from head to foot, he grabbed the door and held it open for fifteen minutes, screaming, "Come on in, flies! Come on in, flies!" over and over. I can just hear him, too.

But right there in the Spangler Park, Jack-Run went beyond too far.

"Hur'm up, Jeremiah," he said, real soft. And in a second they were off in a run. The three lassoed fools began to fall in one piece. I saw the whole thing like it was in slow motion, like the men were falling from a long way up. The day was so sweltering hot and I was so ashamed and excited all at the same time, I was about ready to pass out in a dead faint.

"Timberrrr!" some smart kid yelled from the standpipe.

The three dudes fell — ku-whun-nuk! — on the grass. Two of them on their backs and the other one kind of sandwiched halfway between the other two, facing the ground. All three of them twisting and turning and kicking, trying to get free of that rope. It wasn't any use. Sun had the rope played out taut enough to snap it if it hadn't been as good a rope as it was. And then he dragged those men. He had Jeremiah in a lather in all of the heat, with hooves straining and running, inching along now and dragging those three men over the ground.

The crowd hushed. It had been screaming and laughing up to then. But the three dudes looked like they might be hurting. Big men, the two on the bottom were getting their heads bumped along the ground something fierce. Their faces had turned beet red.

Mom had broken away from my dad and was running back and forth along the taut rope this time, like she didn't know which way to go.

"Sun! Stop it, my god!" she yelled.

But Sun would play it to the end, just the way he had played out that rope.

One, and then two, and a few more men began to move off of the hill, standing up and brushing the new-cut grasses from the seats of their wash-'n'-wears. Then picking their way down through the crowd. They started out kind of slow and self-conscious, but coming off that hill faster and faster. Until they were standing at that taut line of Jack-Run's lariat, where he was still dragging the fallen in larger circles in that open space of grass and field below the hill.

There were some seven men plus the three fallen and lassoed. The seven began pulling at the fallen until they finally had the dudes on their feet. At once all ten of them commenced pulling against Sun's rope. Quickly Sun turned Jeremiah to face them and pulled the other way. It was an uneven struggle even with the power of Jeremiah. For the men were pulling in heaves that seemed to keep Jeremiah off balance. But that beautiful horse would have burst his heart just to help Sun win if the most surprising thing hadn't happened right then.

These young high-school kids, the cut-ups who like to pretend they are some like Sun, began to come off that area around the standpipe just about the same way the older men had come off the hill. Only, these came off faster, swaggering some for the girls that were with them to see. A few of them were big and husky, bigger than Sun, being football boys and the like, rather than track-and-field and horsemen like Sun Run. They were not in his class, but they didn't know it yet. They were soon to find out. Sun always did prefer to stand by himself and fall by himself.

They caught hold of Sun's lariat below Jeremiah and lined themselves out along the rope. So that now Sun had this team pulling one way against this team of ten men pulling the other way, with this ten feet of strained, empty rope between the two sides. It was the weirdest-looking tug-o'-war I or anybody else out there had ever seen. It was done in silence, with the older men looking grim and sweaty and the boys on Sun's side with feverish eyes and that insane grinning just like Sun's own. And with my dad off to one side in his pure-white suit. He was looking out above and beyond Sun's head, like he was seeing something far away, yet something under a microscope, like some scientist.

And Mom. She had come up against that empty space of rope between the two sides. Her chiffon dress was sticking to her now from the heat. She reached over and clutched the rope on one side of her, then reached and clutched it on the other side. To bring the two teams together, I guess, the way she will gather the folds of cloth to cinch it under a waistband.

"Please now," she said. "Jack, please now. Let's put an end to this before someone — "

My brother ignored her. He had his hands full. No one but him and me seemed to notice the danger. The young dudes pulling were too busy showing off their style and trying to win. The old guys had to beat the young dudes if it killed them. Sun was having a time with Jeremiah, who had got himself frightened because of all the human beings closing in on him. A section of the crowd had eased off the hill and that area around the standpipe, too, to close in around the tug-o'-war. Young girls had to start screaming and older women were shouting, either egging their men on or telling them to quit acting like a bunch of city dudes at a farmer's auction.

So that bodies of human beings pressed in around that grand horse until he was near frantic with fear. Faithful Jeremiah didn't want to hurt a soul. Sun knew that and I knew that; but still, he was going to rear. My brother broke out in a cold sweat trying to keep Jeremiah from trampling those boys right in front of him. I swear,

44

I thought Sun's muscles would jump right out of his skin. He couldn't hold Jeremiah back another minute, and in a flash he did what he had to do. I mean, Sun has the strength of a track-and-field star going on across country. And with that last, perfect strength he held Jeremiah steady with one hand for maybe five seconds while he reached over to his side. He pulled out this knife he carries in a trick seam along his leggings. And he cut that rope of a lariat just out from Jeremiah's nose. Honest to goodness, it was like somebody had thrown a handful of popcorn on a red-hot stove. Men and boys flew to this side and the other, and fell in two heaps of head-over-heels and bruised knees. Mom was jostled some, but she was still on her feet. She dropped the rope like it was on fire.

All had happened like lightning, with men and boys flying out and falling back, with Mom dropping the rope, and with Jeremiah almost sitting down on his rump when all of that force gave away. Should of seen those boys scrambling away from there, too. And Dad, in his white suit so spotless, with sparks dancing in his eyes, which never left looking at the sight of Sun. Then, Sun Run wheeling Jeremiah to get out of that field, and the crowd falling back to let him through. All this like each part had been one whole that had to break up in pieces around Sun Run. That was his power.

It still wasn't over, either.

3

The crowd opened up in front of that great beauty
of a horse moving, and Sun with his head held
high and eyes flashing. My brother wasn't quite
smirking, but he was for-sure getting out of there.
He realized before anybody that in the next minute those boys and men he'd caused to fall down
and look stupid were going to turn on him, as
sure as pieces of the day would again collect
around him and become the night.

Anyway, folks get nervous around a kid who'll
carry a knife between his teeth. Sun Run had
clenched the knife in his teeth so he could use
both hands to control Jeremiah. Sun thought he
couldn't get along without that knife, although
he seldom used it for anything. And it was the
hardest thing for my dad to teach him that, to
most folks, a knife was just about as scary as
anything with a trigger.

At the other end of the space folks had opened
up for Sun and Jeremiah came some policemen

out of two cruisers parked in the parking lot at the edge of the green, just in case. It was the Fourth, after all. Any big crowd on a hot holiday could mean any kind of trouble. So these police had been hanging around outside of the grounds, talking to pretty ladies and helping the elderly get their camp chairs out of their cars. Giving themselves an untarnished image.

The cops came walking in, not too fast. Seeing the crowd gather, they must have thought maybe a fistfight had broken out. So they come on in kind of easy, not wanting to get the crowd all excited. What did they have to see but Jack Sun Run struggling toward them, looking for the world like an improvement on Sal Mineo in *Cheyenne Autumn*?

"Wait a minute," one of the police said to the other, "isn't that the half-Indian kid?"

"You mean the half-colored one?" the other cop answered.

My dad always did say that if you could separate the town police from their shiny black cruisers, you'd discover they had flesh and blood from the waist up only. He said the rest of them was pure yellow ether. And if they couldn't solve a crime from behind their steering wheels, my dad said, well then a crime hadn't ever been committed in the first place.

So there was my mighty brother, Jack Sun Run Adams, with the two cops in the lead kind of easing up on him. He had that knife still clenched in his teeth and he had Jeremiah's reins loose but short-up in case the horse thought about rearing. Jeremiah was stepping forward and then side to side, like, given a chance, when he saw an opening he was going to break out of there no matter what Sun Run did.

"Don't you know that knife is a concealed weapon?" one of the cops yelled up at Sun.

"Does it look like I'm hiding it?" Sun said through his teeth, right back at him. "Watch it. Horse got hisself riled."

"Come on down from there, then," the cop said. There were four police and they sure knew that the crowd had hushed and was watching them. They were hesitating just to one side of Jeremiah and Sun, like they didn't know if they should capture them or wait to see if Sun would come down.

"Listen," Sun said, in a gurgling voice because of the knife, and swallowing hard.

Everyone could sense the danger from just that one word. And everybody did listen:

"Getting him out of here 'fore someone is hurt. Now back off."

At which point my brother, the Sun, got Jeremiah true forward in that grand way that horse could move. Jeremiah's shoulders and quarters were rippling under that dark coat, which will look black except under the strongest sunlight, better than the finest war-horse in the best Technicolor cowboy-and-Indian western.

48

Sun and Jeremiah made it seem like the whole Cheyenne nation was parading out of the park right behind them. And nobody said one word. Not the crowd. Not the tug-o'-war boys, or even the police. Jack Sun went on through the parking lot and out into the street, right down the middle, where he let Jeremiah open in a pure, easy gallop. Until the sight and sound of them had vanished into the sunset — except that the sun would go down behind the park. He was headed east, but that was the picture and the "aura" of Jack Sun Run Adams.

My brother was supreme that Fourth of July. The way he could get a crowd and a third of the police force to listen to him like that. And he being just an old fifteen-year-old going on sixteen that winter. I mean, with a word, make 'em understand his deepestmost knowledge in an instant and make them *obey*. I haven't learned that in an entire month of talking.

Nothing more happened. Sun left and the cops moved into the crowd. I don't think they ever found out what really happened out there. The tug-o'-war men and boys were partly guilty themselves for the trouble. And the three dudes who hadn't shown proper respect for my mom or Sun — I never did know which had set my dad off — sure couldn't prove that Jeremiah would've trampled them. It all ended in a kind of letdown for all concerned. Mom just turned and walked out of there with Dad following her. I stayed a minute or two, to pick up what was left of Jack Sun's lariat, and to see if anyone was going to make a lie and press charges against him. Once in a while folks will press charges against him when he lets Jeremiah canter across some lawns. No one did, so I left. Nobody noticed me leaving any more than they'd seen me coming.

One thing can be said for Sun and Mom and Dad. You always know when they are in the vicinity. And that leaves me out. I never did get to see the fireworks, either. I guess I could've stayed, but who wants to sit by herself at the fireworks? Anyhow, I had to get back home to find out what Sun was doing.

That's always the way it is. Just like today on my Birthday. Instead of being happy about my party, I'm worrying just where and when Jack Sun will enter into it and take it over. I swear, nobody else in the world is twelve and feeling the way I do.

When the party girls and I reach South Ekker Avenue, we walk down just a couple of blocks to Ryder Ripple Road. Like I say, they were talking not to one another. One of them would say something and another one would say something that had nothing to do with what the first one had said.

These girls are mostly thirteen going on fourteen.

"Dang it, I *hate* this dress!" Marianne Earley

bursts out, pulling at the new, awful dress hard enough to tear it from the shoulders. She looks to be about twelve, but she is the only one of us who is already fourteen. She has this straight black hair so wispy thin. It just covers her head like some dirty, dusty cloth. Like everyone else, she is stuck on Jack Sun, but he doesn't even know she's alive.

The dress she is wearing is a white, sheer material from the neck to the waist with an underslip to go with it — she'll be chilled in it when the sun goes down. But the bottom half of the dress is this green plaid material. The whole thing is supposed to remind you of 1940 or '50 or something. Seeing the dress, I don't know why anybody'd want to be reminded.

"I refused to go to gym today," said Sue Patterson. "I know Miss Binns is going to flunk me, but I don't care."

"Did all my homework in T-C," Lou Ann Gregg cut right in on Sue. "Usually I can just relax when I get home. Because Mama don't get home until six and Daddy not until six-thirty. I don't have to start dinner until five-thirty."

Who cares? But that's the way they were talking. Every one of them had something to say but Angelica Diavolad. Angel is what Jack-Run calls her. And when he calls *Angel?* she walks over to him just as smooth as you please. He will give her a hand and a stirrup up and off they'll go on Jeremiah, to ride on the paths in the glen until darkness. Now, the fact that Sun Run likes her is probably the best and the worst thing that could happen to Angel. She's a runner just the same as Sun is, and the best basketball player on the girls' team. There is a fight going on in this town at the School Board whether Angel is good and strong enough to play on the boys' middle-school team.

In track and field there's no difference between high-school and middle-school girls' teams. There is just one track-and-field day, and Angel always shows off real well. Boys like to tease and say that all we have to do is put Sun at the finish line of the 880, which is the half-mile run, and Angelica Diavolad will win it every time for our school. It's true. Whenever Sun is there, she wins. He stands there waiting, and when she crosses the line first, he gives her a look that makes the other girls in her group so jealous. We all know she would win without him, but maybe she wins better and faster with him there.

Angel does her schoolwork the best, and she plays the cello for hours, and never fools around even for a half-hour at Gahagan's Drug Store and Luncheonette after school. Sometimes she will stop at the Milktop, which is the best old ice-cream parlor, but she won't talk to anybody much, except for maybe Sun. Her father doesn't much like Sun. None of the fathers around here care for him. For he is the only reason Angel will forget about her cello practice once in a while, or her homework.

One time her parents let Sun take her to the movies. He should've had her home at quarter of ten, but Sun didn't get home himself until twelve-thirty. I know one thing, her dad was at our house the next morning before school, on his way to the funeral home where he is director. He caught my brother just as he was coming out the door. I couldn't hear what they were saying where I was standing behind the curtain. But I sure saw Monserrat Diavolad's face and the back of his hand right under Jack Sun's chin. His mouth was going a mile a minute, too. Then he turned and jumped behind the wheel of his black Mark IV, slammed the door and took off. Ever since, Sun and Angel have to be more careful. Sun never got the chance to take her to a movie again. But I see her with Sun in our secret nighttime, which is another story. In public he will once in a while give her a ride home from school when he takes it into his head to saddle up Jeremiah.

Oh well. I figure if Sun likes Angelica Diavolad, she has to be all right. She never smiles, and I wonder if she knows just why Sun chose her from all the other girls. She is his girl-friend as much as you could say Sun has a girl-friend. Sometimes he will go off with some nobody of a girl in the high school for hours, but most of the time he is by himself or with Jeremiah.

And here I am thinking about Sun again. He just seems to surround my life every other minute. I wish my party was already over.

The girls and I have to pass the Municipal Building on the west side of Ekker Avenue and cross the intersection at Ryder Ripple Road. Mom's studio is south, on the east side of the road. I like best walking home from school so I can pass by the Municipal Building. It is this really huge old brick mansion place, but bigger than that, with white trim, and wings going in every direction. There is a long walk as wide as a street up to it in the middle of a grand lawn. It has a flagpole and an American flag waving. It is so quiet, with just police cars and town-government cars parked out in front. Once I saw this woman run down the avenue and scream on up the steps and inside. I waited to see, but they hustled her back out into an unmarked car and I never did find out what she was screaming about. She wasn't bleeding or anything.

Mom says she went to school in that beautiful building. I said, How come she went to school in a Municipal Building? And she said, Well, it wasn't a Municipal Building then. She said they added the wings onto it. When it was a school, it was the central building, with black fire escapes which they had to walk down from the Sixth Grade at the very top; and with swings and slides and sandboxes and recess periods. She says it was a school she will always remember because of the good times and sweet innocence. Mom and her girl-friends walking around and around the building at recess. Locked-arm, there were five of them — around and around — and no boy could bust in on them, nor no girl who wasn't one of the five in her group, they were such good friends. I said I felt sorry for the girls who couldn't be in her group. And she said, Arilla, you would think of that.

The girls with me going to my party. I bet they sure wouldn't lock arms, being too old-acting. Each has a present for me and I hope to goodness they didn't buy me that rock jewelry that is the sudden rage all over town. One thing I hate more than anything in the world is a kind of polished stone that everyone has to have because everybody else has it. One bunch of kids will discover that polished stones can look like the real thing, and in a matter of days the whole town has them like an epidemic. I bet Angelica Diavolad is the only one of these girls that would spend some time getting me something nice. Her whole family is that way. They don't just go out and buy things, but think about what they want and then buy. People laughed at them for waiting months to buy living-room wall-to-wall carpet and living-room furniture. The whole time they waited, they sat on cushions on the floor and people talked about this rich funeral director sitting in his living room on cushions thrown down on bare floors. Yet, when that furniture and carpet finally did get picked out and finally did arrive, it was just about plush perfect. Furniture custom-made and shipped from some place south, like New Orleans. Angel says it will last forever, and people said they wouldn't want furniture that lasted forever. But people aren't Monserrat Diavolad, either.

Here we are. The intersection at Ryder Ripple and South Ekker is always busy this time of day. Both streets are wider here as you turn the corner. There are two traffic lanes in both directions on Ryder, with a parking lane on each side. Parking lanes are always full, and traffic lanes are crowded with cars and trucks hurrying on out of town. But the sidewalks are mostly empty. Sometimes you come down here just off the main part of town and you'd swear that all of the people had vanished, if it weren't for the cars.

From Mom's studio we can now be seen coming. The front of the Beaux Arts is glass, including the door. We see shadows behind the dark glass, and the girls just all at once go wild, right there in the street. I mean, when they were nice, dressed up and for-sure going to my party a second ago, they become like ponies after a spring rain, shivering and prancing in the ground fog and gliding in the mist. Girls older than me can change like that, from something worse than ordinary into these creatures out of mysteries, and right before my eyes. I don't know what causes them to change. It hasn't rained in a week, and I know for sure not one of them's done any outside reading since the last book report.

There is an alley that separates the building next to Gahagan's Luncheonette from Mom's studio. The alley leads through to the next street, and I swing my head around as we pass it. You never know when a car is going to ease out of there and maybe have weak brakes. "Cars are wicked, feet are true," Mom always will say. For myself, it's my Birthday and I am some cautious of surprises. But the girls — Lou Ann, Angelica, Marianne, Sue Patterson, Mickey Hill and Precious Pearl Wingard — don't even give that alley a glance.

"Hey, Pearl, what was it like at the clinic?" I just remembered to ask her, and even I know it's dopey to ask her now.

None of them take their eyes off that glass door of the studio. Pearl didn't hear me, I guess. I glance again into the alley, for Sun will hitch Jeremiah back there to the rear of Mom's building. Right off the corner and just enough space. What I often see looking down the alley to the next street is Jeremiah's hindquarters and his tail a-switching.

Today I expect I did a second take because I failed to see Jeremiah. No feet stamping or anything. Does it mean that Jack is gone, too? Could I be so lucky as to have my brother, Sun, and his show horse off on an emergency which will keep him away from my Birthday for the whole time?

My Birthday and they have left me. The girls are tripping over themselves at the door. They should wait for me to show them in. Why don't they go on through if they've forgotten their manners? Then the door slowly opens from the inside. Thrust out is an arm with a fist holding a bunch of party hats like a torch.

I come up right behind the Birthday girls and I can see everything. There is that look on some of their faces like a bunch of puppies waiting to be fed. Mom says she tries to get girls into The Dance while they're young; so by the time they're thirteen or fourteen they will think about something other than boys.

Sun Run is holding a torch of party hats on his fist, and holding the door open with his shoulder. He is dressed up in corduroys and a white shirt, with moccasins on his feet, old and soft, fitting like ballet slippers. A white felt band holding back his hair and with beadwork fashioned in the cloud design of the southwest Amerinds. There is no one thing that will always set Run off different from anyone I've ever seen. It's the combination of moccasins, headband, shirt. My brother is gifted, and the girls know it and are caught. He knows it, and he gets it from Dad. It would be so nice to have power that is strange and secret, like theirs.

Sun Run and I have a secret. Deep in the night from our home, there is the sound from the roller rink. Only the rough kids go there, and we are never to go there. But late in the night, around and around we roll; at times, never letting on we know one another:

sometimes, rolling, I am gifted.
this I would have liked for my birthday. better
   even than the rollers.
a name, with power.

4

"Jack. Jack," Marianne says. Breathless and so shy, you know she could die. "Hi!" she says, standing there in front of him. He looks at her, real belligerent for a second, then he lunges at her and shoves her inside the Beaux Arts. She screams. And some of the other girls giggle really high and silly.

"Hi, Jack!" the other ones think to say, pushing each other to get inside. Hi, Jack, Hi, Jack, like it was something new and original they thought up to say.

These are not your frilly type of girls, either, like Patricia prissy Reynolds. Run says they are the ones who are like a no-man's-land coming into homeroom the first thing in the morning. Numb-eyed, he says they bring with them the hurt of the last fight with their moms or dads at the break-fast table; that is, if they were able to have break-fast. Sun Run says you'd be surprised how many American girls come to school without breakfast because they are being punished for thinking for themselves and arguing back. He says it takes them half a day to clean out their heads. And only after lunch do they shiver it off and become some kind of individuals that you can reach out and touch.

But not Angel Diavolad. No matter what happens in her house on a morning, she can bring it to school and work through it. But the other girls, Mom and Sun say, will never be your best students like Angelica. Sun says most probably they are the ones who, after going through high school, will hang around home for two years hoping to get married — I don't know if he's right about that. And if they don't marry, he says they will end up as secretaries over at the air base outside of Dayton.

Right now some of them get tongue-tied around Sun Run and think saying Hi is some new kind of thought. It is just because they are hurt and different by-yourself loners that Sun had me invite them to my Birthday.

"Don't invite some eleven-year-olds in your class," he told me.

"But almost twelve?" I asked him, glad he was going to take over and make up my mind for me.

"No almost twelve, either," he told me. "What you want with them?"

"I know them better," I told him. "They're my age."

"You don't want some know-nothings," he

said. "You want to invite some *girls*. Some ones you can learn from."

"Sure," I said, although now I can see they can't teach me much.

"You know it," Sun had said.

And so we picked them out.

"If it was up to me, I wouldn't have a party for nothing. I hate getting dressed up like a fool."

"If it was you," Sun said to me, "you wouldn't ask for nothing all your life."

"Want nothing," I said. Riding behind him on Jeremiah, we went around to each one of the houses of the girls we'd chosen.

"Moon Mother wants you to have this party, so you are having it," Sun had said.

I sure felt uncomfortable riding on Jeremiah. Never could I get used to the heat of a horse and the way he bumps me so hard up and down. I don't know how Sun can stand it. Give me skates, and cars.

"It's because you're afraid to fail," Sun had said, "why you want nothing. All little kids are like that sometimes, but you take the cake."

I told him, "I am not afraid, you don't know a thing. Because I just don't care for parties. And I ain't a little kid."

"Hah. Anybody keep on saying *ain't* is a little kid."

We went ahead and invited everyone. Sun stopped Jeremiah in front of each house. I had to slide down while Sun sat so still in the Saturday noon light — heat never seems to make him look wilted like it does me. And that day he never even looked toward a house when one of the girls came out. The first one was Angel. She smiled familiar, knowing me from the secret nights. She stared at Sun. The Diavolads have the nicest veranda in town, I'm thinking when I invite her. All the time I talked, she was looking over at Sun Run. Her face so dark and thoughtful. I remember once talking about her to Mom and Run —

"Diavolad," I once said. "What is Angelica?"

"Why, black," Mom said.

"No, but what *is* she?"

Then Sun said, "She means why does she look so different and act different?"

"Because they are Haitian," Mom said, "from Haiti."

"Ferocious Haiti," Sun said.

"Speaking about what you don't know," Mom told him.

"I know Haiti."

"You only know what you read," she told him. "You better believe it wasn't so awful for them with their mystery money."

"So why did they leave?" Sun asked. "Why is it 'mystery money'?"

"So why did we leave Cliffville?" Mom said, looking pleased with herself.

"Illogic. We left so my Moon Mother could rule," Sun told her. Then he was gone on Jeremiah.

All that was some time ago. The Diavolads are still different from me and probably richer than most people around here. I can't even imagine that Haiti they come from, but I didn't bother to look it up in the encyclopedia.

Inviting all the girls is far away next to now. Now we are ready to begin my party. Dad will come to the party, but he'll have to leave by five-thirty to be sure the evening meal at the college is fixed properly. I don't ever seem to see enough of Dad.

We begin my Birthday. Sun Run is taking his time, putting on a show with the party hats. The girls are all bunched around him. They wait their turns. Will I wait that way when I am thirteen or fourteen? I hate boys now. Maybe that's why I hate my brother. Do I hate Sun all the time? When you say brother, you can't hate. You can't hate a kin, Mom says. He is my closest kin. But maybe he can. Maybe that's it. He hates me.

We are standing in the small foyer to the Beaux Arts. Sun puts each party hat smack at the edge of each girl's hairline above the forehead. He takes time with each girl, stretching that thin gray elastic under a chin to hold the hat in place. Ever so gently, he cups a girl's face in his palms and slides that elastic through his fingers along her jowl. That done, he touches the hat with both hands

64

once and then smooths out the girl's hair on each side of her face. After Marianne, Sue Patterson got a hat, green, which tended to make the whiteness of her skin look sick.

"Do I look awful in it, Jack? I bet I look gross." Giving with her giggle that slides up the scale, where it ends before it falls.

Sue is the whitest girl I've ever seen in my entire life. If her eyes were pink, she would be albino.

"You're looking cool," Sun tells her.

Even the hair on her arms is white. I'm not talking about your color, like your black people and your white people. I mean that on a scale of white from one to ten, Sue wouldn't register because she is in a different place altogether.

"Am I sharp?" Giggling out of control into a screech. Blushing wild.

But, like all the girls, she finds my brother, Sun, *fascinating*. But, different from most of them, she won't get tongue-tied around him. She gets kind of loud and mouths a mile a minute, which is okay, since she is funny and kind of sweet.

"Oh, I know I'm ugly!"

"I'm not going to take you fishing," Sun tells her.

I like her a lot. She's a musician, too, like Angel. You can forgive her the way she is laughing and playing with Run, it's not her fault. But in school even the basketball boys will slow down

65

as they run out of the gym past the music room when Sue is practicing. With the violin nestled by her chin and cheek, you wouldn't think she was the same girl. That sad tremolo of hers, they call it, in clean string tones, spilling down the hall and washing over the sweaty ballplayers. The guys just heaving, with their necks and backs dripping wet. The music melts the tiredness out of them, I swear you can see it happening. And she just smiles a little at them, not embarrassed at all the way I'd be, the way she will get with Sun. But seeing the guys and not even missing a beat, but just going ahead and wrapping the music around half the school.

It is sure something to have a first violin like her to soothe the middle school on a heat-aching day. Add Angelica Diavolad joining with Sue at lunch time on her cello to make a bigger, stronger sound that will take in everything you ever thought music could do. The one girl is snow white and the other is coal black. And the two of them are exactly alike, the best of one kind you hope will just live forever.

Arilla Adams, me, is the last to get a party hat. They never even gave me a middle name. Moon-flower? No, but I remember old James False Face used to call me something like that. The girls have on their silly party hats and file inside Mom's studio. You'd think I count for nothing. Sun doesn't take any time adjusting my hat, either.

"Just remember it's *my* party!" I have time to whisper to him.

"You didn't want it," he says, but I pass him by, leaving him to come in last. I hear him slam a door off the foyer and know he is going to waste time in the bathroom.

I never take for granted that Mom is mine, and I sure wonder sometimes how I ever got so lucky. But this I never would've imagined she would do with her studio. Mom's studio is one huge room, all hardwood floors cleaned and polished, and with a bank of windows across one side. There is a mirror the full length of the other side — it cost a fortune to put there — with a bar in front of it for the dancers to extend their legs. Except for a few chairs, that is all the room ever had in it for dancers to take turns resting on. Most the time they lay dead tired on the floor with towels slung around their necks. Mom never uses a piano, just records and a player in the corner, and a tape recorder and a drum to beat with the hands. It's a conga drum with a few maracas on the floor beside it.

But this! Over the ceiling lights there is something that looks like cotton candy to make the glow shimmer in great cobweb circles. There are balloons hanging in bunches down from the cotton candy and on the walls and in every corner. There are streamers all different colors hanging down the mirrors so that it looks twice as much.

There is a table all decorated in bright crepe paper with a glass punchbowl full of ice, with these cartons of ice cream and big bottles of soft drinks. There are paper plates next to the bowl, cups, and there is a big cake. I am just drawn to the table and the cake. I know I am moving, but it's like walking on air. The cake has white icing with pink and green letters and candles. It says: ARILLA! HAPPY BIRTHDAY!

There, right there on that crepe paper I didn't see a present. A big box, I wasn't even looking for it, so I didn't see it. A big square box about five inches high. This present must be from my family. The card without an envelope, I see it says: *Arilla! For you, from Mom.*

Now, that's funny. You mean there are more presents from Jack Sun and my dad? No time to think about it now. For this room looks like a prom night for a hundred kids.

Mom has hurried the girls to put down their books out of the way under the table. She has hurried them to place their presents next to the big one of hers on the table. She is hurrying and arranging them around me where I stand at the cake. I feel her hand and then her arm around my shoulder. I look up and straight into the mirror. Here we all are through the mirror. Seeing us, myself, is like seeing strangers all dressed up going to a party. Looking at us, the strangers don't feel like us at all, but they are still us. Me in one of Mom's dresses she altered for me. I always did want it. It's this soft, combed cotton material with a curled-collar sweater dyed to match. It and the dress are beige. I like the outfit, even if I do look dumpy in it. I always look dumpy in anything on the knee. I look best in blue jeans and tank top.

I wouldn't've known my mom, seeing her in the mirror. She's all made up — not in your regular performing make-up. But like a clown. No — what do they call it? Like a mime! Like those who say nothing and will act out with hands and bodies. Mom's wearing this white paint on her face like a mask, with lines of black paint in star points above and below her eyes. She outlined her mouth in a droopy night blue. I start to turn to look at her, but she holds my head so I can just see through the mirror. Slowly, she performs this wondrous thing.

With her face on a level with mine, she lets her head jiggle and shake until it appears to wobble off her shoulder. It lands on my shoulder right next to my head. All at once I have this sad, painted face with great, round eyes and fluttery lashes. I have two faces. One face is pale and blank, but the other face shows everything I think and feel. Mom, you know so much about me.

The head wobbles off my shoulder and back onto my mom's. She bows to me in the mirror. It gets me so embarrassed but so happy, too. The girls just laugh and clap their hands.

There's my dad through the mirror. I didn't

see him standing off a ways from the rest of us. Then comes Sun Run leaping into the mirror. Sun has black war paint on his face. He wears just enough to make his nose stronger and his forehead broader. Always just enough to make the rest of his skin look sunburnt, of The People. Why did he have to wear a war bonnet? He bows to me in the mirror, and white and black feathers of the bonnet wave and flutter.

My dad has no paint on and no war bonnet. He stands there in just a nice, clean white shirt and creased trousers, with his hands deep in his pockets. He will never take his hands out of his pockets. Looking at me, coming close up to the mirror. I'm so glad to have him always himself.

Through the mirror I say, "I didn't know for sure you would get here."

"For sure," he said, "I wouldn't miss your Birthday. Happy Birthday, Arilla *Nixa*."

Now all the girls say, "Happy Birthday, Arilla Nixa."

Sun Run laughs at them and they know they've done it wrong.

"Not her middle name," Sun tells them. "*Nixa* mean number-two person, and *Nixa* mean boy or girl grandchild; also mean much more." Pretending he's giving them a lesson. "Arilla have no middle name, since I took the sun. She can have moon, but she always afraid of moonlight."

When my brother wears his war bonnet, he has to speak like a dumb actor playing an Indian in some western. Like he's just learning English and he thinks he's being funny.

I know why Dad called me it.

To remind me he has always cared and always will. To say his caring is more than just himself; maybe it's all of his who lived and all who died, caring.

Knowing things and not knowing how I know. Where do they come from like that, even on my Birthday?

Jack-Run brings some chairs for the party girls. All this time they've been watching Sun and Mom and Dad. They've never seen people act the way their own families never would.

I sit cross-legged on the floor with my dad and Pearl. The other girls scramble for chairs.

"You pretty excited, huh?" Pearl says. Everybody is laughing and talking, although as soon as the talking goes in my head, I forget what it was about. Parties are like that, I guess, making you all hot and bothered. You want to open presents right off, but kids here will wait, pretending they aren't thinking a thing about them.

Jack-Run has arranged the chairs facing the room, backs to the mirror, like we are going to have a show. Well, I don't mind. The girls are all excited and not even looking bored. Settling down and acting like young women. Because Sun is now standing so still right next to them and not looking at them. He is at attention in his war bonnet and make-up. And taking them and all of us to a time when many warriors stood that way on flat land, or sat so still on horseback — for hours watching, waiting for buffalo or even war.

He is standing high on a rise watching the sun go down. I have seen it done like that in *Cheyenne Autumn*, but Sun is better than any actor in a movie. He may look like a put-on, but he is for-real feeling it.

Sun crouches and rests his wrists on one knee. Tracking man or animal until the feeling and the mood fade out of him.

The way he can capture us and turn us loose when he wants to. He looks out into the studio and we follow his gaze.

My mom standing there in a black leotard and with the white paint on her face. She takes a walking pose with toes turned out. She jerks from left to right. Her hands flutter together from side to side. We clap in time with the silent flutter. Her hands and arms outline the shape of a large crate at her side. She struggles to lift the crate by one corner and staggers with it down the room to almost drop it on her toe before she sets it down.

My Birthday girls laugh. Sun laughs. I'm sitting with my mouth open and I didn't even know it. I swear, I can almost see the crate that isn't there, and how it almost broke her big toe.

Mom comes back for another crate. By her hands moving and touching, shaping space, we figure out the room is full of crates we didn't even know were there. But now I see them. I see all-different-size crates. Mom picks out the ones that are all the same size, I guess to build something.

She lurches around under the weight of a second crate to finally let it fall on top of the first crate. Standing back to size up her work, going all the way around it. Working faster, and her legs are so rubbery they never take her the way she wants to go in the quickest way. Her head wobbles and is so funny. Now I have to worry about this crate she's lifting and practically running with. It's got her off balance. It's going to slip and pin her — !

I'm practically on my feet when my dad pulls me back. It's going to be okay. She has the crate balanced again and heaves it up on the other two. How she flings it so far — ! Mom struggles until she has I don't know how many crates piled so high, never once asking for any help. Then she stops still.

Mom picks up a pile of something invisible from the floor. By the way she makes a great circle out of it on the floor and the way she takes it and twirls it over her head, we know it's a rope. Next she picks up something heavy and ties it to the rope. She flings it ever so high up to the topmost crate — it's a hook of some kind, tied to the rope. And it holds. She tests it with all of her weight pulling down on the rope. The hook holds. It's in real deep. And she's going — there's something up there — she's going to climb clear to the top to get something! My goodness.

Everyone laughs and claps as Mom begins to wiggle up the rope. Hand over hand she goes, at first so careful. When she is more sure, she goes faster. But the rope begins to sway and she has to slow up again. Still, the trip up there takes her no time at all. She's a good climber, better than I'll ever be. Mom would say that because she has so little weight, she won't have to fight herself going up. If I were to climb it, I'd have to fight my own weight. Dancers are slim so they don't have to fight their weight, which is just like fighting gravity, Mom says.

Everybody claps real hard. When Mom stands up there straight and tall, Jack-Run claps wildly and whistles through his teeth. Watch her bend over to pick up something. Something so little and delicate. She nestles it under her chin. But bending like that and straightening up again has caused that crate to teeter. With her holding something wiggly while trying to keep her balance. My goodness, she can't get her balance good. The crate — !

Falling. Floating and tumbling. So graceful, with one arm held high so's to protect the little small thing in her hand. She falls to the floor hard on her back. Dad holds my arm.

"Just make-believe," he says. "Makes you almost believe she was up to the ceiling."

I see it all right before my eyes. She'd have to be hurt in a fall like that.

I know it's just make-believe and that this is my party. My party is so different, someone could even get hurt — is that it?

Everybody watching my Mom hurt, I whisper to Dad:

"Is it that it's possible to get hurt even at my party?"

"Truth," he whispers. "At any moment. All you can imagine is possible."

Mom's hand and something in it move. Her fingers, opening and bending. Life flows up her arm, lifts her head with the mime's face. Holding a thing in both hands, she rises. Wobbly, legs rubbery, she comes and puts something in my lap.

It's a little kitten or maybe a puppy. We all laugh because we know it's there, only it isn't. Mom bows to me and everyone. All the girls clap and the show is over.

Sue Patterson says, "Miss Lilly, that was wonderful! You ought to teach a course in that — what's it called?"

Mom smiles. "You know, I'd better think about doing that, too." She's talking gentle, like she is out of breath. I see she is perspired. "Now," she says. "Arilla, you open your presents, right? Sun, put on some music."

She has her arm around me as we go to the table. I love the way she holds me close like that, in front of the girls. They can't help see the way she cares about me. Maybe they think I have some hidden something to make her think so much of me. They don't know I have nothing. Nothing at all.

Sun puts on a record of Coyote society, I don't know where in the world he got it. Mom used to send off and get him things Indian — I mean, Amerind — but not so much anymore. Or maybe he just sent off for the record. Sun does so many things like that, sending off clear to some Library of Congress for all kinds of things. He is so fond of Coyote warriors more than any other kind because they always had the power of what he says is cunning and endurance. He says Coyote men always were better at running long distances and could dance better and play games better than any other warriors. The great, unseen power sent the coyote to wander the earth — that's how Sun tells it — and the coyote knew how to talk to The People.

Opening the presents from my Birthday girls. Sun begins to dance warrior in front of them. If I look through the mirror, I can watch him. He jumps and twists, going faster, in time with the music, until Mom gives him a look and he stops. The girls, my friends, don't know whether to watch me open their presents or to watch Run. I could never be like him. He never has any embarrassment about jumping warrior in front of anybody.

The first present is from Marianne. Marianne is not so much shy, Mom says, as she is experi-

enced and tries to hide it, whatever that means.
All I know is that her dad has his own apartment.
Her mom teaches hair-beautician at the technical
school. Most of the time Marianne and her older
brothers are there home by themselves.

I knew it. She got me this necklace of polished
stones. It will fit me like a choker, and that makes
me feel like somebody's dog.

"Isn't that pretty!" Mom says.

"Let me see," Sun says.

I hold up the necklace so they all can see in
the mirror. Sun grins and knows how I feel about
things. The girls all look at one another. Not a
one thought to ask the other—?

The next two presents are stone necklaces. One
is a big pendant on a chain from Mickey Hill. I
could've picked it up in the street and polished
it myself. Good-looking chain. The other is from
Pearl Wingard. She's supposed to be this real
tough kid, but I think she is just overtired from
having to watch out for a lot of little sisters. I
hold each one of the necklaces up and dare not
look at my brother. I see my dad kind of looking
at me in alarm at the presents. I just smile over
the necklaces so he won't feel bad for me. What
is on his mind to make him seem a little too upset,
and where is his present? And Sun's? I figure
they're getting me something together. Maybe it
didn't get here in time, if they got it out of the
catalogue. Wouldn't it be cool if they got me a
real pedigreed dog from Spiegel's in Chicago? I'd

keep her in my room. She'd be a cocker — they have pages of them — and she'd be my own pet. I never had any animals. Sun always did. I just had my brother.

The present I open next is from Angel. You'd know she'd think of something special!

"It's made from lucite," Angel says in my ear. I look at her in the mirror. She is really so kind and always so calm. Just forever knowing how to be her own self. "You can put one thing in it or many things. I put that package of dried flowers in it just to show you. But you can use it for your glasses so you will always know where they are on your night table. Or use it for some special treasure, like favorite earrings."

"Oh, I think it's beautiful," I tell her, looking at the little bag of tiny flowers in it. It is this clear plastic rectangle about three inches high on a plastic base. You really could stand glasses up in it and always know where they were. But I don't wear glasses.

"Thank you, Angel." The words don't come out so well. All of a sudden I'm about to break up in tears, so I hurry to the next thing.

"Yes, O pinme next! O pinme next!" Lou Ann pulling at my arm until finally I understand what she's saying, so I open hers next. Funny how when you open someone's present, what you know of them just seems to be there in your mind. She hangs around Mom's studio, but she doesn't much dance unless Mom decides to do some square dances. She just loves my mom even if she is too closed-mouth to say anything. You can just tell. Her mom takes these courses and goes to conferences to get a Masters-PhD. And Lou Ann wears the same pair of jeans for a week. Mom says she doesn't care if Lou Ann's mother is irresponsible. She says, "That child is old enough to change her socks."

Lou Ann's present is so flat and square I know it has to be a magazine, or something like that. I get myself ready to "be enthusiastic," as Mom would say. I open the wrapping. How in the world did she ever find it — no one would've believed it.

This paper book on how to *Build Your Own American Indian Village* — "Use this book to build the model. Learn about the history of the American Indian. In the village, Indians used the knowledge passed down from one generation to the next. These happy peoples were skilled at building practical and sturdy dwellings."

I mean, it's this paper *punch-out* book. A *whole Indian village* you can punch out and glue together. Punch-outs are always for little kids, but this stuff has to be *tough*.

"Sun," I say, "come take a look at what Lou Ann — " He's already pushed his way right up next to me. Taking the magazine, whatever you call it, right out of my hands to leaf through it.

Lou Ann is acting like she will go to pieces if Sun doesn't like it. Who's it supposed to be for, anyhow?

Sun would never embarrass her on purpose. He'd never pick on a girl because of her dumbness. Except me.

And then my brother had to read some instructions just like they were this ancient warrior song:

"Carefully push forms from the pages
    (Ayaya!).
Square and numbered tabs at the edge of
    the forms must be glued together
(To fall in battle is bold and brave!).
Use a white glue such as Elmer's (Ayaya!).
Leave plenty of time for the forms to dry
    (Attack! Attack! And die — Ayaya!)"

Well, I mean, those girls went into hysterics. You could hear Sue Patterson's shriek of laughing above everyone else. But it wasn't real insulting to Lou Ann or me or any one of us, the way Sun made up the fighting warrior with the instructions. It was just plain funny. Because while my brother chanted, he had to hold up the pages so we could see the little punch-out elk and deer, and the little green forest trees all alike, and long houses and rounded buildings and these tiny domelike huts used for sweat baths during the summer, so the book said.

"Funny thing is," Sun began, and not with

meanness either, I could tell, "you have a whole village, clear down to the eating utensils and the food and buffalo chips [now that was a lie!], but you don't have not one single punch-out red-man."

"Sun, cut it out," I said, but I was still laughing with the girls and happy they were having a good time.

"Not even one old rummy," Sun went on, "and I reckon that's because we are too ferocious, even flat out in one dimension on colored paper."

Instead of handing the book back to me, my brother handed it over first to Lou Ann. "Neat," he said to her, still not mean or sarcastic. "You must've searched ten shopping malls to dig that up."

"I didn't know they was for-real Indian," one girl behind me whispered and was shushed. "I thought they was just passing — " and was shushed again.

All the time Lou Ann's eyes were shining at Sun because of his backhanded praise, I guess. I had to hurry and open the one last present from the girls before she really did fall all over Sun in front of everybody.

The present was from Sue Patterson. And if I'd used half a brain, I'd a opened hers second or third. Now I'd given her every chance in the world to get anxious and upset.

"I *know* you're not going to take to it," she had to say.

81

"Now, Susan," Mom said, "just you relax. I'm sure it's fine."

"I tried," Sue went on, "but I had to take most of the money I made at Gahagan's to help pay for my cavities."

"Susan, you don't pay for *cavities*," Mom told her.

"I mean, for the fillings. I never can stay away from chocolate and I hate milk."

"Will ya let her open the present?" Sun said. "Great thundering hooves, you were sure born with the verbal trots."

"Sun Run," Dad says. Almost forgot my dad was here, he can go into himself so. There in the mirror he was smiling at me, making everything all right.

"Oh, that's real nice," I say, opening up the present. And it really is nice. All the girls want to see. "Letmesee! Letmesee!"

"I hope it's all right, 'cause I didn't know you didn't have a middle name then and so I was worried." Sue says it in one breath a mile a minute. "Miss Lilly, I almost asked you every day last week when I passed by the studio whether Arilla had a middle name. Arilla, I hope you like gold. I could have got it in silver or ebony, but I did like the gold on the pale blue best, don't you? I hope the lettering appeals to you. The simplest lettering is always the best. When I had my name *emblazoned* on my violin case, I made

82

sure the letter was not too *ornate*, but expensive-looking — "

"Great blundering wolves!" Sun yelled at the top of his lungs. "Chee-sus, you're makin' the natives restless!"

Sue's shriek of laughter filled the room. "Oh, Jack!"

Mom rolled her eyes to the ceiling, like to say, what could you do with him?

Well. I wasn't minding Sun now at all. If you forgot about his painted face and the war bonnet, he was almost being pretty nice, like any other brother cutting up at an individual's Birthday. Never kind of scary at all, Sun wasn't, the way I knew and Mom and Dad knew he could be almost any other minute. I was sure glad of that. Anyhow, what it was Sue Patterson gave me:

Some real nice stationery paper, the lightest blue, with my name in gold at the top in the nicest print I could have wanted. If ever I have a letter to write anyone, I'll sure use it, too. I don't think I've ever had any real writing paper before.

"Sue, thank you. I sure do like it." And I meant it, too.

It's my turn to be real nervous. The only present left on the table is the big square one from my mom. I'm about to open it when Mom says, real fast, "Now, girls, I think we will have the cake and ice cream."

I know my mom's voice and the moods that can crinkle or smash it up; that make it tinkle sweet or make it cracked and dried. But this time the sound of it is thin and wispy, like the first sign of dust gathering under my bed.

"I haven't even opened your present," I tell her. The girls looking on and smiling.

"Stony, will you cut the cake?" Mom says before she thinks. At once her hand flutters up, picking at the neck of her leotard. She just forgot how Sun hates to hear her call Dad Stony. Sun will say the nickname is "undignified," but I don't mind it at all. It's Mom's way of liking my dad and the way she will bring him down to her size, which is still large enough. She will say, to take him out of the foreshadow; and I say, on into the for-real.

I mean, Sun-Stone is no more Dad's real name than is Stony. It's really more like Sun-Who-Stone, but who wants to remember all that when even that's not it, either? Then, to have your brother, all of Jack Sun Run Adams, to remember, too.

So Mom doesn't want me to open her present to me just now, with Sun over there cutting his eyes at her for saying Stony. So why wouldn't she want me to open it? Because she doesn't think I'll like it? Because, once opened, I'll have to go on and ask about the other one — the one that's not even there on the table or anywhere I can see?

84

Because Sun and Dad's present is one she'd like never to have me open.

So she is stalling.

My Birthday is beginning to gather in clouds full of foreshadow and for-real, getting darker. My dad coming up to the table to cut the cake, and Sun Run holding himself back in one long straight line of rebellion. Darting eyes, like lightning and a force of thunder.

All at once Sun-Run is dancing warrior again, with just his feet moving. Hands behind his back, he makes a turning, twisted path through the girls. He is in between my dad and my mom before Dad can even take up the cake knife. And jiggling, swooping warrior, he takes up the last present that isn't invisible to lift it up over their heads and place it in my arms. Sweeping white silk ribbon off corners of the present and smoothing his fingers under the edges of the paper. I place my hand there just to help him along. And he forces me to get in a hurry to open the package.

"Sun, we are going to have cake and ice cream now," Mom says. Angry.

"Let her open the present," Dad says, smiling at me.

"Yea," Sun says, "Arilla wants to open it."

I look up just as he is giving Mom the lightning. "But if Mom wants us to eat — "

"Yes," Mom cuts in, "it's getting late."

Sun sweeps the tissue paper off and unravels the hand-done bow. He makes a grand show of wrapping the girls and tying them.

"Pretty presents," he tells them. Jiggling and dancing as they swat at the ribbon. They are giggling and saying, "Oh, my hair, you messed my hair. You, Jack. Get out-a-here, you're terrible. Isn't he awful?" Even Angel seems to enjoy the party ribbon, like a silver scar on the dark side of her hand.

"You, Sun!" Mom says.

"Yes, cut it out, Run," Dad says. "Let Arilla open the box."

I really do want to see what's in the box.

I see Sun walk away like he will leave, and the girls come crowding around me.

"What is it? What'd you get?" they ask me.

Sometimes I think Mom will prove she doesn't favor me. I mean, maybe one time she will forget or be too busy and will hurry and buy me just anything. But she never does.

I open the box to find it is packed full and tight. "Look at that!" I pull out this really beautiful deep-brown suede jacket, a really heavy kind to keep you warm, and real soft, deep-brown corduroy pants to match. Both the jacket and pants have these neat zippers, and on the pockets, too. And this long-sleeved shirt, dyed in the softest yellows and beiges to shape and outline distant geese heading south with a cold winter sun on them.

"Man!" And in the box — I pick them up now

— a pair of dark-brown highboots. Real leather and with an inch heel.

"Arilla, wear it to school," Sue Patterson says, speaking about the whole outfit. "I wish . . ." But she doesn't finish.

I'll wear it to school. After Thanksgiving. Maybe I'll wear it for a whole week.

"Mom." I hold up the jacket and pants against me. "Thank you for everything."

"You're welcome, baby."

"Thank you," I just have to say again and start folding the clothes back into the box. Lou Ann helps me with the boots. I see the girls smiling, but they get uneasy, shaking out their hair. They just seem to stare off. Maybe only Angel ever got such nice stuff for a birthday.

Mom takes the box and makes it neat beside the other presents. "There. Time for cake and ice cream. Stony, what am I to do, the ice cream is hard still."

"I'll slice it. That will be all right, won't it?"

"Noooo!" It's my brother yelling. He's standing, peering around from the foyer. "Arilla! One more present for you."

"What?" I say. He's looking so proud of himself, he doesn't even bother to fool around warrior.

"From Dad and me."

"Really?" I say.

"Now, would I lie?"

"Where!"

"Come on, then," Dad says. I and the girls follow him across the room toward Sun.

"Ooooh!" My Birthday girls all excited, ready for the next surprise.

"Outside?" I'm about to burst. "Really?"

"Really," Sun says. "Stop saying 'Really.' "

I try to tell if Sun has something up his sleeve, but I can't tell. Mom has her arm around me. She and I go out the door last and she holds the door for me.

Outside, there is shade all up and down the avenue. I love shade of an afternoon best. Reminds me of some time when I was little, with shade all around. Just out there on the edge of my memory, it makes me feel strange.

Never even noticed before how hot it is. Why is this town just ever so hot in the autumn? But we will have a lot of late fall rain, I bet.

My dad and my brother disappear in the alley. The girls are following close, whispering and walking on Sun's heels.

Mom gives me this whisper just as we catch up with the party girls.

"Arilla? I'd of given you the outfit anyway. Just try to take it easy."

"What, Mom?"

"Your dad just went along with it. Sun meant well, he worked so hard."

We stop right where Sun keeps Jeremiah between the buildings. And I get this sinking feeling. "You mean — Mom! The outfit, the boots — !"

"Keep your voice down. Now, try not to show . . . Remember how hard they had to work to get it all ready."

I feel like choking. There's Jeremiah, farther back than usual, away from the alleyway. And in front of him —

No.

It's like the party girls fold their arms at the same time. Looking at one another, I know they'll never be the same with me again. Not that we were ever close. But now it's like they're saying it's not enough that I have Sun for a brother, I have to go and have everything else, too. Why do families have to overdo it?

But none of them know how I'm feeling.

So this is my present.

It is a white. More than anything, it's a color breed. They say they color from aging grays to the albinos with blue eyes. And I have seen them almost brown.

It most often is called *spotted*, but people get it wrong and call it a *paint*. Paints are always pintos. My brother never liked the pinto, and so I grew to dislike it. But he can go on forever about the appaloosa called *spotted*. How it came from the Spanish long ago, on through the wild mustangs and was used by the Pierced Nose people against the white-skinned enemy.

Sun tells how the appaloosa was fast and ferocious: "The enemy hated all those spotted war-riors who would fight and kill; people would eat all others that weren't spotted, too."

Sun lies. He says Jeremiah is palomino, but I know better. Jeremiah is too dark, a gypsy no-breed who acts proud and showy. Maybe some palomino bred from a chestnut stallion with a dark mare.

So this is it. This is mine.

"Arilla, how do you like it?" Dad says. I can tell how excited he is. What can I say? He just wanted me to have what my brother has.

Sun brings it slowly forward, holding it lightly by a rope bridle he will use when he is training. He tries to smirk, but he is anxious to see what I will do.

"Is it a boy or girl?" I ask him.

Sun bursts out laughing. The spotted's eyes flare up a sudden. "Horses you call colt for boy — "

"You think I don't know?" I cut him off. "Is it a filly?" Keeping my voice low, but the spot-ted's eyes still flare.

"She's a mare," Sun says, "going on nine and a half."

"What's her name?" I ask him, like Mom says, all matter-of-fact. Just like I've got on the boots and corduroys, I move on up to the animal real slow and take hold of the bridle with Sun.

"You name her," Sun says.

My Birthday girls, Sun and Angel and all the

90

rest. Hear them fidgeting and whispering — " 'S hot out here. We going to stand around all day?" Tired of it and burning jealous, they've had enough. But this is between Sun and me.

"She sure must already have a name," I say.

"Sure she has a name," Sun says. "See if you can guess."

"Come," Mom says behind me, "cake and ice cream!" to the startled girls. "Inside! Inside!"

"But what about Arilla?" It's Pearl asking. I never gave her a glance.

"She'll be along in a minute," Mom tells her.

The mare and me are eyeball to eyeball, with all her strength coiled and her ears active and always moving. I can't help thinking, So I own a horse, just like my brother.

The mare wasn't about to back up from me, either. Still, I knew how to stand quiet and not appear afraid. I stay at her head, studying it. For I've been around Sun Run long enough to know that, like a person's face, a horse's will tell its, well, quality.

She has large eyes with wide space between them, showing that her brain is good-sized and she is not a "dumb" animal.

Good, flaring nostrils. But not so straight, the line from nose to head, looking from the side.

"You looking at the head when you should be looking at the whole beast," Sun says.

My dad just grunts. I forgot he was even there. Next to him, moving up carefully, is Angel. She always seems so interested in things.

"Let Arilla do it her way," Dad says. "She hasn't had your practice."

"One thing about Arilla," Sun says, glad to have Angel for an audience, "she never lets nothing go, but for sure she don't know it yet."

"For sure you don't know even more," I tell him. And then I say about the mare: "Her muzzle hair will never change."

"Truth," Dad says. "And she is a good Palouse."

"You remember I told you," Sun says. "The appaloosa name comes from the Palouse River in Idaho, where the Pierced Nose people lived."

"I recall," I tell him.

"The enemy never liked the Palouse horse."

"They liked the dark horse," I say.

"The blacker the horse, the swifter the course," Sun says.

"So *they* said," my dad says.

"But appaloosa is all its own," I say.

"So this Palouse mare is . . ." Sun begins for me.

" . . . is strong and good," I tell him. I don't touch her, but stand back from her. "Good, shining coat. Strong neck." I stand farther back. "She's some goose-rumped. She's lean over all, but with straight hind legs. I don't know. I don't know something about bone, I forget. But I bet she can run."

"So with her color, can you name her?" Sun wants to know.

Practically giving it away. It's running added to a color — did you ever see dirty dishwater? As far as I care, appaloosa is the purest grotesque horse in the world. And as far as I care, this one is as ugly as sin. Like dirty dishwater after all the dishes are done. And with white soap chips a-floating on the water. This Palouse has a white-spotted rump.

Or think of little clouds way off in the distance of gray sky.

Why does she have to be this different, and apart from everything? Never cared for any horse, and what I care about this one is not far from pure hate. Let me lie down and just pull the covers up over my head.

"Thank you very, very much," I tell Dad and Sun, trying to sound like I mean it.

"A horse all your own," Angel says. She smiles like an older girl who never spent her time thinking about horses. Would never need to consider one if Sun hadn't owned one.

"You can ride her sometime," I tell her. I'm ready to get away.

"So what's her name?" Sun picking at my bones. He has to know so bad. He will never think I have any brains because I'm female.

"It's either full or half," I say to him. I'll never let him know how afraid I am of horses.

93

"Or even new, or quarter," Dad says, smiling so warm at me.

"It's one of them and then running?" I ask. All of a sudden I'm almost sick with the smell of horses on afternoon heat.

"Better the thing itself and running," Sun says, looking at me like he's disappointed I got it.

"Moon Running, then," I tell him, and then: "I'm going." I turn to start back through the alley.

"Let her go," I hear Dad say. "It's too much surprise all at once."

"The other way around," Sun calls after me.

"Running Moon," I say softly.

"You got it. She's got it," Sun says. "Happy hunting, kid. I'll teach you to ride every day on the trail. You'll love it," Sun calls after me.

I walk on back to my party, what's left of it. Sun took my Birthday, after all.

"Palouse is so ugly she's pretty," Sun is saying.

"What's its name — Moon Running?" I hear Angel ask them.

"The other way," Dad tells her. He sounds happy. I'm glad. "Running Moon," he tells Angel.

Either way, I know two things. I hate the Palouse. I'm stuck with her.

5

First time, me. Slipping away from the quiet.

I'll be back soon, Mother telling Run. *You play with her some, you hear?*

Sun Run saying, *You hurry back, you hear? Make me stay all day — you hurry up.*

Hurrying too long and no more Mother talking. Sun Run so high above, throwing his circle. Sun is all, snorting and stamping. Shake the sky with his circle roping. Then I see blue sprinkles cover the hills. Run has done it with his circle? I like sprinkles to touch. Quiet in the hills, and blue dot sprinkles in the breeze. Too many quiet all around.

"You be all right in the shade," he saying.

Never touched so many blues so far away.

"Nobody bother you under the sumac. You stay, you hear? She'll be back soon."

"You going talking?" Never mind him going. But who to keep me from the quiet?

Sun staring down, laughing. "No, you. You

keep talking." He laughs again, saying, "Arilla, see the game?"

Sun throwing the circle on a ground, where catching the green and little stones and one stick I playing with. The circle holding is the game?

"Now. Take your dibble stick and step in with both feet," he saying.

I take my dibble by the knob. Stepping on a green with both feet. The circle holding:

"Me!"

I am the game.

"Yeah, you. Now stay still."

"Keep talking, Sun."

"Okay, Arilla, but stay where you are."

"I am a game."

"Sure. Watch the lasso."

Sun making a lasso climbing up my feet. Up my knees. He stopping it right around my belly. He pulling back the rope. A lasso tighten. Sun Run is hurrying.

"Keep talking?"

Sun Run is hurrying a line over sumac's arm. Tying it.

"Now," he saying. "You can pull on it and even swing on it."

Glad with more talking. Still I am a game.

"You mustn't loosen the lasso around you."

"Sun Run?"

"You must stay in the circle. If you don't, the sumac will fall down and hurt you."

Sumac. Pulling on a line to the arm. Sumac does not fall.

"No, only if you *untie* the circle," Sun saying. "You stay in the shade and be safe. She'll be back soon, you hear? You can swing in the shade."

"Keep talking." Sun Run hurrying ca-loping down the way. Too long is hurrying and no more Sun talking.

Keeping quiet with my stick. Nothing many. Nothing but a breeze. Bright all around a shade. Plenty light by my swing-sling near a porch.

Now, that's the place. Never knowing the swing is there. The house is there when I see it.

Running to get in a house. But circle grabbing hold and pulling me down. So sitting, leaning on a lasso. So tight no hands can get inside it. Hurts. So going on back and leaning on a sumac. Maybe somebody come along to play. Little black ants going up and down a sumac. Fingers standing in their way. Catching ants and shaking them on a ground. Looking like shake a pepper.

Now hold my hands behind me on a sumac. Nobody coming along. Over there. The way through many trees, so many children go. When it's cold. Not now. In a snow, tracks, and with things to ride on. Now no snow with a breeze and a shade.

So many light along the way. We in a yard at an end of the way where more trees. Other way where Mother go and Sun go. So many light up

97

and up to where I can see Sun put sprinkles down the sky. Reach, but never touch them so far away. Leaning on a rope but still so far. Going on back to a sumac. My hands on a circle where it's so tight. Maybe squeeze a thumbs inside the lasso, all along it until it not so tight. Taking a long time in a quiet. Where Mother hurrying? I like a light all the blue dot things up there. Pieces shaken by Sun. Let me go.

But stopping. The sumac will fall down?

Pulling on a line. Reaching up to arm of sumac. Lifting feet off a ground. Swinging but hurting my arms pulling. Stop. And pushing sumac and can't make it fall. Thumbs, loosen a circle some more. Just a little and watching a sumac. Leaves moving. None fall. Maybe when a sumac won't be looking. Keep watching and loosening. Sumac won't make a move. So holding a circle in my hands.

Let it drop? All a time, seeing so sweet a light and blue sprinkles all up and up. Would take a sumac with me if I can.

Standing still. Slowly. Bringing arms down with a circle. Tall sumac in just a breeze. Sumac arms high and leaves shading in a quiet. Can make my arms high. See? Sumac must not make a move. Dropping that circle down around my feet. Watching. Nothing but a quiet and the leaves. Stepping out of circle.

And run!

Not looking back there. And when I do, Sumac

is not so tall. All trees stand still but for the leaves. Shading and waving in a breeze. Me going up and up in many sounds coming all around. Leaving quiet with shade. Leaving sumac not falling way down there.

Sun lies.

Knowing Mother hurrying the town is somewhere. Knowing but so many trees. Looking back maybe seeing sumac and a house. So many trees all around and stand too tall. Keep on going. Seeing some blue in a sky and some shaken down. Getting close and I having something, my dibble stick. Never know having it in a hand. Maybe sit and playing with it.

Sitting. Holding stick tight sitting. Feeling little jumps all over me so tiring.

Mother, I say. But no talking. Just some sound all around better than a quiet.

Lay me down, blinking at the blue. Holding stick straight way up and pieces stick in crumbs fall a my eyes. Sitting. Cleaning out the eyes. Getting a stick and we going on up the way. Big trees keeping me from seeing. Town and Mother hurrying and talking. Keeping on. Maybe will seeing some blue on a ground where Sun . . .

Do see up ahead — something.

Brother? Take care of me.

"Sun Run!"

Sure. Maybe him. Not seeing me in tall trees.

"Wait, Sun!"

For me to follow? Follow. But just trees. No

finding him or Mother or a town. Go on where I saw him. Trees opening. Running again holding stick. Tallness of weeds now. Banging a stick on one tree to another through weeds. And slow down some. Breathing and walking hard and walking for a long kind of time.

Stop. Hearing no ca-loping. Going on. Harder going up and up. Maybe next tree showing Sun hanging around. Up the way, finding there it is everywhere!

All the whole place full of blue sprinkles. Flowers! A-swaying and a-blueing in a breeze. Running to them, me. Must be way far up to be with them. See Sun didn't do the flowers. Him just playing games. Tell him so. Him hiding was a game?

The flowers all clear to one side. And water running real wide place and trees all along where. Dropping dibble and just run around run around. So happy. Pulling hands full a blue tops and some yellow tops way down low. Holding so many bright blue in a my hands, up a my arms. Hold them and smelling them real deep. Breathing them and feeling them nice. Hold and hear them humming. Hear the water stream and humming. Buzzing.

All close a my face and ears to smell them. Which coming the most. Hearing flowers, smelling stream and hum-buzzing.

Oh! So quick, all hurting. Arms! Neck! Everything! All a once, scaring and buzzing. I slip away and no shoes on. Toes sting and making me jump a-hurting.

Let my flowers go falling. Cry, step up high. Get away from so much hurting. Slap! Slap! And see the big ants flying. Cry, and slap fly swatting.

And run! For a stream just put the cold all around me. Run and run.

Hurts. I cry, running for a stream. Tall trees, where it's safe and climb and hide in a leaves.

Tall trees too much for climbing. Have to hurry. Hurting me all up my dress. Can't stop to cry. Just I see tall tree with no leaves at a water's side. A horse by it.

"Sun!"

Standing so. With arms out but no leaves. With horse but no Sun Run.

Standing so, no tree at all. No Sun Run. Man, one arm high up, straight to me, signing. "Stand back! Stay still!" Other arm, high up, hold a long stick at the water. At me looking. And slow, looking along down stick to a stream. And quick, long stick sailing on down the water. And HIT something.

Now moves he and holding up stick through a fish. Push bright fish up fast up a wood and sends stick down the water fast again. Holding stick with two fishes. Bright one two. Other arm straight pointing me, signing, "Stay back! Stay still!"

Looking at me in so many shade. Slowly, at stick quickly down a water many times. So many fishes up a stick and they stop waving. Gray rags so bright. Still. And he standing in a water. Turn away and move out, making real quiet. Walking over to laying stick fishes down. And horse. Horse drinking in real quiet from a stream.

Watching man, me crying. Watching he moving quick way down with a long stick. But now the quiet. Hurting. And cry and cry.

He taking me by hand and drawing me to a water.

Speaking, sounds I don't know. Hands. Speaking hands, he signing, "Wash you. Water you, arms and face where wasp hurt." Signing both hands, "Drink you for to cool the fire that will come." Eyes, caring soft.

How I knowing speaking hands: Father mine always not talking when he sitting me by the sumac: "See you can throw dibble stick out of shade," signing, he not talking. "Throw like the girls and women, who throw the best," hands saying. "You throw, and I will throw like women, too," so they say. Hands.

And all the time father eyes so much soft caring for me. Never know Father is there before I see him. Never just think Sun Father before he standing in my way. Knowing him time I see him. Speaking, hands always with me.

Now. Putting on me the cold stream. All wet, me, falling back on the ground. Feet down in the cool fishes.

Talking, he with the long stick. He, putting

on moccasins and talking so: "Where you travel? Who you and which country? Which town?"

Very quiet, he, and kneel, hand beneath my head: "Where you come from, Moonflower?"

Dress of mine color of the yellow moon. Too much burning face and feet for talking. Holding up hands of mine. Seeing me, fat bumps growing up arms of mine.

"Where, Moonflower?"

"Where it's hurting," Moonflower finally saying.

"Poison going make you boil and fire," he saying. "Get you home. Where — which way?"

"The first time I slip away. Keep talking," hearing Moonflower saying.

He keeping on. Talking leaves a breezing sound, like a tall tree. Still breezing tall, time when we moving. If moving dreaming, I don't know. I know hearing, smelling horse. Knowing a big horse so easy, not a sound. Horse so shade-gray in front. All white on a rump and egg spots a-splatter rump. Rump looking like a white funny blanket. Like somebody splashing mud all over. So funny. Horse not stamping. Walking, not like Sun Run stamping. Me ride the walking, just like Sun. Me, a horse walking Sun.

All the time. The tall tree-man talking sounds I don't know.

"Keep talking you hear?" So hard holding head up of mine. So sick feeling inside. Outside, hurting.

And through the woods a long time. Through the woods and tall tree saying so:

"Take you to Shy Woman. Medicine. Take you home."

A long kind of time, and he saying, "First time you run away? From whom? Stay awake, you! Open up the eyes, for you fall."

Like to hear a talking. And me talking, too. Stay awake and hurting: "First time I slip away, Sun Run. Brother. Ever you see Sun riding high?"

And me saying, "Who you tall tree, talking man? Who the shy woman? Mother — *na' go'*?"

He lead a horse, me. Stopping and still. Slow head turning. See, he wearing glasses, dark a round. Glasses dark shining. And mouth and nose all slanted. Someone press a nose, mouth on a one side. Old face. Grandfather face, still good old face.

"*Yā!*" he saying surprise. Look up at me.

Me a horse and hurting. He make a sign: point-finger draw across other point-finger — one time, two time, three time. Me hurting, make a sign back: point-finger across point-finger, one, two, three.

"*Yā! Shā hī' yēna!*"

Me not knowing.

"You!" he saying. "*Dzǐ' tsǐstä's!*"

Knowing that. "Sure," me saying. "Brother, Sun. Father, Sun. The People. Not me." I know that.

"Then you are a mixed blood," he saying.

"Mama looking just like me," I saying.

"Skin," he saying, "brown and brown."

"Sure. Brown is hurting and hurting." I crying out from the bumps on arms of mine.

Now. Hurrying again and feel so sleeping and dreaming a long time passing.

He still talking. Sometimes talking I don't know. Times he talking true:

"You hear me, grandchild? *Nixa?* One time there are blue-red-yellow birds, but all are one bird. There are black-brown-white horses, but all one horse. It is so with all things living. So with all trees and men. White, brown, black, yellow. Red. Once, only red men. But not now. Now, all. *All*, with peace."

"Keep talking." Me saying nothing more. See dreaming nothing more.

"And yet they all still fighting about it," tall tree saying.

And long kind of time. Somewhere lying flat, waking up. Me somewhere warm.

Moccasin sound so quiet padding by. Food cooking smelling good. Soft-singing sounding so funny and making me warm.

"Where is this?" Me so saying not loud. Nobody come near. Eyes still asleep closed. Not me. Listening. Some a one sitting on a side me, breathing smoke a pipe. All over me hurting so bad.

Try. Eyes staying closed. Trying. Arms staying still.

Way in back of eyes a mine. Me high up in the

air. In a sling and swinging. So nice. Swinging fade away dark in sleeping. Me knowing sleeping.

Until so much time passing late. Me waking up for sure. Opening eyes, look around. This is where. Nobody here in a room. Looking around see a front room where you live. Blanket covering me, pretty colors. Me all slick and medicines, smelling sharp. Seeing in a light on. Raise up arms of mine. No more bumps. One same big swelling, fat hands and arms. No red bumps, little dark specks. Holes where stings go in. Stinging gone and swelling not too bad. Feel a swelling. Arms of mine hot feeling tight.

Night is on a windows. Everywhere sleeping. Light on this room. I turn where is dark. They in the dark somewhere. He the tall tree and mother Shy Woman. Shy Woman who? He told in a woods. We left a woods. We here. Does Mother know?

Mother sleeping. And Sun Run. And somewhere Father. The first time I slip away and sorry. Mother Sun Father. See them all in a wake-up time. Me sleeping again.

I kick the blanket down. Food smelling good and fire burning. Sunlight going. Red and slanting down in a window.

"Well, hi there, baby. You waking up now — yes! Sleep through the whole day! Uh-huh, feeling better now, baby. Sure." Woman loud and close, kneeling down. Big blue bowl, spoon, steaming.

"Eat it slow, now. See, I'll blow on it for you, baby. Sure. Now take a little good cornmush. Yes, baby. See, I blow it for you and you gonna eat some of it. Make you strong. How you feeling, honey? Not so good? Okay? Feeling better, sure."

"Mama."

"Oh, now. Don't you worry. We'll find your mama, me and James False Face. We always find everybody, don't you worry. You ran away — yes, pretty? Nah, you didn't mean to, right? You travel off and forget where you're going. Sure, baby, don't you worry.

"You're lucky, you know?" She laughing. "You lucky you find the little wasps instead of a yellow school bus gonna get you." Laughing more. "When I was little like you, honey. It come up fast, pumpety, pumpety, like a giant gold bug. I sure thought that yellow bus was gonna get me! How was I to know where they take all the children? I hardly ever see them come home. See, because I'd be taking a rest somewhere, or sleeping, and I never saw. So each time of the gold bug I'd run and hide. Never had to go away to school for a long time.

"See, honey?" she saying. Holding up a yellow dress never knew I wasn't wearing. Watching woman so nice and loud talking.

"I wash up your pretty dress for you. Your

mama sure make you up some loving clothes, yes indeed. Amber yellow, like the sunsets back home; like the moon come up here. See? I sewed up the tears. And now you watch me, I'm gonna iron it all up like new."

Eating. Watching woman at a board lying on a table. She take the iron off a stove. Wet her finger, touch the iron. Hearing like a popping.

Woman laughing again. "Sure. Make you real pretty. Find your mama for you. We don't know the people here, so it's going to take James maybe some time to find which hill. We're just traveling, you see. So many of us, all scattered now. Traveling, stopping here and there. Nobody gonna want to stay on the reservation each and every day. James-Face, he always saying the travel, the nomad is in the blood. And you know it, honey. Too much is happening right now for staying in one place. Some places the breeds and the full-bloods are together as one people. In other places they hate fully.

"You know, east of the Mississippi nobody bother you about it. Everybody claiming to be an *Indian*. James, he says if you are one sixteenth or one fourth, well, you are blood-brother. I don't care much about it. Maybe it's more like James want to keep in touch with everybody.

"What do they call you, baby, huuum? Come on now, you can tell Susanne Shy Woman, sure."

She laughing loud and full, like air eating, when I might tell.

"I mean the American name," she saying. "Never speak the *name*, child, so The People say. For maybe a ghost will be jealous and want to take it for his. Ha-ha! But you're a child, maybe you don't have a *name*. James, he give you one.

"So I told you what they call me. Now. You tell me what they call you, okay, baby?"

Watching Shy Woman. Feeling good and warm. Hands of mine around a bowl some shaking. I like talking and laughing.

"See, you maybe call me Enormity, okay? No more Shy Woman." Smiling. "See we head up north one time by Canada. Maybe we will cross over the line; but we get caught up there every time. We stop up there on this side by that most high prairie, where you breathe and swallow burnt heat."

She smiling sad, head shaking side to side. "A gas line runs under the jail there, they tell us, and the line has a leak. The government won't fix the leak — you know what it did? It put a red light in the cells of the jail. The light flashes on when too much gas leaks into the cells. You better believe the prisoners are afraid to go to sleep, for fear they'll miss the light."

Eyes closing and no smiling. Again talking. "We get up there, me and James. He has to go off looking and talking stories with the men. Thinks he's getting me stuck with the women. But he wouldn't believe it — no sir, baby."

Shy Woman talking steady, not too loud. "He

wouldn't know these women. Full-blood Hōhé women. Assiniboin women, some say. But nobody knows what the reservation been doing to the women. No woman ever sign a treaty I know of, and maybe that's the reason a treaty never hold together.

"Hah! *Vího — Wašichu!*" Speaking loud. "*Wašichu*, the white man, never knew how important were the women long ago in the tribe. But The People, they say the *law* was given them long ago by a woman."

She stopping. Iron clear off the board. She looking far out a window.

"Sure, James-Face will tell you all about that."

Staring what she seeing. Maybe ask her when gone the good cornmush. Eating slow, so good and tasting so hot and sweet with honey.

"Sure," she saying, still no ironing. Letting iron go and sitting, hold my one dress nice neat on a lap. Dress looking like me sitting still.

"Sure, men go off seeing and talking. No need looking for work, shoot." She laughing. "And women, Hōhé, tough and poor. They talk tribal politics, you know, baby? Living with self but not for self. Tribal and individual. That's what those changing women are talking about. And talking about today and yesterday, and last wars, all of us against the *wašichu*. Telling stories about all of us, so we will know one another, so we will come together as one. Pass it along."

Holding bowl, empty, watching her. And she very quick laughing.

"Shy Woman is a crazy woman, that's what you thinking, honey? Talking at you to death, poor baby." Now smiling kind and caring. She standing, folding dress. Put it on a board. She kneeling next to me close. Take the bowl and spoon. Staring at me swelling. "Not so much," she saying. Arms of mine full and not so fat. She touching head of mine. Lips. Touching neck.

"You're going to be okay. Right," she saying. "Good baby. Right. You want to stand, test your little legs?"

Head shaking, too tired.

"Well, you rest, then. James-Face, he'll be back soon. James, that old man!" She laughing, and make her big face all lines and teeth. One gold and shine.

"I was just a girl, having passed through the Sixth Grade ten years by then. And then working at the community school at Cheyenne River Reservation right next to Standing Rock. I'm smart, they say. And I'm gonna go to college all in my mind. All ready, in my mind, to leave the tribal behind. Catch the yellow bug to be a graduate, be a real citizen. Ai! I think the reservation is the devil and the misery. I believe it's the bigot. I will come back and change it, and then everything will be all right.

"But James-Face came riding through one day.

A traveling man, he came speeding faster than the dust could settle, driving a truck with a horse in the back (the horse — *shunka wakan!* that holy dog!). So he can chuck the truck and ride. And I saw him riding through on that first great Palouse horse I ever saw. The finest war-horse for miles and miles. James had no thinning hair then. He was standing up on the spotted rump of that horse, with his hands outstretched to all of us and his face bathed in sunlight. He never yet had the stroke that twisted his face into a mask of the Irinakoiw. He was James Talking Story of the perfect face. Strong, lean. Standing up on that horse of high speed, about to kill himself, like some crazed *injun*, yelling his head off, but talking true."

She laughing short, quick, eyes fill of water. "Like the scout come riding fast into camp — you remember that? Ever hear those stories, baby? Come riding like a burst of wind, screaming, *'The soldiers are coming! It's a good day for dying! Make ready!'* So it was when James came, yelling. Only, he was Talking Story, beautiful then, and screaming — eyes closed, golden face, with arms straight out to us, fingers sifting air: *'Chicago is coming! It's a good day for running! Stay away from Chicago — it's a good day for running!'* "

She laughing and choking. "Years before I understood what he meant. But he was telling us the pull of the city was coming at us. He wanted us to fight against the pull. Stay where we were, or run." She swaying me and her, side to side.

"Why you crying?" I saying. Swaying, she smoothing hair of mine. Holding easy, face of mine in her hands.

"Oh, I'm not crying, I'm remembering," she saying. "There was never a question — just hanging around that horse and listening to Talking Story. After a time there was no question for him, either. Ah, so long ago, it must've been written in the campfires. James Talking Story and poor Susanne of the community school."

She all wet in the face. Nose stream. I saying, "You looking ugly, woman."

"Being alone is — remembering. Talking too much," she saying. "I know the end. James-Face working so hard all of the time. Getting the census wherever we go. Finding how many *Indians* and contacting Manpower. He keeps the old ways even when he says we are all one people. Always moving when he knows he is too old for it. James-Face is going to *die!* Then where will I be, one poor mixed-blood all alone?"

Laughing little bit and sneezing. Wiping chin, dripping.

"Mother always crying," I saying, touching on her arm.

Being all quiet, she staring more at me. "Look, tell me where you live, huh?" All hard and no sweet and no laughing.

"Keep talking!" I saying hard the same and no sweet.

"Look, kid, I'm not gonna take this from you!" Quick, by the arms of mine shaking. "Tell me who and where before James kills hisself out there! He thinks he's going to dream it, like the old way. He's waiting for the visions from hunger — God! It might take days. Tell me!"

"Stop talking," I tell her. "Shy Woman, Enormity, stop."

"Then talk!"

Hard and talking. "Sumac. Sun Run leave a rope."

"All right," changing woman, Enormity, saying.

"The way passing by. The house, the yard."

"I hear you."

"A town Mama going take talking. Leaving Arilla, quiet."

"Leaving Arilla?"

"Leaving — my name."

"So," changing Enormity saying. "I hear you. What town?"

"All along the way snowing and children."

"Which town?" Shaking hard and hurting swelling. "Listen! I gave you medicine and I gave you food. I'll dry the fish so James and I will have something anywhere we go. We'll take you back and they surely will be so glad and offer us plenty food — it's the way." Hard hands hurting. "If you don't tell me, he might die out there!"

Me lying down on a side. Lying, feeling so bad and cry, and cry.

"Oh, little baby." Woman always changing. "Hurting you like that, I oughta be whipped."

Changing woman patting me baby to sleep. "What's gotten into me? It's the worry. Never having enough and no place — poor old James! He can't sleep nights, you know? He can't eat hardly anything. Restless, like it was an old time, you broke camp when someone died. You know, everywhere we go now, the people die. All the time now. Hunger, sickness. Dying from themselves — suicide is homicide, so James says. We move on."

Shy changing woman sigh. "I wasn't always like this, baby. Never was I pretty, not like the young girls there who had families."

"Shy Woman just like a mama," me saying, reach for her. "Enormity? Ugly mama."

Woman, taking hands of mine, laughing soft. No changing woman. She patting making baby to feel so sleeping. "I was an orphan child, but it was all right back then. Orphans belong to chiefs. I was so small and scrawny — would you believe it?

"The first and only thing I ever remember was that heat and that land, some shacks looking like log houses. Even a few teepees sometimes for sacred ceremonies. Me always too late. See, the children would run a game. By the time I realized they were playing, why, they'd gone. So there was me, without a game in that burning place."

She so sighing and so listening, head in a lap. Thinking games and Sun Run.

"It was all right," Enormity saying. "They take you in, no matter who. Lotsa orphans. People starve, maybe go to jail. They die then, too. I don't know. I had the same as the other children, I guess. I just couldn't keep up with them. They were too fast for me, playing their games."

"You dying?" asking Enormity. I know dying. Mama saying, "This place is death. You want your Sun to end up like these kind? Cliffville is dying."

"Dying? *Me?*" Enormity saying. "Baby, don't you worry." She laughing. "Too much blood in me for dying, honey. The Lakoda on one side and the Shāhíyēna on the other. The *Indian* Bureau will tell you I am mixed Sioux and Cheyenne. Not the way we call it. But like Sitting Bull, Teton Lakoda, Hunkpapa band. I am Hunkpapa in one heart and them, the most human beings, in the other heart. Only, how can you have two hearts, huh? Sure, sometimes I don't know who I'm talking.

"What was it he said — Sitting Bull? James knows it all — *'The country you gave me you run me from. But it is mine and I will stay. I will stay.'* Something like that. Sure," Enormity so much talking, "I have a yearning for the Tongue River over in Montana, where they keep the Cheyenne. But they say the Lakoda lands at Standing Rock is my home . . . Someday I'd like to see The

Turner of the Cheyenne hanging above the sacred teepee . . ." Enormity saying all slow and far away.

"Enormity changing, Cliffville is dying."

"Wha — ?"

"She going talking to Cliffville, my mama."

"I hear you. So that's the town. You must stay here a minute, honey." She putting me to lie down. "I'll get James, thank goodness. No more fasting."

She putting on a wrap, chilling sun going.

"No! You going talking!"

"Hey, you'll be all right here. I'll be back," Enormity saying. "You must stay quiet."

"Everybody going talking leaving quiet."

"They leave you?" she saying. "Not very nice. Not like old times — take the child everywhere with you."

"Sun Run brother."

"Your brother, huh? Like to meet that *brave*. Leaving you alone like that."

"You leaving me."

"No, I'm not leaving you, baby. I'm just going out for a minute — "

She standing, hearing sound. A horse-coming sound. Stopping sound. When wide the door like a wind blowing, a tall tree leaning there. James of dark glasses all shining, coming through. Leaning, sitting down. So much noise and scraping and bump at the table. Slumping down.

Enormity woman hurry now throw a wrap on

the floor. Hurrying now to a stove and bowl and mush, lots a honey and milk. Quick, down before the tall tree shake the table.

"Hi you, tall man?" saying, glad to see him. Liking him so old. He, head down to a bowl. She, Enormity changing, filling spoon and feeding him one.

"You just an old baby!" saying, can't help laughing.

Some quiet. He eating. Speaking words I don't know. Next, talking true.

"Life goes round and round," he saying. "I am drawn within the circle."

"I hear you." Enormity shy changing.

"Rushing as if to meet the night — a sweep of land," he saying.

"All right."

"Sheer and high, as if the night had eaten some of it."

"I hear you," Enormity.

"That is all. I have seen it," old James so saying. "The child dwells near the height of a cliff."

"Holy earth," Shy Woman whisper, "Cliffville!"

"I know it," old tall tree saying.

"Mama going . . . Sun swing a rope . . ."

Old tall man make a sigh: *I have seen it, I know.* Dark glasses he looking at me. "You children are trying to live, but it is so hard."

Enormity telling, "Now. You just go take a rest, James. We'll start out in the morning."

"How many do you think we will find waiting for me in Cliffville?" he saying.

Shy Enormity him patting and patting. "You just rest now."

I come him patting and patting. "You just resting," I saying.

He laughing. "Such a child! See how she already starts on her own."

"James, she only run away and get herself lost," Shy Woman.

"But such a one!" James. "Come looking for Talking Story of old."

"You sleep now, and I'll make you some cherry cornbread — James, you hear?"

"With some chokecherry and honey?" I saying.

"She knows!" Shy Woman saying.

"Ai! She is," saying James. "To be — " He leaning down, whisper in my ear.

"You naming me a name?" I saying.

"You never say it," James saying. "You have a secret and you will be the secret, for all time."

"I hear you, James, but she is just a baby."

"I be a talking story, too," I saying. Patting and patting.

"Yes! But don't say the *name*." He holding head of mine so close and he breathing like a wind, a heat and mush. He making of signs and humming.

"James," woman saying. "Rest. Tomorrow is soon enough."

"To pass it along," he saying. "On and on in a circle. For all time."

6

I'd even embarrass Mom and anybody else who cared about me before I'd ever show fear. Seven-thirty I get home, too late for everything; and me too tired even to do my favorite subject. I always get A's in Language Arts, but not this time.

The awful orange porch light is on and creams our house this sickly yellow. I come around the corner, afraid any minute something really will jump out of the dark at me. Not some *body* but some *thing* — phantasms of giant beetles or huge crickets out of science fiction. Mom says I just get overcome with the phantasmagorias some-times, and I guess she's right.

I almost cry out with happiness to be safe at home again. Every tree trunk and bush near the porch looks as if they are infected with some yel-low jaundice, I swear. But I am so glad to see the light all of a sudden. It makes me feel better even when I do still feel so bad. I mean from tiredness, and because the roar from the skating rink is now loud enough in my head to erase my brain. I was hearing it and it was beginning to wipe out my mind before I ever knew I was hearing it. That roar never leaves off, even when it stops for real when the place closes at two-thirty in the morning. It never leaves off because after closing I begin to dream the sound of it. And when I wake up around seven in the morning, the real sound of it has started all over again.

The rink is just beyond the end of town on a piece of county land right smack up against the town. We live right near the edge of town with a state park onto our backs, just the way the rink has a piece of the park to its back, and it all suits me fine. At least, it did until I had to start coming home after dark and had to walk so far alone. And had to have that roar seem to creep out to meet me while I'm too tired and too scared to even enjoy the sound of it.

Mom tried her best to get a town ordinance passed so the rink couldn't get water taps and sewer lines from the town. She didn't have a chance. Sun and me were so glad, too. We wanted that skating rink as soon as we saw what it was going to be, hardwood floors and all.

Mom said: "It will bring in the worst element within twenty miles, you wait and see. All the hicks from Greensburg and Marion, and the toughs out of Bell Valley and Northill."

Sun Run said: "Don't the best element ever want to go roller-skating? I mean your slinky daughters of orthodontists who are some slow when it comes to books. Do those kind and the good old basketball boys ever want to roll?"

Mom said: "Not on your life, not. No sir. They stay away, and for good reason. And you're going to stay away as well."

Sun said: "And for good reason."

Mom said: "You have to be a good example for Arilla. Sun, I have tried to give you everything you ever wanted."

Sun said: "And then some," staring at me with those black, hateful eyes.

Mom said: "Everything you ever wanted, and you are going to do this for me. You are going to keep Arilla from going over there by not going yourself."

Sun said: "Oh, we are good at keeping Arilla from doing what you don't want her to do, too."

Sun was right. Once I'd heard that roar, not wild mustangs or phantasmagorias, either, could have kept me away.

Now I'm too tired for anything. And if I live through this, I'll cut out Sun's heart for my survival medal. The trouble is he'd just go on and live without one. Should've known he was cold. I know it now.

I creep on up the sidewalk, up the steps, letting the yellow jaundice-light turn me sickly pale like everything else in its reach. Trying hard not to jar my brain as I move and practically crawl inside the house. Oooh, didn't mean to slam the door like that! Nobody comes to see who is here. Just Mom calling from the kitchen:

"You, Arilla?"

I don't answer and still she won't even come see who it is.

"Supper's at eight. Sun got home forty-five minutes ago."

Think I don't know what time supper is? Who ever heard of people eating at practically midnight when before they always ate at five? And think I care if Sun leaves me to come on home in the dark by myself? I bet I wouldn't be so scared if I could run. But every bone in my body is an aching coward. Every muscle is a deserter trying to jump on out of my skin.

Brother thinks I won't live through this. The fact that just bothers me bad enough now to keep me on my guard. Even when every day I am like peanut brittle, I can still go on concentrating with all of my might. I keep on going and make no mistakes. That's what he can't figure out about me. He doesn't know that I know. Or maybe he hasn't yet discovered about himself what I already know.

One morning about a week ago when I woke up. There were these true-particles — days and days of me and Sun outdoors together. All through the night they had been like dust dancing on the night in my room. All through the night within the skate roar and me hurting in my sleep, the particles — days of Sun and me — begin to pull toward one another. They gather in one sick-ening milligram. Morning, and I wake choking up. Vomit on my fingers, even down my neck and in my hair. Sticky and smelly, like a little kid sick all in the dark. That's just the way I felt. I mean, I woke up and I *was* . . . this kid with all this strangeness in me and the vomit all over me. This . . . this waking up and being somebody else, *somewhere* else, with some clear memory of something just out of reach of my mind. But knowing. *Knowing* now, forever and for sure, so that I'll never forget, not for a minute.

Jack Sun Run Adams wants me dead.

I listened to what he told me from the very beginning. Sure, I was *petrified*, but I never thought of one other putrefied thing the whole time but what I was doing. No "Am I going to break a leg?" or anything. Didn't see the haze in the sky Mom says is an *inversion* of pollution stink over this town for two weeks. Too warm out for late October.

"We get all the crud from Dayton," Jack Sun says one day. "Just look at all of that crud from Dayton." Not a chance. I wouldn't look.

Airplanes, dogs running at our heels — packs of them living wild in the woods — were as good as invisible *and* silent. I didn't hear one thing. Yet, I can recall every second of every three hours we are out there: my heels pressed down in the stirrups; keep a light "feel" of the mouth; shorten the reins; knee pressure, firm; seeing right between the horse's ears.

"Keep your head up straight," Jack Sun Run told me the first time, like I'm a baby and dumb. "Girl, that ain't a passenger train you got under you. You got to ride this Running Moon."

And I did! Rode right the very first time. I'm not saying it didn't get harder to do, because it did. I sure had to work at it, but I kept on riding right. That's what he couldn't understand. And still Run hopes I won't live through it, I know he does. Hoping for some accident. The awful part is, I've known him all my life. I can't even imagine what a life could be without him. He can imagine one without me. You'd think I'd get the creeps around him every time, but I seldom do. Because I think: He's my big brother. It's my brother wants me dead.

Not that that makes it all right. But it makes it all somehow less of a horrible surprise. And I never go on and think the next step. I mean, in words, in my head. Never. I just know it's there, like one of those phantasmagorias waiting to jump out at me.

You enter this house into a vestibule. The floor is this travertine stone slab about nine by twelve feet, which was inlaid there when Mom and Dad bought the place. Mom says it's the best and richest feature of the house. I don't think so, since at the far end of it is the staircase. The stairs have this oak banister that Dad put together and worked from his own sweat just after we moved in. He took that old banister off and he went out and cut him down an oak tree somewhere in the woods. And got two lengths of wood out of the tree, and put them together so they look like one length of wood. Then he carved the whole thing with some odd-looking designs which Jack-Run says are from his tribal memory, whatever that is supposed to mean.

I say to Sun, "Which tribal is it coming from?"

And Sun says right back, "Little Moon, it won't matter so long as he's got one and he makes it work for him."

So now I creep on upstairs, leaning hard on the carvings of the banister. Not touching them with any pleasure at all like I used to. Seems a long time since I've enjoyed anything in this house; only it hasn't been so long. I take the putrefied smell of horses upstairs with me. I just want to get into my room as quickly and as quietly as I can.

Going away from the stairs down the hall to get to my room. Mom and Dad's is in the middle of the hall on the other side. Directly ahead of me is a big window that in the daytime lights up the whole hall. Sun's room is right there to the left of the window.

The hall light is on. I'm not even off the stairtop when he hears me.

You, Sun!

Standing right outside the door. Not looking at me, but with his face turned ever so little toward the window. Standing there like something carved but truly lifelike.

Just the coldest wave of sickness slides over me. That smell of stalls mixed with hay and making me weave right there at the top of the stairs. Seeing him like that all of a sudden has me back, feet planted in the manure again.

Not looking at me, not moving. Not even a quick reason, like he just happens to think about it weeks too late, why he shouldn't wait for me. He says,

"Did you sort the leathers? Did you use the brush and the combs? Did you cool her out? Did you pick her feet good and clean?"

"Did you sew your mouth shut yet, too?"

"Moon, it ought to be fun by now."

"Shut up calling me *Moon!*"

I'm about to burst into crying, like it's rising on top of the sickness. But instead I laugh, short and sweet. "Call me whatever you like, ugly brother, but guess what? I've got her running to me when I clap my hands!"

"My, my," he says. "Just like that, you turned her into a puppy dog."

I just smirk and look tough and strong as I turn the corner. "I'm taking me a shower." Know he is watching as I slam into my room.

Letting slide an armful of homework onto my bed. I love my bed. But if I lie on it now, I'll never get up again. So I just stand a minute, looking. I love my room, the only place where Sun can't get to me. I've seen other girls' rooms with all that white frenchy furniture. Mine has a big old bed. A desk made from a door, and books, and two chairs. A window. Looking at the light blue curtains.

Sound roars over me like I'd just learned to hear it. I go to the window, looking out. Slide the window up. By craning my head around, I can see lights from way over there. It's funny how land dips and turns when it looks all flat with trees. If I were to walk straight out from here, it would take me hours going east through the state park to get there. But if I go out the front and through a little bit of the town, it doesn't take long at all.

Seeing the lights, I get hungry for it. I hurry and close the window. No more than a minute passes and Mom comes in like I knew she would with some clean clothes.

"Whew, that's an odor, I tell you. Get yourself into the shower," she says. "Supper's almost on. Five minutes."

"I can't make it in five minutes." I let my face give her a hint I'm hurting. Too busy with getting supper to notice.

"Ten minutes, then. But come on now. How was it today? Fun?"

"It was fun," I lie.

"Bet you're tired out."

"Yes. Mom, I hurt."

"Well. Maybe tomorrow I'll come out and take a look at you all riding. I'm so glad you and Sun . . . I'll come watch you, would you like that?"

"Sure."

She been saying that for weeks. How's she going to get there with all her classes and with Dad at work?

She leaves me alone, all at once, like she can't keep her spirits up or focused on any one thing too long. Never even noticed it before, but Mom is as strange and different as everybody else in this house. Or maybe *I'm* just strange and different. She didn't notice that I hurt, even when I told her. But then she's a dancer and she says dancers always hurt. Every minute of every hour. Maybe if I'd done The Dance, I wouldn't hurt so much now.

Taking up my clean clothes and head for the bathroom across the hall.

Jack Sun, I think. And take a split second to look. Still standing there! He hasn't moved a hair, waiting to hear me moan in pain. I walk on out with strength. Give him a backhand wave and close the door behind me.

Inside, I get out of my stinking clothes. On into the shower as hot as I can stand it. I stretch out full length in the tub. Let the shower water beat out the pain. I can't hear the rink roar with the door closed, with water beating, and steam like it will fill up my eyeballs.

No thinking in the tub. Just letting my mind go fallow like a field. Fields don't know pain. So I go blank, hoping muscles will stop jumping. Blanking out horses, jumpy and making me so sore.

It seeps in, how other people can live every day without having a phenomenon like Sun Run around. Mom says a phenomenon is a happening you can't put a name to. And I said to her, Yes, you can put a name to it — a phenomenon! But she didn't appreciate my sense of humor. That's because I never show much of one, I guess. Sun has one; and that's how I know a sense of humor is his way of showing he is better than anybody and that he couldn't care less about anybody's feelings. I know my life has been some trouble with him, but it would be just forever dull having an ordinary boy for a brother. Even when he and I never have been like the kind of stuff you see going on at the basketball games and the soccer games.

Girls will never mind to bring along their little brothers as what they call the chaperone. Meaning to keep what the girls call going with a boy a secret (where do they *go* with the boys? — I never see them *go*, other than Angel). Girls will button up their little brothers' coats and buy them popcorn and wipe their noses, even slap some little faces when a kid may need dis-*i*-pline. And the whole time keeping the little ones close, so they won't get lost or trampled in the excitement of winning and losing. I never will figure out how girls can concentrate on older boys, chewing gum, varsity cheers, crossing their legs and swinging them — always their right legs swing back and forth, back and forth, in time. And never once forget to take care of their little brothers. Their little sisters always seem to sit still between their moms and dads, which is a cramped way to watch some game.

I wish some older sister could of taken care of me once. Whenever I see those girls with their little brothers, I wish it. Not something I think about and to bother me. Just that I wasn't a little boy and Jack Sun wasn't ever a girl. Naturally, I never had the chance to show him off by taking care of him. Even if I had been oldest, I bet he wouldn't be the type of kid who'd let somebody treat him like a baby Ken for a grown-up Barbie. But in true life Sun Run never took care of me the way older brothers stand in front of their sisters to take up for them. Thinking back, Run all of the time seemed to be fooling with me. Or Mom was there in the middle taking up for me so Jack never could; or telling him how to do something so I would do the same. Maybe that's why we never got the crinkles worked out between us, I don't know.

I can't quite make the way it was more exact because thinking back hard always makes me feel ready to have a fit of some kind. But girls I know feel free to talk about when they were little and stuff. They will just go on remembering about anything, man! I never even want to think about when I was little.

"GIRL! *You get your own private country club, you can stay in it for an hour*." Sun is always hungry. Banging on the door, trying to make out I'm holding up the supper.

"Okay, ugly, I'm out!" Off with the shower and I'm out, drying with the towel. Did I wash with soap? Sure, but I was so busy being a blank and when I was little . . .

Maybe we were so poor we were partway hungry when I was little. Nobody talks about it, like my dad will never talk about when he was in Korea.

I don't recall being poor or knowing what poor was, or years, or anything like that. Because I haven't lived so long, I guess. I can't remember whole times from one year to the next. Mostly, I bring back something from when I was little all in a flash. The way the flash works is like heat lightning around the skating rink, outside but way off dead in the darkness. Do all kids lose whole times and most of years like I do, and then see a little bit of them all in a flash? Like heat lightning flashing and quivering way over in the earth's curve.

Your eyes keep coming back to the flash, so big in the dark you get blinded by it. Until all at once you know you are seeing many flashes rolled into one. You take one of the many and it grows into one great big flash. You watch it repeat itself, echo itself and give off more than one image of itself in the dark. But watch out, you have to work fast. Heat lightning only flashes a second. Work fast and you can hold on while it gets deeper and deeper, just the way I turn a flash of memory over and over. I let the flash echo in my brain again and again until I have grabbed every piece and particle that is in it.

I get this flash of wood planks laid out on cement blocks in a long, crooked row. The sound of water rushing around the cement blocks about six inches below them. And all these real little girls and me having to walk the crooked row because the school basement has got flooded. The sound of that rushing water makes us have to go to the bathroom more than ever. I mean, a flash of *boards* just inches wide and we are walking them class by class because they wouldn't let us go in the basement one at a time. Like, you raise your hand and ask, "Teacher, may I be excused?" and the teacher will say *Yes* or *No, not now*, all up to her if she thinks you really have to go. Most times she'd guess right, with what I recall to this day my mom said to her when she brought my lunch was an *uncanny accuracy*. I remember Mom saying that just as clear — I thought it meant a taste of something that wasn't home-grown and put in a can. And if the teacher had an uncanny accuracy, then I wanted some of it, too.

It was true, too, because most of the time the

teacher guessed right about a kid having to go to the bathroom. But once in a while some little boy or girl would have an accident right in their seats. A bad accident. So that the teacher would have to clear the whole room. And some little kid would be stinking and bawling, and some embarrassed mom would have to come and get the kid.

I mean, a flash of the whole thing in detail, almost, just as clear. The water wasn't as high in the girls' bathroom because there were drains in there. I can see the water rushing down the drains. Hear it. There weren't any planks up high, but boards laid out on the floor so we wouldn't have to step in the wetness. We stood in line and I watched water rush down the drains. I was *happy* there with all of the girls in one place. The only time I can remember being together with a bunch of girls, feeling close to them. All in dresses, like it was special being a girl and I was special, too. With these women teachers standing taking each little girl by the arm oh so carefully, like one might break if they didn't. And when it came to my turn, they did the same to me oh so carefully, and leading me into the cubicle with the swinging door; and then *guarding* the door on the outside while I was in there. Even to think about it makes me feel like I was something special.

Water gurgles down the drain of this bathtub right now just in the same sound as when I was little in that flood basement of a school. And I remember watching water gurgle swiftly down a large drain. The chance to see some easy working of indoor plumbing forever opened my brain, like a trapdoor sliding back. Even sweeter than being close with a bunch of little girls all alike, and it was awful nice being all alike.

Because seeing and hearing that drain, I would never again fear sitting in the cold in the dead of winter. In the world, there was a way of draining water — and I know I remember thinking that. Someday I wouldn't have to freeze in the out-house.

My head is like that. A flash of something clear, but the rest darkness. Nothing. Kind of scary. I get a scent of trees sometimes, and a flash of cool pale bark of a tree. I appear to be floating past it, back and forth. I get kind of weak, either with the floating back and forth or with the scent of the tree. I wonder if somewhere, sometime, I have lived another life.

Downstairs, thinking so hard I'm in the kitchen hearing the skating rink like it is the sound of home-fried corn with bacon I see sizzling on the stove. My head gets mixed up like that when I'm real tired. I have to blink a few times to make everything clear again. Mom's at the stove putting supper in bowls and Sun is sitting on his side of the table like he is saying, This side is mine, I own it.

I sit down on my side. I notice that Jack Sun's hair is still damp from his shower he took before I got home. He is forever letting his hair drip dry and never catches a cold.

"Thanks for coming home with me," I tell him. Right away I'm sorry I let on I didn't like coming home alone.

"You never said you wanted me to wait for you," Sun says, as polite cold as he can be. He's sneaking a fork of coleslaw in a white bowl.

Without a headband, Sun's hair just flows shiny and black. Prince Valiant in some old comic you see in the shops around here. He is dressed clean in a white, long-sleeved T-shirt with a feather decal, and faded jeans.

"Get your fingers out!" I yell real fast. But he keeps on sneaking the slaw. "Who do you have a date with?" And, naturally, he doesn't answer.

My voice doesn't sound like me at all. Me so tired my head feels light. Either I am sick or half asleep, something.

Mom puts a bowl on the table — heat rising from fried corn in a yellow bowl, color-coordinated.

I know. I'm jealous of Jack Sun, I can't help it. And why don't I look like that, with that way of living now and long ago? Who am I? Why do I have to be the ugly one? Why does this table seem like the worst place to be this evening?

Everything is on the table, a platter of lamb chops, which I haven't seen on our table for the whole summer. End of October, when the lamb chops fall off the lamb, and I look like Leslie Rainy.

Leslie Rainy is the singer they blast from the loudspeaker outside the rock shop on weekends. The rock shop doesn't mean rock-and-roll shop, but a place where you can buy leathers for weaving or braiding, and beads and all kinds of polished stones to string on wire. They blast Leslie Rainy, who can do some strange skating up and down octaves with her voice — hard on one edge of it and sweet on the other. Oh, I love that Leslie Rainy, but I don't like looking like her.

Mom says Leslie Rainy looks just like the Taylors in this town and says I look just like Leslie Rainy and the Taylors in this town. All of them are plump with this complexion that Sun says is from-the-moon fair. And I hate fair because it is yellowish or it looks unhealthy. Taylors and me with lumpy hair that is not quite kinky. No Red Indian anywhere. I must of said the "Red Indian" out loud because Jack Sun suddenly says, "The Red Indian is a misnomer, Little Moon."

Mom clucks her tongue and puts full glasses of Kool-Aid, no, it's pink lemonade, next to our plates. "Jack, don't start up," she says.

"What's a missed number?" I ask him and he has to laugh.

"Dummy!"

"Jack, you start up and you leave the table," Mom tells him.

"Yay, whoopee. Leave the table so's I don't have to look at you," is what I say.

"Oh, my lord," Mom says. "The two of you can just make me sick."

"I said 'misnomer,' " Jack says. "Not missed number — oh, forget it."

"No, now you go on and explain it to her," Mom tells him.

"Story of my life," Sun says.

"A misnomer?" I ask him, getting it right this time.

"No. You. Explaining to you."

"You don't have to say nothing to me for the rest of your career, too," I tell him, "get smart with me."

But he's patient. Proud he's so smart.

"The Red Indian is a misnomer. I ain't going to give you a half-hour course, which is what it would take," smart-mouth Jack says. "But, quickly, it means a mistake in naming something. People think Amerinds are red-colored. What it was, the first Amerinds ever seen by a white land thief probably had red paint on them. They liked the bright colors. And they got to be called 'Pull up the wagons, here come the Red Men.' "

"That's very dull," I tell Jack. "That's the most dullest, uninteresting, made-up story I have ever been forced to listen to."

But Jack is looking satisfied with himself. And I'm amazed at how easy it is for him to turn any conversation to himself and Indians.

"Who you going out with?" I say real fast, hoping to catch him.

"Never you mind," he says at last.

Mom sits down at the head of the table between us. "Sun? You must have homework to do."

"Too early in the year for homework," he says to her. Words slide out of him like moss agate strung on silk.

I fill up my plate. "Bet I know who," I tell him. "Bet it's Angel Diavolad. Because she is darkest. Sun don't like nothing that has any light on it."

Mom fixes Jack's plate like he is a baby. "A sixteen-year-old promise is going to trip and fall in a seventeen-year-old dead-end if he's not careful, too."

Jack Sun gives Mom a glinting look she missed but I caught. Before he can be smart, I butt in: "And no dark angel is going to catch a falling star — hoo!" That was pretty good for someone as tired as me.

I can see I'm getting under his skin. Smile is tight. He orders his plate like always, but in quick, jerky motions. He moves the corn so it is not touching the coleslaw, and shoves over the coleslaw so it won't touch the lamb chop.

"Never you wonder about it, Moon Child," he says to me. "An angel will know how to wing it."

"The two of you," Mom says. She is eating, watching her plate. "Your father ought to hear this brother and sister."

She's only irritated. She don't yet know she is surrounded by TNT.

"I *like* Angel," Jack says. "It takes class to run the eight-eighty at two minutes. I think I'll walk her through the dark to the roller rink."

Watch it, Sun!

He did that deliberately to get Mom started.

"She is a thirteen-year-old child and she has no business over there at that skating rink. You know that, Sun. Her father finds out she is over there and running with you — "

"She was fourteen about ten days ago," Sun says. "She running the four-forty and me running the eight-eighty. I'll wait for her at her finish line. Have to. I like the angel. Better than a moon maid." He gives me the eye, like an arrow flashing past.

"That's enough," Mom tells him. "Eat. I haven't said you are going any place. Eat."

Sun eats one food at a time. Corn, then cole-slaw and finally the lamb chop. How can he eat like that? One food hot, the next lukewarm and the last cold. I can't stand to watch him.

Quiet and the muffled roar of the rink is on my mind. Skating is dangerous to talk about, and I hope Sun will leave it go.

His glinting eyes on me. Oh, no. Sun, leave

it alone. I take it all back. I'll clean your room, I swear, for a week.

Down at his plate, eating so carefully, like he is wearing his headdress. He says, "We'll just skate some waltzes to the loudspeaker and listen to some rock records during intermission."

"He just wants to walk in the dark with Angel," I say to get Mom's mind off the rink.

"You ever learn to skate, Moon Child?" One smooth stone at a time.

"Now that's enough!" Mom says. "I'm telling you, you're not going over to that skate place. Arilla can't go and you can't go. Now that's it."

Be careful, Sun.

"How you going to stop me?" Sun says, just as nice as he can be.

"You just don't defy me," Mom says. She's getting angry.

"I think I'm too old for you to tell me what and when, Moon Mother." Still so pleasant, but his face seems to close.

"As long as you are under my roof," she says.

"You all stop fighting," I say.

"As long as you live here," she says. "And I'll tell you something else, Jack. You're too old to be playing the brave warrior. It was all right when you were twelve or so. But you aren't a boy any longer, so stop pretending."

"Who's pretending?" Jack Sun says. "Aren't I my father's Sun?"

"You all stop it," I tell them.

"Do you think you're the only one with blood of Indians in this town?" Mom says.

"I'm the only one that's my father's Sun."

"Your father is *interracial*. And you are *interracial*." Mom says it like it's a tribe all its own.

"Don't give me that," Sun says. "*She's* interracial, if you want," not even looking at me. "But a blood is a blood. Dad's mother was a fullblood."

"We don't know that for sure," Mom says.

"You look at her picture and you know."

"We know how she married," Mom says.

"How?" I ask them, looking from one to the other. I've never heard any talk like this before.

"No, you don't know that, either," Sun says to Mom. "I say she married only part colored in the first place. The rest was hers and it was blood."

"But your father married me. So that gives you less than a sixteenth."

"Or as much as three fourths," Sun says. "Anyway, Dad and I look Amerind."

"Looks don't mean a thing," Mom says. "It's what society says."

"Society has said it all wrong forever. And looks mean everything, and who cares what society says? A blood is a blood."

"No sir."

"He may be light-complexioned," Jack Sun goes on. "He can be dark with blue eyes or blond with coal-black eyes. But if he wants it, he's a blood and the law will back him. You have to agree with that, Moon Mother."

"Stop it," she says.

"You have to agree," he says again. "You wait and see. One day the restless bloods here will reclaim what's theirs. They'll build a nation house and the Feds will give them funds, it's happening all over. And some will be blond and blue-eyed just like country farmers; some will look like Little Moon there, and some will be like me. Because some of the mothers and fathers, grandmothers and grandfathers and even the great-grands never left when the tribes were forced across the Mississippi."

Jack Sun smiled, looking like he was seeing it all. "They stayed, but they melted away into the countryside. And for generations they looked like poor white and poor black farmers. They looked like you, Moon Mother, and they looked like Dad. But they were just waiting. They were bloods, waiting."

"So now everybody's an Indian," Mom says.

"Just maybe you and her and me and my dad," Sun says.

Slowly, Mom shakes her head back and forth. Slowly, Jack Sun nods his head.

They look deep into each other's eyes. Something between them not quite friendly.

This is the strangest dinner table I've ever sat at. All the days of dinner tables being just about

143

the same, something you could depend on to be ordinary, with all kinds of usual, ordinary nourishment. And this time we are the first time like this, with these words and eating.

All at once Mom says, "You always were a brilliant boy. Always different, though, and set apart."

"Yes?" Sun says.

What about me? What am I?

"When you called me Moon Mother, I thought it was your sense of humor, that's all I thought it was," Mom says, looking at him so deep.

"No," Sun says.

Who am I? What part, on which side?

"I see that now," Mom says. "You mean Moon Mother, just like you say it. And Moon Child for Arilla, just like you say it. To differentiate, to set us off from the Sun."

"Why name me the Sun, if not to differentiate?"

"No," Mom says. "I had a dream. The night you were born, and I'll never forget that dream. I was walking down this very dark and lonely road. There were streetlights like question marks about half a mile apart. They couldn't keep the dark back. There was no moon."

Sun smiled.

"Suddenly I stopped in my tracks," Mom said. "I could see the whole earth in the dark. You know the way a harvest moon will come up big and orange? Well, this time a really gigantic *thing* began to rise up from beyond the earth's curvature. It was orange, but it wasn't a moon. It filled the whole night sky with its fire. It was terrifying and it was beautiful. It was the sun.

"The next morning you were born. I couldn't get the dream out of my mind for a minute. So I said to your father, 'Let's name him Golden. Golden Adams.' But Dad saw your long, skinny legs and he said, 'This sun has to run.' That's how you came to be named Sun Run."

"Nice," Jack said. "People shouldn't be named like Jack, after your father. People should be named like Sun Run, by prophecy."

"It was an accident," Mom said.

"No," Jack Sun Run says.

"Oh, yes, Jack, come on."

"No," Jack says. "Maheo, the all one, spooned you that dream just for me."

Mom laughs. I laugh with her.

Jack Sun smiles at us, but his eyes are not laughing.

Mom sips her coffee. She is smiling just a little. "I can't wait to see where you end up," she says.

"Yes?" Jack says.

What about me? Can you wait for me?

"Wish you had a dream when *I* was born. Mom? Then I could be Arilla Jump Over The Sun or something."

Mom laughs. I don't know why I even say that.

Jack-Sun is looking at me. Like a shadow falls over him. The look gives me a chill before it is gone.

"Moon Child is some interesting sometimes, too," he says.

" 'Course I am," I tell him. "Want to hear how interesting?"

He backs up from the table, taking his plate to the sink. Just like that, he puts an end to the meal and keeps from talking to me at the same time.

Sun takes my plate to the sink and Mom's to the sink. He clears off all the dishes and puts warm food from the stove pots on a plate in the low-heat oven. So it will stay warm for Dad. Dad may eat when he comes home or he may not, depending on how he feels. But we always keep food warm for him.

Jack-Sun is such a good waiter he clears the table in a second and with hardly a sound. Always clearing from the seated person's right.

"I don't think I'm finished talking with you," Mom tells him. Looking at me, she smooths back my hair and runs her hand over my cheek. I like when she does that.

Jack stays busy and says nothing to her or to me. When he wants to end a meal, he can be as silent as a thief.

7

"We will have to finish this conversation sometime," Mom says to Sun Run.

She is holding me around the shoulders in her nice way. I lean against her, ever so tired. We stay at the dinner table.

Sun keeps silent at his work. He can clear a table in fast time, but he never will scrape a dish. Mom says, if you ever expect Jack Sun to do more than pile up dirty dishes at the side of the sink, you'd better have the proper flat scrapers on hand, and a barrel for the garbage. She says you'd better have a square vat of scalding water to rinse them — three feet across and four feet deep.

Sun wipes off the table and begins to set out a clean plate, a napkin and silverware for Dad. Looking just like the best waiter in a dining hall.

I've seen my brother waiting on tables with his silver tray. Now, with school on, he works only Sundays. I'll work some Sundays, too, when I'm fourteen. But I have seen Sun carry that oval tray full of dinner plates of food on the flat of his hand. One dinner in the center of the tray for balance and six more surrounding it. Seven on a tray — turkey or chicken dinners with stuffing, and roast lamb with mint jelly and mashed potatoes on a Sunday. Sun holds an eighth dinner in his left hand, with all of the dinners steaming up to the hanging lights overhead. He is so quick the meals stay as hot as when they left the kitchen. Sun can balance that heavy tray of food like it is nothing. He can move through a crowd of diners whose chairs clutter the aisles as if the crowd weren't even in the way. Eight dinners for a round table of evening diners. Sun has already served them their rolls, water, coffee, or tea.

I have seen him trip over a chair leg in that big dining room. The full tray he carries jars out of his hand. It seems like forever that the tray is falling. But Sun catches it before it hits the floor. Not one plate of food is spilled. The whole room of diners starts in clapping for him.

Once I saw him slip on a piece of ice and the whole tray of food flipped and fell in his lap. Gravy and mint jelly dripping down his fingers. And Dad rushed in at the sound of the crash. Dad stopped still when he saw who had made the noise.

"Well, Sun, at least the silverware didn't break."

And all those college diners laughing.

I have seen the college kitchen, where the refrigerator lockers are so large I could roller-skate inside them or pull up a couch in there to lie down. Next to the lockers are metal cabinets about waist high, with round holes in their counters. Deep cardboard containers of ice cream fit into the holes, ice cream that the college makes. Never in my life have I seen so many different kinds of ice cream and that taste so good. And college boys in a line in front of the cabinets, scooping ice cream onto pieces of apple, cherry, pumpkin and berry pie in season, and lining up the pies and ice cream on still more counters. So that waiters like Jack Sun can scoop them up and serve them out in the dining room. Those fantastic pies are made by women and men who are fine cooks. A lot of them are related to me on Mom's side of the family. We have lots of cousins in this town, but few my own age. Mom says her family is now about middle-age and will die out. She says the relatives stayed in one place too long and that the college influence and zero population has sifted through the sand in their brains.

The cooks sure know how to pull fine meals together in that huge, hot kitchen. They always greet me nice when I come in once in a while before the busy dinner hour. I have Dad's permission to get me some free pie and ice cream — man-oh-man!

"Hi-you, Arilla-honey?" the cooks will say, like a bunch of bells chiming Arilla-honey, Arilla-honey, on down the kitchen. Most of them with time for a smile at me — "Hi you doin', Arilla-honey?" Sometimes with some signifying at what Mom says are my *origins*.

"Arilla, you sure you want some fattening pie? Put on a little weight this summer, dint cha, honey?"

"Takes after her father's side."

"Well — " and soft laughter.

"How you know about her father's side!" And snickering.

"I know which side it *am not!*" And whispering and more laughter.

It don't bother me. I know they like me better than they do Mom or Dad or Jack Sun. They think Mom is strange for wanting to dance. She came back home and that was a plus on our side. But if her studio had failed, she says, they would have called her a dreamer-woman to carry on so. Ought to know there's no business in that kind of thing, they'd have said. Now they can't say a thing, with some of the women joining in exercise classes and inching what Dad calls their *ample figures* into The Dance.

They tolerate Dad with some respect because he is good at his job, all will say, and plays no favorites. They used to call him Old Stone Face behind his back because he was so polite. Maybe distant is better, and they couldn't tell what he was thinking, couldn't read him. But they stopped it when one day this weird couple with an out-of-state license came to the dining hall driven by this black chauffeur. Nobody had ever seen a black chauffeur, not even in the movies, usually, and for certain not in for-real life in town. Anyway, these folks out of state wanted a peaceful evening meal on the dining-room screened-in porch, which is really the best place to eat on a summer's evening. They asked Dad to please give their chauffeur — Mr. Bushnell D. Walker was his name — anything he wanted to eat, but, if you please, to feed him in the kitchen.

Dad blew a righteous fuse. I wasn't there, but Jack Sun told how it all happened. He said Dad stood stone still. Didn't move for a full ten seconds. And then he began to shake. After he shook, his face turned darker, like he couldn't breathe. And then he spoke in a steady three-minute rage right up to the out-of-state dude's face:

"Even the cooks don't eat in the kitchen. I wouldn't *have* them eat in that hot kitchen. How dare you enter this establishment with your offensive trash? Everybody eats right out there on the porch before the evening meal, right where you want to eat. Their fingerprints are on the salt and pepper shakers. Their elbows have rested on the same tables. No need to speak about what of theirs has warmed the same chairs. The food you eat will be cooked by their hands — and you come here with . . . with that offensive, that stupid nonsense, when no one has ever come here with it. The black man eats in the dining room or you can take your hunger elsewhere . . ."

Anyway, that was the best part of it. Sun said he was hoping Dad would go ahead and punch out the dude. But Dad never would do a thing like that. Sun said the black man was an old guy afraid he might lose his job. So he felt he'd better fix things by eating his dinner in the dude's car. Dad sent a waiter out and a busboy, and even one of the hostesses to hand him a menu. He sent Sun out as the waiter, to serve the old guy. That's all Sun had to do the whole time — waiting table on the old guy in this white Lincoln Continental. I was always surprised that the out-of-town dude and his wife didn't just leave when Dad started on him. But Sun said he was too scared and embarrassed. And probably too hungry. Anyhow, they all got to eat. After, they paid and they left, with Sun, the hostess, the busboy, my dad and a nice bunch of students that had gathered watching them leave. I don't expect we'll ever see them again, either.

From then on, my cousins — the finest cooks in the county, too — thought that Dad was just about perfect. Still, they don't much like folks close to them to be too perfect. What's there to talk about, to make up gossip and tales about, if the point of interest, Mom says, is above it all and can do no wrong? To them, Dad is much more like a relative at those times when he pulls one of his disappearing acts and is nowhere to be found for a few days. They can't find him. The college jeep he uses is missing. None of them have seen him. The college wants to know where he is. So they cover for him, but they don't know a thing. They think they understand disappearing. Mom says they think they know why it happens — just another poor fool with some weakness in the flesh. All kinds of excitement and they can make up stories. Call him Stony, just the way Mom does.

But when there are strangers around, new people working in the summertime, or a pick-up kitchen crew for the overload of out-of-towners, they call Dad Mr. Adams. Mr. Adams to all outsiders. That's funny because we, Dad and Sun and Mom and me, are always the outsiders at other times. Goes to show that blood is a closed door against the wind.

They hate Jack Sun Run Adams. They hate him with a pure, perfect hate. Because Sun decides to be whatever he wants and as weird as he wants, any day he feels like it. They can't get a handle on him, the way he enters into a world he makes for himself. They do these little mean things to him. Like, they will shun him by never saying a word to him directly. They talk around him when maybe for a few minutes the counter has no pumpkin pie, or something. They know they need to put out more of that kind of pie. Sun comes rushing in wanting the pie. In a minute he knows they know he needs the pie. He waits while they make him wait. He won't ask for it, knowing they know it's their job and knowing they know their job. He's always ahead of them, knowing that if he's too long from the dining room Dad will notice.

"What's he standing there for?"

"Like a fool, too."

"Like a idiot."

"Stealing some time. Tired of working."

"Just lazy. Too big a shot to ask."

"Hair falling all in the food."

"Couldn't pay me to eat his dinners."

And whispering and laughter. Not looking at him or putting out pumpkin pie.

Until Dad comes in. "What's holding it up?" he says to Sun.

"No pumpkin pie ready," Sun says, looking at them, the cousins.

"Pie's been ready for hours — get those pies out there! Now! Do I have to do it all myself?"

Sun laughs. He has got them again. Every time. They put the pies out, flinging them, once Dad's back is turned.

All of it small-minded, Mom says, just spiteful. She says Sun shouldn't even go down to their level. But my brother always does. He knows what to do to beat them in the littlest thing, too. I wouldn't even *care* to beat them. But Sun will play any game, any time. No game is ever too low. And that keeps me on my guard.

Here, still sitting, leaning on Mom. Thoughts jumping over things, with dozing off a few seconds in between. I'm so tired. Our kitchen is always so cozy with its yellow curtains and yellow paint. It's the best place to be when my dad comes home, although I sure should be thinking about bed. I can feel all the little aches in my ankles and in my calves. Legs are going to hurt me tonight. Sometimes they get so muscle-tight they hurt me the whole night through.

Seems like we've been here at the table a long time. But it's not much later when Dad comes in. Bringing a swirl of fresh night air with him clear into the kitchen. I must have been dozing good, for Sun isn't in the kitchen. Everything is neat and ready for Dad. Sun is waiting for him in the hall there. He always waits for Dad like that when he's wanting to go out somewhere. Sun is neat and casual with just the thinnest silk headband tied in a knot just above his ear. I've tried to wear headbands knotted like that and they look awful.

He and Dad stand in the light of the hall, facing each other. Standing close, Dad is on this side, and flings an arm over Sun's shoulder. Sun is looking down at the floor, talking right in Dad's ear. They talk low and for a long time. Most often they have this long, private say between them. I wonder, does Sun tell Dad about his whole day? How he is going to hurt me? Or does he make up a whole day like my dad would want to hear? Does Sun say that Mom doesn't want him out of the house?

Dad eases his arm away. He stands looking at Sun. Sun Run is not quite as tall. Both of them have their hands deep in pockets now. Run can meet Dad's gaze, but not for more than a few seconds before he has to look down at the floor again. I get the feeling more than once that Sun has these layers. Thin, like onion skins. And the longer he looks at Dad's eyes, the more skins peel away. Brother has this wall of respect for Dad. You can see it the way he stands there. Layers peel away and Run lets Dad see him as some sixteen-year-old waiting for permission.

"Hi, Daddy," I have to say. Dad turns toward the kitchen. It's awful to see him, for a split second, have to think who I am. So deep he has been into Jack Sun Run. If he stood somewhere on a beach, I'd be just a small wave around his ankles.

"I told Sun he couldn't go out," Mom says. "I told him he will just make problems for that girl."

Mom hits Dad like a wave behind his back.

"We kept the food warm for you again," I say.

"Arilla, you should be in bed by now," he says. "Did you do your homework? You should be sleeping."

"I told him he'd better start studying and leave the night alone," Mom says.

Wave upon wave, we hit him. Sun is easing toward the front door.

"You let him have his way," Mom says, "and that just makes it worse."

"Makes what worse?" I ask. "You want me to fix your plate, Dad?"

Sun is out the door.

"You see?" Mom says. "How am I ever going to teach him anything when you let him always have his way?"

"It's nothing to think about," Dad says. So handsome in a dark suit. Hair falling so soft on his collar. "You can't tie him down," Dad says. "You can't keep his spirit in forever."

Dad, hi, talk to me.

Dad is slowly moving around the table now, as if he's trying to find his place. Never does he take his hands from his pockets. You can see them knotted up, holding keys and change. He gives Mom a nice kiss, but she won't be taken in.

"You know there's curfew not two hours away," Mom says. "You know he'll never get back in time."

"He has my permission," Dad says.

"He's supposed to be with an adult if he's out after curfew, you know that. He's no different from any other teenager. He has to obey the rules."

Dad says, "The trouble is, my kids *are* different. They will always be different." A great sadness.

He is talking about me, too. Talking about me, different.

"Daddy, are you hungry? I'll get the food from the oven."

He touches my shoulder, meaning for me to be still.

Mom says, "If he breaks the curfew, he's going to get the girl in deep with her father."

"Diavolad won't even know she's out of the house," Dad says.

"How can you be in favor of that? That's even worse," Mom says. "Supposing they get caught? What then? You are going to have to do the apologizing. I wash my hands of it." Mom sighs. "It all will get worse just because you never want to say no to him."

"Nobody's going to catch the Sun," Dad says.

"Oh, stop it, please. He's not a god. He's just a kid."

Dad says, smiling at Mom, "You know better, but you won't admit it."

Where am *I?* What about *me?*

"I know the law polices that skating rink. And eleven o'clock comes, all kids under age better be out of there, too."

I could tell Mom a thing or two about eleven o'clock. I could tell her how you manage the law.

"Sun has strong medicine," Dad says, touching Mom's face. That does it. She looks like she is going to punch him, but she won't.

"Arilla," she says, "go to bed. You'll be tired in the morning."

"I have homework." I haven't even seen my dad. Now I lean on his shoulder. "I have to write this paragraph." About my first friend from the time I was very little. "We are doing our autobiographies."

Dad pats my arm. But he is speechless now. No words for me.

A great sadness stalking the table.

"All right, then," Mom says. "You take twenty minutes to do your homework and five or ten to get your nightclothes on. Then, into bed. Stony will tuck you in."

I don't need tucking in, but I don't say it. I like my dad to come into my room, pull the covers tight around my neck, brush my hair back. Like putting parentheses around The End of the Day. Putting a period after the parentheses. I never feel the day is done unless Dad comes to make sure I am ready for sleep, parentheses, period.

"Go on now," Dad says. Lifts his head away from me. "We'll talk tomorrow," he says. He knows how I feel. "You go on, study. I'll be up there in a while."

So they make me leave. "Good night, all." Sounding lighthearted.

"Good night, Arilla."

"Good night, baby."

I go on up to my room. Turn on the light. Hope to goodness I can do a paragraph when I'm so tired out. I stack all my books on the floor and open my notebook on the bed. Kneel on the floor. Not so comfortable, but better than falling asleep in a chair. I have this really neat notebook. It's heavy cardboard front and back, and covered with real blue-jeans material, and with a blue-jeans pocket on the front cover where to keep pencils and pens. Jack Sun got me the notebook. Every fall he goes with me for my school supplies. Mom makes him, so I won't buy out the store, she says. Nobody trusts me to do anything well. We, Sun and me, came back with all my supplies except for a notebook.

"She wants only the one notebook," Sun told Mom. "And it costs six dollars."

"No notebook can cost six dollars."

"Well, the one she's heart-set-on is six dollars."

"You mean, six dollars empty, with nothing in it, not even a slip of paper?"

"Six dollars empty," Sun says.

"Never," Mom told him.

"She wants it," Sun says. "I'll chip in a dollar fifty, that's all I can spare."

"How come you are so willing to be nice to your sister?" Mom, teasing him.

"Moon never wants anything," Jack Sun tells her. "But this, she wants."

Mom thought about it awhile and finally gave in. Giving Sun a good, hard look to see if he was kidding. He wasn't: the notebook was six dollars. We went on back downtown and got it.

I knew he wasn't being nice to me or anything. Without me saying too much about it, Sun knew I wanted that notebook. If he'd a wanted something, he'd a got it. Somehow. So he was just doing for me what he would a done for himself.

He organized the notebook for me. Putting in all the separate subject dividers and writing in the subject names on the little tabs, so I could keep my homework in each subject section. And put in all the three-ring, lined notebook paper. Glad to have him do it because I would've just messed it all up. Brother is the best organizer of anything. His mind is like that, ready to put things together before you know you need them put together. Mom says, "I'm out of potatoes for potato salad!" Or, "Darn it, I forgot to buy eggs." Even before she stops talking, Sun is going down the street to get what she needs.

Well, I know I'm thinking about Jack Sun Run so's I don't have to think about what I'm going to write for my autobiography. 'Course, the best way to write anything is just to start writing. Mrs. Donley of Language Arts says I am most *energetic* and full of fresh imagining when it comes to some written word.

Keep talking in my head so I won't think what to write. I only had one friend when I was little, is what breaks in on my head talking. So I write it down:

I only had one friend when I was little. And he was an old man. To tell you what he looked like is something I can't remember too well. But I think that to the small child I was, he looked like a tall tree standing in shadow.

Nice. Now make a paragraph. Don't think.

His name was Mr. James.

That's a lie.

He rode a horse that was Appaloosa, just like the kind I have myself. He rode all across this country with his wife.

Me tightening inside. Feeling peculiar, the way I always will when trying too hard to remember. Maybe I was never a child. I mean, I was born grown-up but never even knew it. The grown-up just waiting to get out. And is still waiting.

Her name was Mrs. Susanne James.

That's part lie. I don't want to tell their names without telling who they were. I'm not sure who they were. Don't think about it. Just write. How James-Face was my friend.

Mr. James took care of me while my mom worked.

Another lie, but write it anyway.

He was a neighbor and too old to have a job. Mr. James would take me riding on his horse and show me some streams and the fishes. And show me flowers and good plants for healing, along the water.

End it. It's long enough. Don't tell anything about your feelings. Me. I'm talking to me, telling me to be careful.

Mr. James was a great baby-sitter. I remember we used to gather apples right off the trees in the woods. And cook fishes right out of the stream. Mr. James would make a fire and we'd cook the fishes wrapped in special leaves. I don't know the names of the leaves. And we would bake apples between two hot rocks shaped like bowls. Or we would bake fishes between two clumps of clay, like you make a mold for something. And the clay would get hard with heat. We would let the clay

162

get cool and then we'd open it. You can believe that was the best hot fish ever I did taste, too.

Oh, there's more, if I could just think the good things and not feel so bad inside. But end it now.

I never had another friend like Mr. James. And I'll never forget him.

The End.

Good enough for Donley. She'll write on my paper, something like "Arilla, tell us more! A." We will have weeks and weeks of writing our autobiographies. How am I going to keep from telling about this family? It'll take so much work, making it all up. But don't think about it. Get to bed.

Put my notebook on the pile of books. Kick off my shoes and pull on my riding boots again. And putting my nightgown on over my clothes. Roll up my sleeves so's they won't show under the three-quarter arms of my blue nightgown. I'll get too hot in all these clothes, keeping the blanket up to my neck. But I'm used to it. Maybe I won't need to stay dressed. Might not even wake up. Anyhow, I'll be ready.

Close the light and leave the door open a crack. Get in and pull the covers up. I'm full of little jumps of being so deep of tiredness. But I sink on down. The last thing I know is of keeping covers up over me. And I'm gone to sleep.

8

Saying that kids can sleep the sleep of the blessed. Mom. Saying that sleep is the best medicine for healing hurts. And she is right on. I come to in the dark, knowing that Dad has come and gone. I am wide awake at once. Haven't a hurt anywhere in me, not even my leg muscles. I've slept as easy as a little babe, if only for three hours or so. I figure the time is around twelve-thirty. What I need is my own clock with some numbers lit in the dark. I just stay relaxed in bed and wait.

Jack Sun says the best way for to wake someone is not to hit the bedroom window.

He says, "If you use small stones against the glass, you'll never hear them. And if you use larger stones, you'll perchance to crack the glass."

What he does is to take a clump of dirt, like a clod, and throw it at the house right next to the window. It's enough of a different sound so's to wake you up. That's what must've wakened me. I wait and, sure enough, there comes the soft

164

thud so like throwing a rubber boot on a wood floor.

I get up easy, not too slow, not too fast. Throw off my nightgown. Cross the room and out my door. Not opening the door real wide, but just so to get me through.

Jack Sun has warned me — walk down any hall and down any stairs like you walking it in daytime, when you are full of strength but walking lightly. He says if you tiptoe or move real slowly, someone is bound to hear you. Because tiptoeing is never natural. Walking slow, afraid to be heard and of every sound, is not natural. Says nobody is going to wake up when you move the way you always move.

Know he's right, too. But it sure is hard not to slow down and get up on tip-toe. I force myself and I don't slow down. Take the hall like going to the bathroom. Steady and easy. I get down the stairs, making whatever little noises are natural.

Comes the hard part. Getting the front door open without clicking the lock. Sun says any house-owner is primed to hear locks clicking.

But Sun is there. He has used a plastic ID card on the slip lock. I see the doorknob turn. The door slides open an inch as he holds the knob just so and holds back the clicking. All for me to do is slip off the night chain, and that isn't easy. Sun has to close the door near to the whole way. My hands shake and the chain will clink if I'm not careful. But I catch hold of me inside and calm me down. I'm out the door.

The night air, so crisp. No stars above looking like little gems. Cloudy, and no moon tonight. A dark night and I'm going to be cold. But they've brought an extra sweater for me. She puts it into my hands. I can hardly see her. Angel Diavolad. Dark Angel. I know she must be smiling at me like she's a big sister. Big brother and big sister.

We start out at once. Everyone staying quiet, staying in shadows. I never even wonder anymore where they go and what they do before coming to get me. I just am full of going.

We know how to move in the dark. Jack Sun and Angel lead the way. He has her by the hand and she has my hand. That way, if we have to hide, I'll know it in a moment. Sun will jerk her by the arm, and they won't need to pull me down. But we have no trouble. We stay along treelines, off the sidewalks and streets. It's not far. We will not have to cross the highway up ahead, near the rink. We will use the way of the Little Egypt River that runs the boundary of this town. Really it's not a river. More like a wide stream; this time of year, cold and not near as much water as in the spring. We'll walk under the highway. We'll go through this viaduct, along the edge of it, where there is no water rising. And we are all of us so full of nerve at being in the night and going. We are safe and unseen, with Sun leading.

What it is. Is a truce between Sun and me. I

know just the way he has made it out, that the world he makes up for himself he fits for-real in his mind. Sun is that much superstitious to need me along with them.

The day is his. But the night belongs to me. He is the sun. But I am the moon child. I give him the safe passage through darkness and whatever danger. He'll never want me dead in this time. So it is a truce, with him letting Angel hold my good-luck hand.

I'm catching a scent of Angel's perfume as we go. It's so sweet but not strong. I'm scenting it and noticing how the rink sound changes as we get closer. We are very close now. We've been on a curve, all the way down from the house to the Little Egypt. We walk along the sides of property, behind bushes and hedges and in between trees. Only coming out for an instant where properties end and we must go out on the sidewalk to get around fences. Just need to step around a fence and into the next property. We can stay hidden when there is a front-yard hedge. Where we have to cross side streets, we have to turn the corner, still hidden, and go down the block. Find enough darkness to cross in the open. We do that, coming up the other side, turning the corner, and hidden, walking steady, with a careful eye for cops, the way Sun knows how to do it. Sun says the police stay in close to business buildings, or out in the south plat where all the money is in big houses with alarms. Sun knows the rounds of the police as well as they do. One time we had to stand like trees for maybe ten seconds while this squad car slipped along the side street. We watched it go, a lone policeman behind the wheel.

Where's the other one?

Maybe having a sandwich and Coke at the rink.

We'll go in slow. Let Sun make sure before we bust in.

We have come out in the open in the light so's to cross the dead-end road in front of the old high school. Not a school anymore, but a community center. Big and dark. Silent, and no one around this late.

Sun leads across the dead-end pavement onto grass and weeds at the top of the riverbank, right under the streetlight. He leads us fast. In an instant we are over the bank and hidden again. At the edge of the stream my brother stops and leans his back against the viaduct. There the opening is scary black where the stream goes through.

Sun says, "Hurry it up," so softly.

Angel says, "Only a minute." I can hardly hear her or him, the rink being so close on the other side of the viaduct.

The sound of it is a steady grinding. Here you can't hear the music as well, for the air carries it off toward home.

I'm about to die with excitement.

"Stay still," Angel tells me. She always tells me that.

"I'm *trying*."

"Keep it down," Sun says.

I want to tell him, who does he think can hear us way down here and with that roar going? But I don't say a word.

Angel clips these large button earrings on my earlobes. I hate the way they squeeze. She ties a silky scarf around my hair, letting it hang low to my shoulders so I will look older.

"Match," she says.

At once Sun cups a lighted match in his hands, and she presses the make-up to my lips.

"One second and I'm putting it out," Sun says.

She is rubbing some make-up on my cheeks. "It stinks," I whisper.

She giggles.

The match goes out. "Okay," Sun says. Checks the water. I see him bent over. "Arilla in the middle this time," he says.

"You mean Moon Child," I tell him, but he says nothing.

We take hands again, with me in the middle. We go in the viaduct. It is pitch black in here. The air is warmer. You hear the music and the grinding skates and some gurgle of water up close in your mind. The water smells of iron. I can't see a thing. Angel's hand is tight over mine. Sun has my other hand so strong. Oh, Sun, this is the best old time! He knows it. And which do we like the most — skating or within the night, being dangerous?

We face the water with our backs to the wall

of the viaduct. Creatures scurry ahead of us. My eyes wide open, but I see nothing. We move along in a slow-dance shuffle. All around is dampness and the smell of iron. But the Little Egypt waters never touch us. We move in rhythm with — never touch us; never touch us. Left right-leg; left right-leg.

Darkness always seems to take longer. But then we are out of the black viaduct. The highway is right above us, with lights and cars. The skating rink is just below us, a short ways ahead.

We've come all the way along a great sideways S curve of land downhill to a final low level. Home is at the left tip of the sideways S. The viaduct and the Little Egypt are along the middle curve of the S. The rink is on the right tip of the S. It sits there below, to one side of a flat level land with the park behind it.

I shiver all over at the sight of that ten-foot neon sign flashing — SKATELAND 68. SKATELAND 68. The rink is named after the State Route 68, which is the highway above us. Beyond the rink lights, there is darkness. The park is a timber forest. The part of it where Sun will ride Jeremiah, he will call the glen. And when you look down from here toward the rink, you are looking through tall and scattered forest trees.

We follow a path worn along the slope of a gentle ridge. Jack Sun is leading, of course. Hurrying on ahead now, he is out of sight in darkness.

Angel and me have to take our time for fear of slipping and falling.

"I hate this part," she says.

"I sure do, too," I say. But I don't. I love all of it.

It begins to rain down on us so gently. All around, the sound, like wind starting up high in the trees and many leaves falling. That's why it's so dark tonight. Rain clouds. I don't mind rain. I like the sound. A fall rain and no warning of its coming, but for clouds.

Angel is right with me. We take our time going off the ridge down a slope. And now we are getting wet enough to make us chilly.

"Will it cause my make-up to run?" I ask her.

"It'll be okay," she says. Never saying, Girl, you think of the dumbest things. Just like a dumb kid.

We are down. And walking through grasses and weeds getting slick with the wet. In a minute I wish I was back in my bed. But not for long.

People are running out of the rink with their skates still on. They skate on down the sidewalks. Making a lot of noise rolling to the parking lot to make sure their car windows are closed. They are mostly older and some younger ones finished with high school.

Sun waits for us in front of the entrance to the rink.

We come up close and he says right in our faces, "It's all clear. But be ready in case of an emergency." We don't have to say anything back. We know what to do.

We all three hurry inside, laughing and swaggering some, like I am older, like we've been having this great time somewheres else and are giving this old rink a treat because we've come here.

We get inside. "We couldn't be luckier," Angel says. Jack Sun nods, and it's the truth.

We have come at the Snowball Time. The Snowball is spinning and spinning. This lighted ball, huge, and covered with mirrors, hanging from the ceiling and turning. It spins to make spots of white light and mirror reflections of light all over the floor and walls, and on the skaters. It makes skaters look like they are speeding in the dark through falling snow swirling in a whirling wind.

"Let me get in there! Hurry up!" I tell Sun and Angel.

But they take it easy. There is this cashier's cage with a woman in it right near the entrance. I keep an eye on her and all around, too, but nobody looks at me closely in the Snowball.

Sun walks up and buys the tickets. Tickets cost a dollar each. The reason why we can't come here more than once a week, or once on weekends. Sun has to pay for all of us because I have no money and because Angel is his date. It costs fifty cents each for skates. Sun has his own skates which he bought from the rink. He keeps them here so Mom will never know. And so the rink maintenance can oil them and take better care of them.

Jack Sun has the tickets and we go over to the left where you pick up the skates. The Snowball is still going on. Noise is so loud, and music and snow falling. Skaters whirling around. Late at night, Sun says, this place is crowded from workers off the night shift, or laid off from machinery and tool plants. They hurry in here for the need of unwinding. Some little bit of smart skating for to relax tensed-up muscles. Sun says, for some fun going around the rink and messing around with chicks and dudes before home tired and trying to sleep.

We take our skates to a bench right up front by the rail of the rink. Sun's skates are fine-looking, with maple-wood rollers like the sweet maple wood of the rink floor. Mine and Angel's are just good shoe skates for stroking along. I'm a pretty good skater but not as good as she is or as Sun is.

Seeing her in the light. Like a wheat stalk bending in a field. She has on wheat-colored pants and shirt, I think. Hard to tell with white spots of the Snowball over everything. She or Sun, either, don't give me a second glance, so my costume of being older must look all right. Sun always looks like a rich boy from some big-deal school in Hawaii or some place of tropics. In a place of lots of people from towns, he doesn't look American or even like a blood. But some special breed from some special place. People always do look him over hard. Especially when he has Angel on his arm. They make a combination of grandness, and I think they must know it.

The hardest and the slowest part is getting my shoelaces tight enough. Angel gets Sun to tighten them for me. He does and then he tightens Angel's.

I love the truce with Jack Sun Run. He loves Angel. She likes me. And he doesn't hate me in the truce. We are ready to skate into the rink.

We are cars going on a freeway. Only, cars have these lanes to travel. We have just an invisible space between ourselves. You have to sprint fast to get into the rink. You have to find the pace of everybody moving in the same direction and at the same speed. It takes no time, and I am stroking along. With each new stroke, one foot or the other touches lightly on the floor. Real smoothly, I glide in my curve of travel. Left skate curves toward the center of the rink; my right skate curves toward the railing. Toes pointing down for to look so graceful. I lean in and I lean out, and to tilt in a straight line sideways toward the floor. I have lost Sun and Angel in the stream of skaters in the Snowball Time.

I am free and rolling free, with nothing holding me back. This is the best old time. Wheels under my shoes tickling my feet. I can hardly stand the way it feels so real funny at first. But soon that tickling goes away.

A dude coming up on my right. We call him a referee, dressed in black-and-white-striped shirt and black pants with black shoe skates. There are usually two referees. They all of the time skate to make sure the pace is just fast enough but not crazy. Anyone who spills they take quickly off the floor.

The referee right beside me. I make myself look straight ahead. Make some long, graceful strokes. Looking peaceful and bored, until the dude strokes on ahead of me.

"Good. I'm okay." To myself.

A woman in this really short skating outfit has two men stroking on either side of her. All painted up with a pink ribbon in long, very dyed black hair. Looking like she is a high-school girl, almost. Older people behind me and all around.

Music is loud. The skating is so loud. All of me is skating hard and there is no unhappiness in my stroking. All the tired and all sadness rolls away behind me. A pure, sweet feeling is rolling with me. Ahead of me, I think rolling I will come to something stroking that I have never come to before. Someday.

In the center of the rink is this really huge area marked off by a black circle. Early evening, and skaters who are still learning skate within the black circle. Tonight, no one skates there except for an old guy. Sun says they call him Long Neck Sport-'em-O. I've seen him a couple of times, too. Because he dresses sporty, although he is all of seventy-two if he's a day, and because he strokes along with his neck thrown way forward. So really weird and funny to see.

But Long Neck is a supreme skater. What they call a purist because he follows all the rules of skill. He can do the School of Figures, all the positions and combination figure eights without ever changing a one of them. They say he can. No one I know's ever seen him. But we believe he can, because what we've seen him do is letter-perfect. Right now he is finishing up a serpentine, which is a three-circle figure. In the final circle he changes his lean super cool to the center. Now he's in the primary outside forward edge. He is going to complete letter-perfect, as folks say here.

I just go around, not racking my brain much to figure out the names and stuff of what he is doing. But just watching the old guy, wondering how it feels to be old and to skate with everyone secretly watching you, to learn it from you. I wouldn't mind to grow old and die on rollers, I sure wouldn't.

Come Angel and Jack Sun stroking me by on the outside. They do what is called a tandem dance position but without touching. Sun is stroking directly behind Angel so that their feet are in line. They are skate-dancing through the music, which is the best way. Never touching, they take the Snowball in what is the precision time, and they look wonderful. I race to catch them, they took me so by surprise. I catch them and skate all around them, always keeping a stroke ahead of them. Not too cool, going so fast.

Sun looks worried, glances around for the referee. He and Angel open a space for me between them. Sun is in back of me, and Angel in front. We skate precision. We are tight not touching on cornering. It feels like we stroke faster and faster in the snowballing. Snow falling all over us, all over the ground. We skate all around. We skate on down the snow, getting smaller and smaller. Faster. Taking off from a hilltop and watching yourself go down, getting smaller and smaller.

"We're going to fall over! Sun!" But he doesn't hear me. Angel hears it and slows the stroke. Soon lights come up, not too bright. Ends the Snowball Time.

Sweating in Angel's sweater, I am cold with this creepy fear.

"It felt like I was going over," I tell her.

"Going over what?" she says.

"Going . . . to fall," I lie, I don't know why. Then we break out of our three-some. They skate on away. I slow down. My legs feeling shaky.

"Okay, folks, settle down." Coming to us over the PA system. The voice of this manager who plays some of the records.

Everybody skates along without some music, getting used to lights without the Snowball. The roar is steady, without a swing to it. All of rhythm goes out of me. I'm tired.

"Okay, folks, get in the groove. Time for the

Couples' Skate." Up come some soft lights called the Moonlight.

Meaning for singles to find partners. I hate the doubles skate, and to think it makes me all out of line and leaning wrong. Can't make up my mind to be on the sidelines and maybe seen, or look for Sun or Angel to be my partner. I know they will want to skate couple together.

Jack Sun coming up fast beside me, black hair flying in the breeze skaters make going around. "Moon, find someone or else get off the floor!"

"Let me skate with Angel."

"No. You find someone!"

"Who can I find?" But he is gone, stroking up to Angel ahead of me. Taking her in this full-face waltz position. The music comes on loud in a blues fox-trot. Sun changes their position to the blues prime. Which is just him and Angel standing side to side. Her left arm across his chest to hold his left hand. His right arm behind her back and hand holding her right hand at her hip. They begin the dance with a real pretty four-step corner sequence, with the first two strokes one beat each and the third, on their left feet for two beats. It's more than pretty, but I've got to get off the floor.

When this person grabs me in position for the blues. "Now, girlie, what er you doin' out here all by your lonesomes?"

Oh my lord, it's Long Neck Sport-'em-O. With nobody to stroke with.

"I can't do the dancing too good," I manage to

stammer at him. Just scared to death and thrilled at the same time.

"Girlie, this is easy as pie."

A good thing he isn't so tall and I'm not any shorter, or I'd never get my arm across his chest.

Well, he is expert and it is pie-easy when you have him to follow. There's Angel and Sun stroking alongside. Giving me and my partner a look, with Angel giggling at us.

Old Long Neck smiles right back at them. "Sure. Now ain't we something?"

"Pure pleasure!" Sun yells back. He gives me a look, which to say that me and my partner are a queer sight. I could have killed him.

It's strange dancing on skates next to a seventy-two-year-old man. Not that I have much experience, but once in a while one of the younger guys will turn me a few dances. But Long Neck is much lighter on his feet and so smooth. His grip is strong, but he will breathe in real short breaths down on my arm. And he sometimes grunts with all of the moving. What would I do if he passed out right there on the floor with a quitting heart? Don't even think it! I concentrate on LOF's (Left foot on the outer edge of the skate and forward motion) and RIF's (Right foot on the inner edge of the skate and forward motion) and the XB's, which are strokes sliding the right foot back and crossing behind the left heel, and stepping down on the forward half of the right foot. In a short time I don't have to think the move-

179

ments at all. Oh, that blues dance is pure pleasure for sure.

I don't mind who sees me dancing with him. Barely care if they see me as a kid trying to be older, and him ancient and trying to be younger. Why shouldn't he roll himself on into heaven if he wants? That sure must be the best way to go, too.

Sun and Angel pass us by in long strokes through the music. Suddenly we are up on them again and they move in close. I can hear Sun yelling something through Long Neck's funny breathing.

"What?" I yell back across to Sun.

All I hear him say next time is something like "urgency." He gives up yelling over the blues and the roar of skates. He mouths the word: E MER GEN CY.

Oh, my lord. Oh, for heaven . . . I'm out of step, out of rhythm. Losing my balance!

You are responsible. Me, for killing the old guy.

The next thing I know, I contact Long Neck's left foot. Pure and simple, I trip him.

We are going down. He's down, flat on his back. And me down hard on my knees like I'm going to give a prayer.

The shame, and with referees all at once all over the old guy, dragging him in a split second out of the line of skaters. Bodies hurl away from me, not missing a stroke. I have messed up a whole floor of rhythm. And all of them staring at me. Some angry stares, and maybe seeing I'm only a kid that shouldn't be there. Because kids don't know how to have some respect.

Somewhere in that awful spill I had a second to see this policeman standing at the rail with one of the men who run the place.

E MER GEN CY

And somewhere in there I know I've hurt my knees so bad the pain is terrible. Ref's going to get me. Coming, and no more than a second or two from the time they got my partner.

I'm up on my feet and rolling. Skating like crazy. And off the rink. No time to look for Sun and Angel. I'm off the rink down the ramp full force to the girls' restroom.

"Hey, young woman!" The last I hear someone calling. The cop, for sure. Will he come in after me?

I bust open the door just as this large woman in a green pantsuit is preparing to leave. I clip her arm, spinning her around, and I hit one of the swinging doors of the cubicles hard.

"Well, for pity . . . Whyn't you slow down afore you wreck some hav-oc on somebody!" She's a right to be mad, too.

"Sorry. Dint mean to hurt you." I lock myself in the cubicle. Just for a minute until the woman has skated on out of there. I skate to the bench under the window. Have to hurry. I picture the policeman easing up on the restroom and I have to get away.

"Oh, my goodness."

How'm I going to get anywhere on the skates? I have to, and scramble up on the bench under the window next to the sinks. Holding tight to the windowsill and happen to remember the restroom is above ground level. Because you roll down the ramp to it. But when you stand on the floor, the window is above your head. There's got to be a drop from the window on the outside of the building.

Try to remember what the outside looks like coming down from the viaduct. No great big falling off of land, as I recall. Probably more like a six-feet drop.

We always knew this would happen one time. So why didn't we figure how far one of us would have to leap?

I force the window up and I climb over, one foot at a time. One skate scrapes my ankle. Hurting myself and feeling rain on my face, sudden.

And jump. Hands holding my stomach when I should've had my arms out for balance. Too late.

The ground comes up so fast and hard. The worst kind of shock. A blow that shoots straight up my legs clear to my scalp. Can't breathe, skates flying out from under me. My behind hits so hard I'm going to die. Seconds, seeing sparkles.

I come to, cold and wet and hurting. Angel's sweater must be a mess. I can't move until I can breathe. It is the awfulest feeling, to wait for breath and know you might die.

When finally I can get up, I remember the skates and so I crawl as fast as I can. Know where I am, in the flat meadow place next to the rink where the Little Egypt used to run through. I crawl on and on with my knees hurting, killing me. Soon I get on my feet, walking and rolling a little bit at a time. Making so much noise, but the rink roar must cover it. Have to get to the timber of the park. Maybe I won't get busted if I'm on state property. Me clinking through the weeds takes so long! It's so dark and rainy — supposing somebody is hiding!

Don't even think it, so I go on in the dark. And scared, about to cry like a baby. Oh, why did I get into this? Just need to moan and whine, like a baby. Somewhere inside, I know what it's like to be all alone. And lost.

"Sun? Is that you?" It's only a tree coming up on me fast. There are lots of trees now, and I must be in the state park. I have to stop because land does these strange dips into gullies and ravines. I hide myself behind a tree, just shaking to death.

I'm way far out behind and to the side of the rink. I'm far out and can see the lights and just hear the loudspeaker, but I can't make it out. The voice sounds like an echo of God or something.

Scary. I can't help shivering, getting cold as ice. Just sort of crying with my voice against the tree bark. But not really crying, I'm too scared.

Oh, no! I left my boots. I've got their skates! Now they will bust me for stealing. And I do start to snivel like a baby, I can't help myself.

Sun? Whyn't you come on? Oh, I just feel so awful and afraid. The dark is the worst thing in the world by yourself. If Sun would just come this one time, I swear to Mom, I'll never run off like this ever again. You know you don't mean it. Yes, I do, too. No, you don't, either.

Wait. Wait forever holding the tree and jumping at every sound. My knees hurt me so bad.

Wait. I know he will come get me. With my shoes? I know he will. Does he think I'm lost? Does he figure I'm gone on home? On roller skates? Maybe he will get even, to leave me here to die. But I remember, it's a truce.

Wait. Forever. I'm going to be sick for sure. My throat is just closing up on me.

All at once, somebody. Moving through grasses. I hold death-still. Let it come clear by me. It's going past, my lord, maybe six feet away in the dark. You can always tell in the dark when something's moving. Sun says you hear a little and you see a little, but mostly you feel it. Rain rustling like leaves.

"Arilla?" Just a whisper.

"Angel!" I leap out and scare her half to death.

Didn't mean to. Her skates and mine sounding like a car wreck in the quiet.

She grabs hold of me and I just lean on her, half-crying and -laughing for happiness.

"You poor kid, are you hurt?"

"Yes."

"Where?"

"My knees, mostly." My voice is shivering. "I thought you all wouldn't come find me."

"Your brother was sure mad."

"I'm sorry."

"But they don't know who you were or who you came with. Man. This is the dumbest thing I've ever done."

I like Angel better when she is quiet, looking special on Sun's arm.

And then another sound through the weeds. Coming on fast. We stand still, and soon I can tell it must be Sun. He is there with us.

He says to me, "You really did it this time."

"I'm sorry."

"No time for sorry. Come on, get the skates off."

"You get my boots?"

"How can I get them without the skates? Take 'em off!" He screams at me.

"But my feet will get all wet!"

"Come *on!*"

Nothing but to sit down and take the skates off. So I sit and I work, just all wet from the rain, and muddy. I bet he hoped I'd killed myself jumping down.

I don't bother to peer over for either one of them. I bet he's holding her and kissing her face. He's always got her in the dark and kissing her face. I think teenagers in love very much are stupid. I kick the skates off, hard, and get to my feet.

Jack Sun comes to take the skates. "Man, what a mess. I'll have to try to clean 'em off before I can take them back." Right away, he rubs them with his shirt and scrapes them along his pants.

"You knew sometime we'd have an emergency," Angel says.

"But she didn't have to run out," Sun saying it to me. "All she had to do is keep dancing, or go off and get a Coke."

"The cop yelled right at me," I tell him.

"Yeah, because you went out of the rink like someone had set fire to you. If anybody'd been coming up that ramp, you'd both be in the hospital. The cop was just trying to get you to slow down."

Sun was moving off toward the rink. A second of silence. Then Sun's voice coming from the dark:

"Better hope the skates aren't ripped or anything. If I don't come right back, Angel, you take her on home."

Angel makes a mean sound in the dark. Know she must hate me now.

"I'm sorry for everything."

But she is silent. We wait in the cold and rain, neither of us saying a word. I feel just awful, like I will vomit. My head aches so bad and I'm so cold now.

But I have skated again. And there's nothing can beat the feel of stroking along so free and easy.

A long kind of time before Sun makes his way back. Yes! He has my boots and I don't ask him anything. I know he's so mad at having to get back and forth through the wet. I'm pulling on my boots and it's a shame to get the fine leather all wet inside. My socks are soaking.

When I'm ready, we head out into the vast dark of the forest park. We get up high on a ridge opposite of the rink. It's going to be a long way around and a hard way to go. But nobody will chance to see us.

Sun has to find this twisting trail they say was once for sure a Shawnee Indian trail. He finds the path at last, after wandering us through weeds and stumbling us into sticker plants. Good I've got boots, too. Nobody bothers to hold my hand or help me. Is it still a truce, with my luck so bad? I could cry, but I don't. I just follow as close to them as I can by the sound of their moving.

She and Sun holding on to each other and probably smooching. You'd think they'd be serious about having to walk a couple of long miles and even more to get home. Maybe their way is what kids mean by "serious." Jack Sun Run Adams and Angelica Diavolad are getting serious. That's most probably what kids will say when they find out. I wonder what Monserrat Diavolad will say.

Thinking like that, and about Mom and Dad, all the way home. How'm I going to get my wet clothes off and into the hamper in the bathroom, and into my bed? Thinking about everything and skating; then, feeling really awful and alone. No one to hold on to. But think about anything except how long it's taking us. My legs almost refuse to walk. I trip and nearly fall; no one to stop for me. I have to hurry in the dark to catch up, and nobody cares.

It feels like hours and hours until I know I have had it. I'm not going to make it. When, all at once, we are home, coming up on the back of the house. No lights, it is all dark and sleeping. We go quietly around to the front. Sun strips open the door. Whispers, "Hide the wet clothes in the hamper. I'll take them out when I get back. And tomorrow I'll take them over to the laundromat so Mom — "

"I know it. You don't have to tell me!"

Then, inside the house and not even hearing Sun and Angel slipping away. Up the stairs, like walking in the afternoon and no tiptoeing. Into the bathroom. Slip off all my clothes and Angel's scarf wrapped around the earrings. Clean up myself a little. And hurry out with a towel around me and into my room.

My room. My room. Thank goodness, so warm and safe. Oh, I'm tired!

I hide my boots way back in the closet and hope they will dry before I need them by tomorrow after school. And hope Mom will never have to see them so cruddy wet.

I have to chance the light by my bed. Take the towel and wipe off some wet and stuff. My knees, ooh, they are bruised so. They are going to be so sore in the morning and I can't tell Mom how they hurt, either.

Quick, into my nightgown and off with the light. Into my bed under the covers. Sheets. Oh, so sweet. I'm warming up, but feeling my cold feet and legs cold as ice. Shaking all over. I'm shivering and hoping to goodness I don't come down with the flu. Slowly, I breathe easy and get calm. Somewhere, within a shiver, I fall asleep. Dreaming — not on rollers but just the feel of rolling. I am dead to the world.

9

There being this day for all dressing up, they say. Being still cold but snows not so deep. Not so good for sailing sleds. February melting, so they say. I am ready.

Do we go now? Been a long kind of time since I seeing old James-Face.

"I am ready."

Mama banging around the cooking stove. Closing lids, banking fire.

"Never in my life," she saying. "Never in my family do we take the child."

She being so angry at the house, at everything. But she buying for me this Christmas real kind of pretty coat. With blue night fur all over some sleeves and some collar. With some buttons shining fasten good. I'm still wearing the coat to be ready.

"My legs gonna get some cold, too," I saying, sitting. Looking outside windows, where Jack

Sun horsing around. Wishing to be out there with legs warming.

Sun Run busting open the door and cold air.

"Close that door!" Mama saying. "Find her leggings for me, will you, Jack? Be a good boy, so we can get started."

"Find her leggings, find her leggings — that's all I got to do."

"You, Sun," I saying. "Wishing you would just stay to home. Old James not be speaking to *you*."

"What's she talking about?" Sun Run says.

"That's what I mean," Mama saying. "In my family we never, never take the child."

"This time we are going to take the child." My Stone Dad is saying.

He is there, so quiet. My Stone Dad at the kitchen table, even in the dark night when I being tucked into bed. And still table sitting when I am up and dressing.

Rushing him around the neck and sitting next to him. "Being time to go now, I'm ready. Can we go to see James?"

"That's what I mean," Mama saying, hearing us. "I'll stay home with her, please."

My dad, head shaking. Jack-Run coming up with leggings, acting up games. He pushing my feet in the leggings. I giving him no help because he is silent mouthing like *I hate you. I haaate yooooou.*

"Hate you back!" I saying. "Hate you. Hate you!"

"Stop it, Arilla," Mama saying. "Jack, don't annoy her."

"Oh, don't she look pretty in her mis-matched clothes."

"Jack!" Mama yelling at him.

"They're just playing," my dad saying.

"I don't like these leggings brown," I say.

"See what you've started, Jack?" Mama saying.

"Taking them off, too," I say.

"Mom, she's taking them off," Jack saying. "It ain't my fault, either."

"Then you see she keeps them on."

"Get your hands off!" I saying. Jack squeezing my toes. Squeezing so hard to make me yell loud.

"Jack, why must you annoy her? Stony, can't I keep them both here with me?"

You can see how Dad going stiff from the neck. So Mama stopping with the talk. Stopping silent, she throwing herself in a rocking chair by the stove. All dressed up, my mama, looking so pretty in all her long pants but for big old boots. Miss-matching my leggings.

"Wish you wearing my leggings," saying to her. And then: "When will we go, Father?"

"Soon. When first light enters . . . here." Raising a hand all around the kitchen.

We all silent sitting. Now Jack sitting at the table, too. Mama off rocking, looking where she sees my dad. They looking back and forth.

Coldness outside still in the house. Glad for

my new coat and even some leggings. My dad's hands being gray like ashes. Being stiff, like out freezing.

Cold hands, Dad, holding this letter. Long yellow sheet from a white envelope. Hands holding them so careful like an egg and baby chicken. Never seeing him with a letter.

"That letter coming from old James?" asking.

"Nothing to do with him, Arilla. Know that James would not be . . . writing it down."

"Who, then?" asking. Knowing not to ask so much.

No one saying a thing. I shutting up, too. Dad like he just learning how holding a letter is. Letter and his face so clear. Everything like being in a dark but them. Black, shiny hair of Stone Father falling straight, almost. Almost oil-wet falling to shoulders but caught behind ears.

Dad. Lips moving again. Me sitting below the letter. Watching hands holding and lips to move. Sun being there on the other side higher than hands holding.

"When am I getting to go!" saying to hands. "Dad?" saying to lips moving over and over.

Jack-Run making me so mad, quiet waiting. So still and waiting, I don't see why. Just any old yellow piece of paper. Not a letter from old James.

Jack-Run saying so much to my dad all a sudden. I not caring to hear so saying and never even listen to him. Just caring when Stone Father done with holding and lips moving so we can go see old James.

Dad saying to Sun Run and I caring to hear.

Sun saying something I don't care. And my dad saying, "He was inkerea the same as me, my staff sergeant."

("   .") Sun saying, I don't care to hear.

Watching Stone Father, hair so long and face breaking full of these little skin jumps. And eyes like to shine wet and so sad.

"Now he is a dead man," Father saying.

("   ?") Sun, I don't care.

"When we were both inkerea, we knew we would die," Dad saying.

Both you having sores, sickness of inkerea, is that it?

Dad saying, "We were ready for war. We were warriors prepared for death. In Korea or here, so many of us wanted to go to war."

"Being a place, isn't that so? In Korea," saying.

No one saying a thing to me, making me so mad. "Why can't we begin to go!"

"Arilla, keep still," Mama saying sharp.

Not caring to hear you, too, Mama.

"Now, so much later, this man, my staff sergeant, he is dead," Dad saying.

("   ?") Brother, I don't care to hear.

"*They* sent the letter," Dad says, "after he passed." Putting letter flat on a table, pressing hands on it.

"Twenty years ago! I lose track of him while we're still in Korea. He got wounded bad and so they ship him home. After it's over, I come home in one piece, not a scratch. Do you know the percentage in that? Most men lost part of their hearing, at least. But not me. I had nothing to show for it. So I . . . I had to find him. We had been young. He was the fallen warrior, you know?"

("   ?")

"In the VA Hospital. Very bad there. So many men in all the annexes and wards. It took me a long time to find him. He knew me, like we had lapsed into silence over the fire and he had just thought to ask me something."

("   ?")

"Yes. Like we had never been apart."

("   ?")

"Well, your mother always knew. It's easy to forget, not to talk about it, when letters come a year, two years between. This letter comes a week ago.

"They say passing comes in threes. Then, something happening like old James. I wonder who's next, and I'm reminded of . . . connections, I guess you'd say."

You talking about James-Face. Something happening? He going to move again?

"Let's say goodbye to old James. Dad, see, getting light," I saying.

"There," Dad saying. "She understands. She knows."

("   .") Mama saying a thing, I don't care.

("   ?") Sun asking Stone Dad. Still I don't care.

"Yes. Hurt so bad," Father saying. "His face was all shiny, one crease. You know, a scar tissue from explosion and fire. And when I find him in the hospital, it was like we had never been apart. He says to me, 'I got to get going — get me outta here. I got to get purified. You hear — you hear?' He couldn't sit up by himself. He couldn't stand. What could I do for him? Nothing."

("   ?")

"He wanted to get to the reservation just once. I told him, I promised him, I would go there and pray for him to Nimhoyah, The Turner, to turn sickness and death away from him. I promised him I would purify him in symbolic sacrifice for return of the warrior."

"It is so the truth." My dad, eyes so round and black shining. Hair so long and black and blue.

"Koreans look like Navahos. When you are over there, you believe you are with your own. You believe things have got confused. You don't want to leave your own, or fight them. My sergeant was a brave warrior, but he didn't want to fight those who he had come to believe were his own kind.

"Got it in his head, and I nearly got it into

mine, that the whole place over there was one great stockade. That we were only warring against ourselves. We had been tricked again. So my friend would crawl away from a fierce battle. He would crawl off and paint the death and dying he saw."

("   !")

"Paint it, that's what I'm telling you. He could paint beauty from ores and dyes he found in a hillside. With these, he painted on dead trees. On bits and pieces of clothing found in the field. On the side of a howitzer and on empty cannon shells. Miniature, tiny paintings on flat pieces of shrapnel."

Dad. Why being your face so creased up and wet?

"Somewhere in Korea," he saying it slow and softly, "there are buried treasures of his pain of painting. I like to think they are safe there, on the buried shrapnel and the dead trees — think of it! If I hadn't been assigned to his platoon, the blood never would have gathered behind my eyes. That part of me would have remained sightless. He was such a remarkable man, Sergeant was, not unlike old James. But I worry that it comes in threes."

I loving old James a remarking man. What are threes?

("   ?") Sun saying, I don't care.

"No, he never could write to me. But I'd get a letter from someone there, telling me he wanted

197

to see me and could I come there. But I never did go back after that first time. I think I must have made up my mind even then I should have remained sightless. And no use in any of it."

Dad. Head down, holding ears, and hair so black and blue.

"I never prayed to Nimhoyah. I lost the belief between there and back here. And yet I know my old warrior friend has walked the Hanging Road."

("   ?")

"That the Hanging Road is the path between earth and heaven? My friend taught me so much about it! But do I believe you cannot go home again from war until you are cleansed? I believe home is in your head only. Oh, there are times when the young warrior in my head holds open the flap of his teepee. I cannot help but walk within.

"The time is now to pay respect." So saying, Stone Father. Rises, leaving letter. Leaving table. We all rising. Jack Sun Run and me, Arilla. Mama rises, leaving chair rocking. Light of morning holds the room.

Quickly now. Sun and Dad head for horses. I and Mother mine walking out where my sling-swing so wet and broken. There is the sumac, no leaves on a tree. So wet dripping. All is dripping wet. Snow wet on a my shoes.

"Hur'm up, Strider," hearing Strider and

seeing horse and Sun Run riding high. Looking like a warrior boy and war-pony.

"Sing me a war song, you, Sun!" I saying loud in a mist of quiet.

"Shhh! Hush!" Mama saying, hiss and soft voice.

"You shoo, Mama, shush, yourself!"

"Arilla, you'll wake the — " Mama turning, climb on up a ride on Strider. Getting behind the Sun and holding on tight.

"Here come Dad, better than you two and old Strider!" Rushing Dad. And gentle him, he swinging arm down. Scooping me up high. And I like a bird sitting high on a sumac. Sitting on a saddle in front of Dad and the new Jeremiah.

"I wanna holding the reins, Dad, please?"

"Hold the top of my hands, Arilla."

So holding, just the finger my tips touching the reins.

"Horsing not so bad with you," telling Dad.

And we ride. Not so bad up high with him. Through the wet all down the road. We picking our way. Catching up alongside with Strider. Eyeing them.

"Wanna sing a song?"

Nobody talking and laughing. Nobody want to say nothing in a so strange quiet. I don't see why.

Leaving a road behind. Into crossing country land. First around Cliffville, quiet around houses.

Some smoke coming from some roofs.

Dad saying, "People waking. We are late."

Jeremiah faster. Riding up and up in hills. Many trees wet and no leaves. Dripping everywhere and on a my head. Feet getting chilly. And wish I could be sleeping. Faster now, Jeremiah, in the snow melting. Maybe we gonna slip down.

"Dad? Taking care now."

We loping so fast and afraid we gonna fall all down in the wet and mud.

We climb and climb. "See the stream, Dad?" With snow in the weeds. With black water and running along the grasses of snow melting.

"Rememory, see, Dad? Where first I meet old James. Where I'm stinging, right over there."

"Not so long ago, either," Father saying. "The summer comes and goes. A man enters, bringing a lifetime of riches. Goes, leaving you poorer."

"Why, Dad? That old James have to travel so far and much. Rememory, I been walking and running with James False Face. And now he too sick all the time."

"Don't talk. I'll sing you a song."

"You will, for sure? Thanks, Dad."

"Oh, James was always so right about you."

"So what right about me?"

"It was a young woman who talked stories to the tribe and make the first chiefs."

"So saying?"

"So saying, maybe you will be the one to talk stories again."

"And so saying, making chiefs again?"

"No, it's just a dream. But when James tells it! Maybe only to save the words in a memory pouch. Now and then, take out the words and cause us to be strong and not afraid."

"And so saying. Being Talking Story given in a pouch from old James," I say.

Father singing.

"So saying, enter the teepee, bad luck, stand
    outside.
Enter the life-giving way.
On this sad-luck day, stay within."

Leaning around, me. Look up, seeing Dad. Touching a face so cold and cold breath blowing. Patting Father mine and turning back to picking our way, many black trees and no leaves. Wind coming and many mists blowing. Mists as one mist falling on us, making us slow. Jeremiah picking our way.

Mama and Jack-Run on Strider in a mist. In a mist Strider carrying them going in so much white, like a cave-place. Seeing them go in mist and we going in. I think never coming out. Then see Strider come out, picking along, and we coming out and going through a cave-mist. Quiet, and no wind again. Everything fall on us white and stripes of trees. In and out. In and out so wet and, oh, so quiet.

So sudden, James-Face saying, *Fear not the mis-*

tai *derived from the dead. They are making dark noises in deep places. They are the small noises of the woods, which tug at your leggings and whistle in the brush. Be not afraid of the* mistai.

I saying to Dad, "Old James-Face. He talking to me all the time now in a woods. Telling me like always. You think he be getting well this misty morning?"

Dad holding me tight and tighter. Stiffen, breathing hard, tighten reins. Jeremiah faster now.

"You listen to me, Arilla." He whispering down in a my ear. "We get there, and you say nothing about talking now to James. Stand quiet and not near a thing . . . maybe will be there. A thing . . . you stay away from It and do not look at It more than once. Twice, at most. You be silent — you understand that?"

"I know standing quiet," saying. "You going tie me to a tree?"

"Be still, we are coming closer."

And coming closer a long time with sounding in a woods. And a long time, distant sound come closer. Noise, sounding so high song. Noise coming, crying. Meeting us — is it a *mistai*?

My day of dying is come, and gone. All things come and go in a circle.

James? You going show me along the water this springtime. Never seeing with you the water when grass beginning jump up.

Jeremiah coming on Strider fast. Stopping fast

in a clearing where the small house facing us. James and Shy Woman house. I don't see James. Just a Shy Woman. Enormity woman looking big and wide. Walks around and around the long blue bundle roped and lashed. She seeing us. Stop the noise singing cry and stop the circling.

"What took you so long!" she saying.

"Oh, my lord," Mama whispering, "look what she's done . . ."

Jack Sun turning, touching Mama, making her quiet.

"I couldn't stand it," saying Enormity. "Thought I'd go crazy in that house with It for two nights." She crying, saying, "I'm not a believer, you know I'm not a believer! But he would want it this way, and his finest clothing."

"They won't box him that way," Sun saying. "They'll have to undo . . ."

All a once he stop talking.

Dad talking low, "You, Sun!"

She, Enormity, not hearing a thing. No seeing me; she not speaking to me.

So saying Enormity, "You know I'm not a believer, but I swear to you, all yesterday and last night. All he taught me for years and years came down upon my head. I swear to you, I know his spirit walks around me and all around the house. You must remove It to beneath the ground, or he will not leave. He cannot go on his way!"

"Hurry," Mother saying low. "She's losing her mind. Let's get it over with."

We staying on horses. Dad jumping down so easy and no sound to it. He going up to where blue bundle all lying down. Where Shy Woman Enormity woman standing on a side. Dad standing on a side by her side. We sitting horses watching it all. Dad on a side to us, side to little house facing us.

Dad so standing. And so saying.

"Dear James! Old James! Standing here in the circle the woman makes. It is the circle of the teepee, but there is no longer a teepee. Nothing can be saved that no longer exists. It is gone and forever, as you have gone, and forever."

"No!" Sun-Run have to say, but saying no more.

"Oh, James! There are no words to give thanks to you for all you have done. So many warm days riding with you and my little daughter. It was not only having someone with great knowledge with us. It was having you with us, and there has been no one like you with us. It was the truth you said to me: 'Great Wolf, you are two warring men. You must become one.'

"And it was truth you said to me: 'Great Wolf, can you live being one of us and Moqtai-viho, a black white-man, as well?' You said, 'Don't be insulted by that description, for when the old tribes first saw the dark-skins, they had only the white-skins for comparison. But what man can walk on four legs?'

"Oh, James! I have decided I can live as one

204

only. I will hope that my children will live as one only. We will leave here, as the mother of mine wishes, to become Americans. I don't think it will work. And we will probably always remain separate. But I will go as one man; we will live as one people. Release the child from the Talking Story. For without your support of day-to-day learning, she will never remember who you wished her to be, anyway. Why make a war within her?

"Goodbye, James! Never after this time will I make the signs: Go in a circle. Go in peace."

James saying, *Come along now, follow my shade and we will live in a new place and have a good time.*

"I hear you, old James!" I saying.

Enormity come peering at me in a mist, and coming closer. Me to smile with some surprising. Enormity seeing me and clap her face and covering mouth.

"Back! Back!" She backing up Jeremiah, going into trees. Father comes beside me, climbing up and taking reins.

She yelling, "The danger of it — and you brought her here? Don't you know he will want her with him?"

Come along now!

Me climbing down the saddle, trying to. Dad holding me tight.

"Let me down, I want to be walking with old James!"

"Get her away!" Enormity saying.

Mama quickly coming and taking me down. Holding me tight, walking back away. I feeling tired and sick all a sudden. "Let me go!" But she grabbing and pulling. Screaming, me, and hitting.

"No you don't, Mother!"

Freeing me away from her, too. Running to shadows by little house and never even making it.

Tripping, falling over long bundle all blueing in the way. Hands and knees hurting on a ground. For sure, taking a look at bundle so long and such a blue. For sure and seeing. Way deep down, a knowing all suddenly. A deep knowing so heavy and such a deep sad in me and wishing for to go away.

Enormity yelling, "Get her away from It!"

"I'll get her," Jack Sun saying. Jumping from Strider and hurrying, coming fast.

Wordkeeper?

Listen, a long bundle saying my secret name.

"Get her *away!*"

Wordkeeper!

"Hearing you, too," I saying.

We will offer the first pipe to Heammawihio, *who long ago left this earth to live in the sky. We will have a good time. Come.*

So blueing bundle and so deep sad in me. Wanting to lie there. And smelling It so new and almost making me feeling more sick with Its new and wetness. And so still, and nevermore moving.

"I tell you, It will make her sicken and die!"

Jack Sun grabbing me up where I just want to lie.

Shaking and cold, I am. Leggings wet and mud, shivering in a my arms.

He grabbing me up, handing to Mother. Holding me, Mother, in a her arms.

"Get her away from here!" Shy Enormity loud saying.

"Oh, will you shut up, Susanne, please?" Mama saying, not mean, and softly. She carrying me and into house of Shy Woman and James False Face . . . Once.

"Don't take her in there, get her away!" Woman pulling at Mama. Mama pushing at Woman. Never seeing Shy Woman with so big eyes black. Mother going in with me and slamming a door. Mama pushing on inside door, holding Shy Enormity out.

Looking in a room. Rememory. I looking and smelling smells. Rememory a good kind of time not so long gone, too.

"See his coat hanging in a corner?" I saying to Mama. "See him, moccasin so soft he making all the time? See? This is the place. This is the place of James-Once."

Mother carry me to low bed and laying me down. She holding hand over mouth and swallow hard. Gagging, stand there, looking around and swallow again.

"You understand, then." At last she saying something.

"For sure. This is the place." Lying there, me, in a warm place. Why I have to be shaking so?

Mama covering me. "This is the place you love so much?" she saying. "This place has never had a window open. I've got to get a window open and get some air in."

"Don't do it," I saying. "Warm all around, but me being so cold, Mama."

"Let me get those leggings off," she saying.

"Making so more cold, don't do it."

"Arilla, the leggings are wet. Your feet are all soaking with mud. You're getting dirt over everything. I'm taking them off."

She taking them off, too, and no kind of kicking to stop her. Too tired for any more kicking today. Feeling so deep and sad.

"Not so good feeling, Mama."

"Baby, you're not sick."

"Yes."

"You are tired from the long ride. And you got chilled. Maybe you'll catch a little cold. But you're a strong baby."

"No."

"Now hear me! You are not going to be sick just because she says you will be."

I am not. But so saying, I am sick. Way deep

and heavy. So sad and sad. Being sick with it.

Then. Coming in a door quiet. And with caring coming is my friend of a friend, Enormity.

"Old Shy Woman," I saying so soft, hardly a sound to make. And she looking at me once only and holding herself there so still, right with Mother.

"All that out there," she saying to Mama. She not so tall but being round. Liking her so short and round. Holding hands together way down on her dress.

"I'm sorry about that." She rubbing one arm with one hand. Looking Mother and then away. All the time, trying too hard speaking. "I don't know what got into me like that . . ."

"You don't even have to think about it," Mama saying, kind and caring. "You sit down and rest awhile."

Still standing, Woman holding hands down her dress. "He, James, was so sick so long. Had to do all his chores plus my own. There were people always wanting him with work for him to do. But he wouldn't let me tell them he was sick and going to get well soon. He made me stay here and not tell a soul. All the same, I was afraid to leave him."

"Here," Mama saying. She pushing Woman down sitting at the table. Like the table. Rememory, James-Once so sitting with a pipe and smoking, talking stories.

Mama taking bowls and filling from pot cooking on a stove. A bowl on a table for Woman. A bowl Mama holding next to me.

"Have this. Arilla? It will make you feel better."

Looking and smelling. But feeling like being close to a wall. So turning, no soup now. Wall resting, tired feeling, so sick.

"He gets to coughing," Shy Woman saying, so sudden. Voice so shaking. "And I know I better go get someone. I get all ready. But he stops coughing and he says no, let it come to pass."

"Come now, Susanne," Mama saying. "Eat the soup. You'll need it. There's so much to do and such a long trip ahead."

"Yes." Shy Woman. "Box him and take him back home. Have a ceremony."

Mama being so nice patting her and Mama never even wanting to come.

"But I do run out," Shy Woman saying. "Thinking he's asleep, I run out to get somebody. Going on the horse all the way on the hill behind us. Haven't ridden by myself in a long time."

Mama sighing: Shut up, shut up, Susanne, but she saying nothing. Getting a hand under a my head and making me slurrping some soup all hot and down my throat. Not too bad. I eat it.

"There. Good," Mama saying.

"Oh, I can ride a horse," Susanne saying. "The second thing they teach you is to ride, even when you don't have a horse. On a reservation, someplace, somewhere, you learn, knowing someday you will need a-ride."

Mama saying, "What is the first? The first thing you learn?"

Round woman look at Mama. Slowly shake and smile. Looking away off above a stove.

"The first thing," so far away, Woman saying, "you learn you don't grow up. You don't grow thin or fat, or tall or old. You grow hungry."

So saying, nothing shy about it. Changing woman hard all a sudden. Looking Mama hard and staring cold. "But you don't know about things like that, do you?" Woman saying.

"You know better than that," Mama saying.

"Not feeling so good," I saying to Mama. She putting bowl down so much care. She pats and rubbing me. Sitting next to me right on a bed. And curling up around her back.

Shy Woman, "They don't take from you every growing thing and leave only hunger. They don't take the land. Take the wheat, the fire and smoke, the children and chiefs. They don't destroy you completely."

Mama saying, "No, we had a breathing time."

Changing woman only smile.

"We weren't expected to survive the cold," Mama saying. "We were to die out in the cold north. But we learned how to use the time, and the cold."

"And so," changing woman. "You sound much like Hōhé woman. Assiniboin woman, now."

211

Quickly, Mama rising. Hair smoothing into place. Shivering, looking around.

"Talking like this," Mama saying. "I never do. It's this place! I'm sorry, I don't know much about your . . . your people."

"No," changing woman hard. "You still don't. You don't want to."

Mama saying nothing, looking around. Sitting down again. Patting me.

"Well," Woman saying. "It won't matter now. James is gone and everything is over. I did ride the horse to get help, I want you to know that."

"Of course. We know you did everything you could." Mama.

"I didn't just let him die."

"Of course, we know that."

"I come back here. I was gone so long, rigor mortis had set in."

"Susanne."

"He was over there, trying to get his moccasins on. Wonder where he thought he was going. Sitting there, knee bent and with a moccasin half on. His two fingers in the back, pulling on the moccasin. That's the way he went. And I found him just like that. All stiff. I have to get a sledge hammer and break — "

"Susanne!"

Shiver all over me.

Mama walking away to the door. Looking through a window and staring. Watching something.

Changing Enormity go standing and watching.

"Mama? What you all seeing? Come on, sitting down again."

She giving a glance. "You just stay there and rest," she telling me. And she not coming to sit.

"They are waiting for you. I'm going to let Arilla rest. They can come later for us."

"I got to go, then," Shy Woman again. Friend of James-Once.

"Shy Woman, you staying!" I saying, feeling cold and tired.

"Oh, baby." She rushing fast to me, kneeling. "I got to go, honey, but I'll be back to pack up the things. See you then."

Crying, "You won't be coming back!" And holding her hand.

"Don't think that, honey. Because of James? Hey, she's all feverish. This child . . . this child is sick!"

Mama coming. I closing the eyes. No more talking. Everything jumping in a my head. Hearing them moving and whisper. Bringing me something to swallow. And I swallowing. Never knew the taste before. Sweet, like cherry and medicine not bad.

Someone rushing around and then out the door. Mama calling from a door, "You all go on. Go on. Arilla has a cold, tired out. We would just slow you down. I don't want her in the wagon with It."

Wishing them wait. I wanna be going with

them and old James. James, he coming talking again. I hear him coming.

Wordkeeper?

"Hearing you, too."

Think of a time, any time, and I will be with you.

"But you going now?"

Yes.

"Can't I going with you?"

Yes, if you want to.

"Is it far — going?"

It is only going in a circle.

"Then you coming back again?"

I am here and now, then and there, in all things.

"You just going around."

Yes.

"Then I thinking to stay here."

Stay, then. Live with honor. And Wordkeeper?

"I hear you."

Remember who you are.

10

Riding through November-dismal is about as dull and damp as anything can get. It's so gray with wet everywhere. The horses stink; the ground and air stink. You can smell pig farms and cattle-breeding clear on the other side of the park, miles away. You can smell some perspiration — truth — from people in town shopping in overcoats of some kind of re-processed wool that, when damp, has an odor of awfulness like no other. All of the smells hang above the ridges and then seep down through the dark pines like a full-blown calamity.

This is where I'd want to be, though, if and ever the world's worst disaster hit. I don't know what it'd be, but I'd like to be right here down below the ridges in what Sun likes to call his glade of a sweet glen. Not a soul is down here in this kind of weather but us. That's what Sun Run likes best, having the whole sweet place to himself.

They say it hardly ever snows in these parts

before Thanksgiving. It never snows on Christmas, and there is never any brightness to Easter. What is even more peculiar, it can be dawn and zero degrees, with frost on your windows and folks scraping it off their cars. The ground, hard like a rock. But by noon, ice is melting from roofs, and dripping. Mud splatters your legs as you walk. Two o'clock and it's forty degrees. They say weather happens like that — a quick-change artist — for fifty, sixty miles in every direction from this glen. Sun says the weather *emanates* from right down here, along the Little Egypt River where it comes up from underground. He says weather updrafts for miles from down here. That it climbs the ridges with a lot of warmish air and mixes up there over the ridges with cold currents. And makes some fast-changing weather for fifty, sixty miles, swooshing storms through flat valleys. He's probably making it all up, too.

Nobody ever bothers with this kind of weather. With all the reporting they do out here — the winter blizzard watches and the summer severe-thunder-and-wind watches, you'd think at least a few old farmers would pay some attention. Nobody pays it any mind. Because, I guess, it all changes too fast, so they go on and do what they had planned to do. Just like weather wasn't going to happen to them or anyone else for half a hundred mile.

I have seen girls wear their fur-collared winter coats to school, their new high-boots, their little wool hats and scarves, when they know full well it's a January thaw and going to be fifty-five degrees by lunchtime. They don't care to even notice. Or, end of October, the farmer will get on his tractor to plow under what's left of cornstalks. The ground should be firm enough for him to good and well turn over the earth. You watch him sink down in the mud, but he keeps on fighting it and plowing until dark.

"Let's make it on over to the pond," Sun says, all of a sudden. "It ought to be full up to level with all the rain we got. See what is wintering there."

"That's another two mile," I tell him. He doesn't pay me any mind. Just going along on his grand horse. In the grayness all around, Jeremiah is some Technicolor space of rich brown in the shape of an animal. A peculiar mistiness down here today that don't so much rise off the river as it seems to come out of the ground and out of the trees. Rising so's you can't really see the top of ridges. You can kind of see through it all up to a metal path of sky in the opening above the water. If I didn't know my way out of here so well, I'd swear Sun Run wanted to lose me down here forever. 'Course, he knows I know how to get back. Just follow the Little Egypt. Or take to the ridge and follow it toward the sun.

Jeremiah stops to take a drink of cold river water, and Running Moon comes up to do the same. That steams me up all at once, the way my horse will always follow Jeremiah. And every time I try to make her lead, she'll fall back no matter what. She's knowing pretty sure and well I'll never dig her sides to hurt her. That kind of force just isn't in me, though I know some girls are cruel with their mounts. Sun can dig into Jeremiah and that grand character will shoot out from wherever he'd been thinking of moseying along. But Sun won't even have to dig in him. Just a movement of his wrists, his knees pressing and a sound of squeaking in his mouth. Jeremiah is gone in a black streak. If I tried that, Running Moon ud probably shoot out from under me to catch some weather five miles ahead. She can run pretty, but I have to be thinking in front of her every minute of the run.

Brother takes out the green thermos from his saddle bag and pours us each a cup of steaming coffee.

"Now, that's all right," I tell him. Nothing like pulling off leather gloves gone clammy on the inside but with hands still cold, to warm bare fingers around the hotness of coffee. There's nothing I like better to drink than steaming coffee made just the creamiest brown with evaporated milk. And sweet with sugar. Sun gets Mom to heat up the coffee again once he's added the evaporated. Or I heat it up, like I did today with it being a Saturday for us to be just out here for hours. While he messed around with little cans of oily deviled ham mixed with mayonnaise on some bread.

I don't mind us sitting like this. I've got my leathers on. My jacket and this real funny hat of Dad's, so old that the leather can be molded tight around my face. Makes me feel like looking cute, almost. I have on the boots that are the best riding boots you could want. My Birthday boots.

"Take it easy. Relax," Sun says to me.

I don't bother to look at him, sipping at my coffee. He's right, my leg muscles are quivering and jumping, since being mounted like this for so long.

"What time is it?" I ask him.

"Don't worry about some time," he says. "We got another good two hours."

Mercy. Well, I don't actually mind, even when I get chilled all the way through. It's not so bad once you can ride well. It's probably colder out here than the dampness makes you feel. Something else, too. Going along downriver. Slowly, my hands aren't cold anymore. Then, going along again for a time and I realize my hands are cold once more. Because of pockets of warm air and, next, cold air, in no kind of pattern. Probably, if I concentrated, I could feel it all over when it changes. The horses sure can feel it. They've not been so calm this entire ride. Sun has taught me that, when river-riding, stay alert for any sudden thing that might startle the horses. Small animals flashing across the path. Snakes maybe sliding along the rock bank. Even a fish jumping out of the water. They will do that sometimes. A lot of fish jumping out and flashing quicksilver, startling the tuned-up horses.

My brother just kind of pokes his hand holding a sandwich against my arm. It's a funny way he does it, all kind of formal and gentlemanly. Have to take the sandwich even though I'm not so hungry. I never am when I ride. I take it, I guess, because he's gone to the trouble of making it, bringing it along and offering it to me.

For sure, Sun and me are some different and going through something this November-dismal. It's like when we're riding side by side down here or maybe out in the grasses where it's all flat in the park, I catch him looking at me. What I catch for real is the look on his face after he'd already been watching me. His face will look worried. Also, sort of weary.

Or we are up there riding the ridges. This area is actually fifty or sixty miles of flat land, valley land, with ridges on one side of it. Like somebody taken a sharp blade making some quick, deep slashes, causing the ridges and some strips of deep land below them.

Up there in the snow, along a ridge lip, is got to be the most dangerous game I've ever had to play. Although Sun tells me riding up there isn't dangerous very much. I *know* it is, way up there, following the edge of a rocky ridge. In and out of trees with patches of snow all underfoot, with everything so slippery. I'm seeing myself fallen all the way down to here. Falling and killing myself. Lying crumpled down here, and dead. I'll be up there with my mind full on the horses. Have to be, but I'll also be watching every move of Sun in front of me. Keeping myself cool, but scared to death something will fright the horses and knowing I never have a total degree of control over Running Moon. She is such a quick and awake horse. I wonder if she is ever scared up there, too. But then it's over. We come off the ridge with Sun starting in watching me, like he is hurt about something I've done.

Maybe he's tired of having to not like me all of the time. Tired of the habit of wanting me out of his world. He almost seems to enjoy being out here riding with me. Now that I know how to ride so good, he isn't smart-aleck half as much.

Maybe we both are bored with worrying over each other. School, and weeks of writing my autobiography has made me the sorriest girl anybody'd ever want to see. I get myself enjoying writing the compositions before I go to bed. It's something sure different to do. Easy enough when I stay loose and don't think about what I'm to write. And saying things in class I never would think to say.

September 30 came and I just blurt out: So ends the Plum Moon. Everybody liked that. And come October, the kids have to say, Which moon is it now, Arilla? Up to the present — which moon is it now? And I tell them, as easy as anything: It's the leaves fallen. The ice forming. It's the hard face, the time of the Freezing Moon. November-dismal, which is what I always like to call it.

Sun says, sudden in the quiet, "You're awful mum today."

"Huh?" I'd been thinking so hard. I got embarrassed, like he can read my mind.

He slides off Jeremiah to wash the cups. He smiles, taking mine. "Want some more? There's some left."

"No. Thanks."

Both of us stiff and formal.

Watching him bending, hands swishing water in and around the cups. With a red bandana twisted into a band around his hair, he looks like the first Indian.

Or the last.

We are still brother and sister.

And being he's the Sun.

Don't get it in your head he's changed.

Watch him.

Thermos back in the saddle bag, Sun mounts up and we start out again along the river. Water sounding cold, rushing. Branches are so still, not a creak. Me and Sun are side by side where the shore below the bank widens rocky and almost black.

"I've been thinking about you," Sun says.

It surprised me he would say it out loud. "What about me?" Just as ordinary as I can sound.

"Not about being this or that," he says.

"But what?"

"But that all of you," he says. "Mom and Dad, too. All of you are so Midwest. You the most. A Midwesterner."

Now that leaves me blank; or it stuns me, I can't tell which. "What do you mean by that?"

"People in the same place have some clues about one another," he says.

"Clues," I say. "You're really wild today," I tell him.

"Well, I'm working it out," he says. "See, people of a certain manner give off with some signals that they all understand."

"Signals," I say. "Okay, I'll bite. What signals?"

"Okay," he says. "The kids in school may not comprehend why you drag around by yourself all of the time. I mean, you won't even try to get close with some certain kid. But the *signal* they get from you is one of thinking. Of the smarts."

Now I'm listening.

"You get the good grades," he says, "and that makes sense to them. They understand being alone when it's a bright girl with an arty mom."

"Is that what they think?"

"You know it," he says. "You have the clues, the signals. So does Mom and Dad. Everybody has got the clue to the way all of you are. They accept Angel and her old man, too."

Sun laughs. "But they don't accept me," he says. "They think I pull the grades because teachers are scared of me. They think I'm a hustle. I ignore the clues, or I catch the signals but I refuse them. Something. That's why I'm breaking out of here."

"What? You're lying!"

He looks hurt. "Wouldn't lie to you, Moon," he says, real quiet. "You watch if I don't."

We veer up above the riverbank and Sun goes on ahead of me. The trees fall back from a path worn along the side of a clearing. We go single file with the horses trotting when they can. Sun's shoulders are hunched high. I see that at the same time I feel my hands cold and stiff holding the reins. I can see some of my breath, but I pay no mind to it. I'm on Jeremiah's tail, as close as it's safe.

"Sun? What'd you mean — are you really *leaving* here?"

"Just what I said," he calls back to me.

That gets me really upset. "When? For how long?"

"I made up my mind," yelling over his shoulder. "I'll make it through in three years. Be finished with school by June."

"This June?"

"And then I'm leaving."

"What?" Running Moon gets jittery with my yelling and I slow down a minute.

"You heard me!" Sun calls back, going off.

"But what about me! Sun? Slow down!"

Sun laughs. He slows to wait for me. Turning, he grins at me.

I come up, just full of the worst scare I've ever had. "You *were* lying, too," I tell him.

" 'Fraid not, Little Moon."

"Don't call me Moon!" I can see some teasing on his face. We sit there with the horses close and us turned in the saddles to face each other.

Some sound. Rising. We look up.

"Sun . . ."

"Shhhh!"

It makes no sense because it's so sudden. I just want to get back to all this new stuff about him leaving.

"Sun . . ."

"Listen."

It's a confused sound. Not rising, it's falling and it's going.

A wind comes up, like you open a barn door and what had been gathered there in the dark comes out. Easy, first, and then gathering and marching, fast. Up the river, westward comes this wall of smoke at us. Only it is wind with all of this wetness on us all of a sudden. You can't see through it.

It's not rising, it's falling all through the trees and all over us. We are pelted with it. Slippery, making dark wet hits on our jackets and sliding down.

"Ice," Sun says, "and rain."

"It sure is." And something else. "What's that . . . noise?"

We are looking all around and look up again. The slippery stuff is coming down in the funniest sound. Feeling like rain, only it isn't. It's cold and it gathers white along the edges of the path.

"Sleet, too," Sun says.

"Man, we are a long way from home, too," I tell him.

We can't see much up above us. But we sure can hear all the squawking.

"Birds," Sun says.

"Are they ducks?"

"Ducks or geese."

"Where are they going?" I ask him.

"A lot of 'em get caught by the warmish weather," he says. "Maybe ducks, all trying to make it to the pond. They got caught. And we're going to get caught, too. Come on."

He turns Jeremiah and heads on, going fast. I follow fast with Running Moon moving easy, hardly any effort to her wonderful drive.

"Shouldn't we climb on out of here?" I call out as loud as I can.

Sun motions his head over to our right. I look that way and up, through all the freezing rain and sleet falling. Man, I am covered with the stuff. The ridge along here is close up and steep. We'll have to go on to the pond, where the high-line breaks open into clumps. Another mile or so and we'll be there.

The first half-mile isn't too awful. How tall pines do sway and sound! I've got Running Moon close up with the reins. Patting her often, she is being so slapped by the freezing wet and wind.

I hunch down in my collar. Make myself smaller so I won't be such a target for wind driving the stinging ice drops.

The squawk-cackle of birds comes in waves.

Wonder how many are there. Maybe hundreds. But that has to be too wild.

I hold in Running Moon, feeling all her strength wanting to rip wide open.

"Easy, girl. It'll be over soon."

By the time we close in on the pond, every tree is wearing this slick of ice. Unbelievable. Each stalk of weed has a tube of cold coating around it. This storm is going to build into the prettiest winterland! But I won't have the time to admire it.

The Little Egypt has narrowed into rapids of small size. We've been on a downslope most of the way. Just the gentlest downward trend of land. And now it levels out and opens up into the pond. Too small for a lake, but it's big enough for water birds to settle along the banks and to nest around it all through the seasons. Oval, the pond is like a huge teardrop. They say kids like to swim here. I was never much for swimming.

It sure is just the quietest place when Sun and me come in on a Saturday. Today it is in an uproar.

We come up to it on a rolling bank and just sit there side to side. The horses are kind of moving in place and both Sun and me have to pat them calm. My back and shoulders are tight, hunched against the ice falling. Sun has his collar turned up. He's taken his bandana and made it into sort of a pirate's headcover. The bandana is soaking with ice and Sun's hair isn't any dryer.

We just are stunned with the pond. The sleet and rain sounds like sizzling as it hits the water in sheets. Birds, ducks and geese, keep landing and hugging the water's edge in this grand necklace of white, and green-and-blue-shining mallards.

"Ain't it something?" Sun says.

"For sure — man!" The honks and quacks rise and fall in a kind of sound rhythm.

"We can't fool around," Sun says, moving again.

"Can't we wait it out?" I ask him. "It just might warm up and turn into rain."

Sun says, "This stuff will just get worse. Come on."

He turns Jeremiah and heads over to where the ridge is formed in clumps of height. The steepness is broken up into more or less levels where you can get a hold. I can tell that the first rounded rise is ice-coated good.

"Not too bad," Sun calls, "if I can get this animal to get his hooves through. Once we make some mud. But if we wait," Sun says, "it's going to get tricky."

"Looks bad enough already," I tell him. And it does, with all the stuff falling on us and in our eyes. With all the riot of noise.

Another bunch of ducks hit the pond. "Man! Did you see that?"

Sun has Jeremiah halfway up the first clump, then works him back down again. That great horse cracking through the ice and making some tracks on the second try.

"Them birds ain't even taking the time to land!" Which is what I'm seeing. Birds plopping down on the pond without wasting any time at all.

When it dawns on me.

"Sun!"

He is making his way up the rise another time. And turning, "Come on!"

But I'm looking up and seeing these birds falling out of the sleet. Falling through trees.

"Sun, they're not landing at all."

"Get on up here!" he yells. When this bird, like a streak of green and blue, hits Running Moon right across the neck.

I mean, it took all my strength of rigid muscles to hold her. "Get away! My lord . . . Sun?"

And I shake the bird off just as Running Moon bucks and knocks me crooked in the saddle. I get off fast, but I hold her. And the bird flopping all over the ground. Think it has hurt its wing. "Get away from me!" And Running Moon trying her best to drag me out of there along with her. "Sun, I need some help!"

I get back to her flank, thinking to mount up again.

"Watch her hooves!" Sun yells. Because I'm not seeing the bird flopping under, right between Moon's hind-quarters. Running Moon kicks straight back and the dumb bird flops out of there.

Sun is starting back down and birds flopping everywhere in this real hard, freezing rain now. I get on Running Moon moving forward, ready to climb. It's like all of a sudden I realize how serious it all is — that this stuff is getting worse, and fast.

When all these mallards fall right between Sun and me, but closer to Jeremiah's path. That grand animal lunges to the side quicker than I've ever seen him move.

"Sun!" I scream out and all these birds on the pond make a giant commotion. Feeling this fear turning my stomach.

Just when a big white thing hits Sun's head in a crashing thud. I swear, you could hear that hit like a muffled bomb. That bird hitting Sun and lifting up again like it was leaping out of the red of his bandana. The look of shock on Sun's face.

One of his arms flung back, and then the other,

as if he'd just taken a hard blow between his shoulder blades. Jeremiah, still in his side-stepping lunge; and Sun, out of the stirrups, falling in the same direction as the lunge. All in an awful flash before my eyes. When Jeremiah slips to his front knees and falls on his side, right on top of Sun hitting the ground.

Screaming, I'm seeing it all.

Sun's head hitting, and the rest of him hitting the ground on his shoulder. Jeremiah like a black boulder rolling over, covering Sun.

Screaming.

The bird flopping in the pond. Jeremiah rising, black and fierce, heading straight for me.

Screaming.

He veers away past me. A great, swift brown, southward along the pond. And disappears in the forest of the gray icing.

Running Moon gives a supreme pull of her neck. The reins are out of my hands. I know I am panting like I can't breathe. But I have sense enough to slide off out of the way. Moon moves and is gone, melting into the sleet, following Jeremiah.

This is no such thing. It can't be for real. I'm here, making sounds of screams through the ice fall. Until I can only swallow and grunt, trying to make sense. It has happened so fast. I've got to do something.

Sun is moving.

Suddenly he lifts one arm straight out. Trying

to lift himself on his knees and off the other arm he is lying on. Turning, he looks right through me and crashes over on his face. Sliding an inch or two on the ice and mud, face down.

He doesn't move again.

It's like I'm frozen in one place. "Sun." Whispering.

His legs are spraddled uphill. One arm still twisted under him.

The worst of all feeling. Cold and sickening. My brother is down. What am I going to do? All alone here.

"Help!" Sounding trapped and useless through the freeze. Birds still flopping and awful noises from the pond.

Sun is down. Some way I make myself go on over to him. Kneel down. There's mud all over him. I get close to his head. "Sun!"

His breath is so ragged. His eyes are half open. They close and half open again. Like maybe somebody tries to wake him when he is deep tired and he can't come out of it.

They say in an accident, best not to move the person.

I can't believe this.

"The dumb birds. Jeremiah never would've lost his balance!" But it was the ice caused him to slip.

Think what to do!

It's moving and doing. It seems like forever happening only in a few minutes. He's hurt, so you've got to do it. He won't wake up, you've got to do everything.

And take off that wet bandana. I put my hat down over his head. Easy. Don't move him, just put the hat down low to cover. I tie the soaking bandana over my hair. Not even a blanket. He'll maybe freeze out here. Lord.

"Help!"

But nothing and no one. I have to do it before he freezes.

Taking off my gloves. I clap as hard as I can. Blowing into my hands and clapping until my hands hurt. I know the animals are nearby. Clapping until my hands sting and ache. Breathing heavy mist and clapping.

Until Running Moon parts from grayness and comes moving over to me.

"Oh, what a beauty you are!"

A slick of ice like some armor over the saddle and down her sides. Her tail hair is ice-stiff. Jeremiah looms black at a distance.

"You scare me so!" Whisper it. Don't want to run him off. No use thinking of getting Sun up on him.

But I get Running Moon by the reins and flake the ice off the saddle. Put my gloves back on and flake it away some more. I mount up.

"We can try it," I tell her. "Hur'm up, let's make it!"

I take one last look as we pass Sun so still. And I lead Running Moon upriver, westward. I know horses have the best of balance, but I never would of thought such a small upward trend of land could be so scary. But I know to be careful with Moon. And I know we can make it as long as we don't have to climb steep.

Yet I hate having that grand character to my back. I know he is traveling with us, keeping his distance. Jeremiah, so big and grand, terrifies me without Sun to hold him.

Sun is down. My brother. Arilla, you got to hurry. But how can I with all the slick? How much time is gone? Ten minutes? Twenty minutes? He's got warm boots; his warm jacket. Gloves. Maybe he'll wake up. But better he doesn't move if he's hurt real bad. Oh, don't think that. Sun is so down. And that awful great black horse to follow me. Arilla, Sun. Down.

Away from the pond, there is near-perfect quiet in the freeze falling. There's no high wind now. The trees are black and still, iced over and shining. My reins are coated good. The bridle iced. All over me, every part that isn't moving every second is coated. I can feel the stuff in my nose thicken, so I breathe through the mouth. My hands are cold but not too frozen yet.

Into a dismal quiet. All alone and walking with just two horses. It will take us forever walking like this. Let's see to trot a little. Horses have such balance; even knowing that, I am scared to death! Force trotting easy and steady. Running Moon has to be talked gently and coaxed. The grand horse is coming on behind us. I steel myself and look around, ever so slow. He's some five yards back. Following his lady-friend. And maybe following me, too, because I am a familiar scent as well. I don't like it, though, with his fierce eyes and nostrils snorting smoke. He's a fire horse, a sun horse. For sure. I never look back again. But pick our way sure and careful through the blinding storm.

And a great, long time of silence so alone. Past where we stopped for coffee. How long it's been since Sun fell? Don't think it's forever and don't quit.

We are walking again. Forcing, coaxing Moon to go on. Now she is so cold and skittish. There is strong danger now, where we walk on nothing but the straightest slick ever.

Walking the flat stones of the Little Egypt, which is better than before because it is bumpy. Seconds fall into strings of minutes. We are in one place and then to the next place. Soon we are where the river ends to stream underground. A wide, low bank with grasses.

"Okay now. You can take it easy in the grass." Running Moon seems to know. The grass is long and the ice crunches and mushes up. Grass gathering under her hooves, and so easier, and not such a risk to fall.

The forest trees space apart. There is silence in a near-twilight, all is so misty. I get it in my head we're lost. But I know better. I know we'll soon be all right if I just keep my head and hold Moon steady. I feel better when I moan with the effort. A little dizzy-feeling, from being so deep tired and so frightened.

So all alone, I get it in my head the great horse is right on Running Moon. And I get it in my head . . . someone. Behind me. Someone's riding Jeremiah.

A chill of spasms all over me. Making me tighten my knees. Moon thinks to trot awful fast. But I pat her down and we go slow and careful, through the ice falling.

I get it in my head we'll never ever get out of this. Oh, but I will. I will get help for Sun after this long time it takes. It was an accident he had. I thought it was going to be me for so long. I never would have dreamed it'd be my brother.

Watch her hooves! That's what Sun told me when the bird flopped under Running Moon. Oh, there must have been a hundred birds out there, wings all ice-coated, but I don't see any now.

Sun tried to save me from the hooves. So how could he ever want me dead? Did I really make it all up thinking he never cared for me? Is it all a lie? I'm going to get paid back in these woods, too.

Oh, there's somebody riding Jeremiah and there are things all around, I can feel them. Who's there? I'm so awful scared — get me out of here!

I can't stand it. So I dismount and lead Running Moon for a ways, until I can dare look around at Jeremiah. It takes such a long time to get up the nerve. I tie Moon's reins to a bush. We are almost there, anyway. You can see the top of the Skateland above us, over to the right. I'll have to go around to the left, following the land-curve to get up there. And sudden, like a breeze, I tune in on the skating. It just makes me feel so good all over.

I turn around. Jeremiah is there, big and real. Never have I ever tied his reins. He knows me. I'm the one always with Sun. There's no need to be scared. There's no one riding him. How I make up things! Jeremiah knows my scent. It's just that I've never led him before. Sun always leads.

I go up to him easy, the way Sun always does and like I've been doing it forever. Jeremiah backs up. Above me, big enough to trample me into nothing. I force myself forward and take the reins ever so lightly. Next, to lead him so careful over to Running Moon. Tie him there next to her so their heads can nuzzle. So long as they're together, they'll be all right in the shelter of the tall trees.

"I'll be back!" It comes to me that I still have to get them stabled way over in the barn of Trebiens! We pay charges every month for the right to stable, and for salt, water and hay.

Get going! I don't take the long way around. I take the hillside going up in front of me. I can slip, but if I dig out holes with my boot heel.

Find a stick and pound holes in. I can climb with this stick that is too short. I can do it, even when I slip down and get myself muddy. And the ice stuff still coming down.

It's warmer again up here. The stuff freeze-falling is slacked off. The weather won't know what it is or what it's doing. And in no time I've made the hill. Dragging myself on, breathing to burst my lungs. If you think tired, you will be tired. The Skateland is growing bigger and bigger in the slowest of ways. Through those trees where I hid that night when my luck ran out at the rink. On past the window where I jumped. Must be the one, and from that high! How long ago it was from now!

On around and up the steps. Going in to where it is so dark coming in out of the daytime. Just a group of senior citizens, like a club of them, going around and around. They must've got themselves caught and maybe decided to spend the day. Some few of them are back on the side benches talking.

I come in all muddy and try to tiptoe so as not to make a lot of tracks. Taking off my gloves, and head for the cashier.

"Need some change for the phone," I tell her. "We had an accident. My brother is hurt." Sounded shaky, but getting it out. I won't cry.

"Oh!" she says. And quick, giving me change for the only piece of cash I have fished out of my corduroys. Fifty cents.

"Must be awful out there," she says. "We been hearing the sirens all down the highway for the last hour. Jake? Jake!" She calls for the manager. After a second he comes out from the skate rental.

"This child's been in an accident," she tells him.

"Out on the pike?" he says.

"Her brother's hurt," she says, before I can say a thing. "Did the car overturn?"

Both of them staring at me. "No."

"I'll call the police," Jake says. "How far's it at?"

I'm shaking all over and the woman comes out of her cage. She puts her arm around me to take me over to sit down.

"Where'd you say it was at?" Jake is getting the police, and that just scares me to death.

"It wasn't a car," I manage to say. "We went riding our horses down by the pond. These birds — a whole lot of birds came falling out of the storm and everything is so all slick . . ."

"Well, for heaven . . . I saw them ducks go over!" the cashier says.

"And my brother's horse is spooked and my brother got hit and falls and Jeremiah, the horse, falls on him."

I sit there and hold my head. "I have to call my mom!" Trying to stop the shivering shakes.

Jake is talking on the phone and telling the cops what he heard me say. He comes back over after hanging up. "They're busy," he says, "but they got it and'll contact emergency. They say they got fender-benders clear to the next county."

"I got to call my mom."

"You tell me the number and I'll get it for you, honey," the lady says.

But I'd rather get it myself. They stand and look at me getting up like a senior citizen myself. Getting oozing mud all over their hardwood. I get over to the skate rental and they say it's all right for me to use their house phone.

"Go on ahead," Jake says. "Call your mom. You sure you're all right?"

He is this guy I've seen before in the secret nighttime. But he don't recognize me at all. I nod at him and call Mom.

He has to talk at me in the middle of my dialing. "You walk all the way back from the pond? Where's the horses?" Just real nosey and I get the number wrong.

"I ride back part the way," I tell him. "Left the horses down over there, where you come up to here."

"Must be three or four miles!" the woman says. "Your brother still out there?"

"Yes." Where's he think Sun's gonna go?

"Is he bad?"

"He wasn't moving." I dial some more and get a dial tone. Mom picks it up at the studio on the fourth ring.

"Mom, it's Moon. I mean, it's Moon." I can't get my name right.

240

"Arilla? Yes what is it?"

I start as fast as I can. The man Jake motions to take the phone to tell her, but I can do it.

"Jeremiah gets spooked from the ducks falling. And Sun falls and is hurt. The man here called for the police, but they are busy. Sun is still way down there and knocked cold, I think." I don't tell her his breathing is bad, like it will quit.

Mom says to stay where I am. She'll get Dad. She says not to worry, she'll take care of it; says to stay at the rink.

Mom letting me stay at the Skateland. I almost laugh. She hangs up quick.

"She says to wait here," I tell them. "My dad will get some men and get my brother."

"Well, the emergency is on its way," Jake says.

They watch me go off to a bench by the rink. I really can't sit up anymore. I slide on down on the bench. The lady comes with a little pillow for my head.

She touches my arm. "Honey, how we know you're not hurt yourself?" she says kind of nice to me.

"If she come all this way, she has to be all right," Jake tells her, somewhere behind her.

"Oh, I just forgot! It wasn't no car they was in."

I lie there facing the rink, with just these older people going around and around. My eyes close, but I open them up on the movement going around. That music so fills me with restfulness.

My chest is aching from breathing so hard. I'm warming up, though, and easing my boots up onto the bench.

"No. Thanks," I tell the lady who has come back with a cover for me. And she goes away.

I close my eyes and I'm still on Running Moon. Still riding up and down in a sickening motion. I open them up fast.

Thank goodness it's over. Don't think about Sun out there. Dad will get there quick. I did it. I got help. I rode well and did it all.

I'm following a skater. Eyes glued to his tan jacket and green bow tie. It slowly dawns that this is my friend, old Long Neck. Riding close up to the rail every time he swings near me. I raise up to see better. He gives me a long look and does some beautiful pulls and lifts. Gives me a wink on the go, stroking through *Waltzing Matilda*.

But I can't keep my eyes open. How in the world did he know me like this? Probably didn't. Just him winking at any young woman.

Me, a woman?

And I'm out like a light.

11

We had started out on this old two-lane, which probably wouldn't have been such terrible bad news on any average dry day. But this morning it was black and sleek with wet. It was snowing again and I had visions of us hitting this streak a ice and going into one of those long, horrible skids that end in an explosion. I had sure wanted to start out on the I-75, the divided highway that most cars and big semis will take going for the long haul. But once you're on the interstate, you don't often come off; and I had to make a bus change for the one that could make my stop. And it's still snowing. Has been ever since I barely made the change in time back down the way. The first bus was that late coming off the two-lane.

I said to Mom this morning before I had to leave, "Why do I have to go out that way first when it makes better sense to get down there and then go over?"

She said right back, "It's as broad as it is long. Better that you change at a smaller place than at a station as confusing as the one in Cincinnati. It's bad enough to send a twelve-year-old."

That's how I knew she was so worried by my going.

"Arilla, you will be just fine, I know you will," she said, hugging me. "Don't worry about bad weather, the drivers are used to it. And when you have to make the change, don't get upset if you have to wait. Even if the bus is an hour late, you wait right there, don't take a ride with any stranger."

Only, she didn't warn me that maybe the first bus would be late, with the second one about to pull out by the time I get here. I had to run like hell, and I never curse, either. Didn't have time to get some food, or look around, or even to buy a magazine. I just had time to throw me and my bag on, and lucky to find a seat in front.

I am by the window and I notice I'm holding on to the arm rest hard enough to cause a backache. I ease up and try to relax. Just stare at the back of the driver and try not to look down the highway. It's the divided I-75, which I thought would be a whole lot better but it's not. I still worry about skidding and I wonder if we stay on it for the whole way. I tried to ask Mom every detail, but I didn't know to ask her about the route. So I have to go and wonder if my overnight case is on the rack above when I know full well

I put it there. What if I didn't? What if I left it on the other bus? If I make it through this without a hitch, will I ever be the same again? Wasn't even the same before I got on the first bus; the first bus I was ever on, too. I haven't been the same since Sun Run got it in the ice storm.

He was so lucky. They said he could've broken his neck. And lying out there for so long until Dad and some men got there in the jeep to cover him and keep him warm. They wouldn't dare move him. Until this emergency crew finally comes to lift Sun on out of there. That squad can just about get anybody out of anything, even from out of deep wells. Sun didn't have not a bit of frostbite. That was because the weather kept warming and cooling in that awful day of pure strangeness and disaster in November-dismal.

He had a concussion from falling and not from that dumb bird. The bird just must have shocked and stunned him. He had a broken arm in four places from shoulder to the wrist. Multiple fractures, Mom said. And a badly sprained knee that swelled up bigger than a cantaloupe.

In the hospital for over a week, mainly because of that bad-swollen knee and partly because his head hurt him for about three days after his fall. Wonder if he'll ever be able to run long-distance like he use to?

I just keep going over and over it, like it is on this track in my head.

The doctors make sure of everything by doing

some observations of his brain. Some X-rays of his skull to see if it was cracked. I could've told them Sun had always been cracked in the head, but I didn't have the nerve. Mom came home the first full day he was in the hospital saying Sun couldn't remember falling off Jeremiah.

I told her, "Well, he did too fall — do you think I would lie?"

And Dad said no, of course not, they knew he had fallen. And Mom said it was just that Sun couldn't recall anything about a bird hitting him and then him falling.

I don't think a soul believed me about them birds falling like some toy planes out of the sky until Sun was better and able to tell them how true it was. Or was it that some of the rescuers discovered some dead ducks under the brambles — I can't remember, exactly. Anyway, Sun was remembering everything by the second day and we got Mom to lie down for a while. Even if Sun hadn't remembered and even if they didn't find some dead ducks, they'd a had to believe me by what Dad and me saw all over the town after the storm. That storm finally was over. It turned for-real cold, and the ice over everything got as hard as granite.

Dad came by to get me at the skating rink, still using the jeep. Come to get me after I slept there for a long time with all the music and skate noise like it was *Rockabye Baby*. Nobody could rouse me, and the skate people were getting kind of worried I might have fallen myself. But finally Dad got me awake and up and out in the jeep, which was covered with mud icicles clear to the windows. He said he'd already got some men to take care of the horses and I was glad of that.

We went toward town and all around, trying to find a way home that wasn't too bad with ice, and wasn't uphill, either. We finally had to go by way of the cemetery roads, and it almost getting dark, too. But light enough still, because the sky had cleared to this cold white light. And coming around that back way was when we began to see something queer.

Birds, but little sparrows this time, just lining every telephone wire. We could see them from a distance, just sitting up there in endless rows trying to keep warm. Only, when we got close, we could tell for sure all of them were stone dead. Frozen to the telephone wires in little ice shrouds, Dad called it. Frozen stiff in rows, like plastic packages in the supermarket.

It was the most awful thing I'd seen that day. Even worse than Sun getting himself hurt, because that really hadn't hit me good. But all those little birds trying to wait out the storm; and then trying to get out of there only to find that all those tiny feet had got covered and frozen right to the wires.

The next day it warmed above freezing. You'd see sparrows with one foot sticking straight out from the wire, like they were going to walk off it. But when the other feet melted loose, the birds started plopping to the ground. Garbage crews had to go around with big cans and shovels to scoop them up. I don't know how many of them in big cans taken to the town incinerator.

Something about those birds frozen like that that day really got to Dad. Or else it got him to thinking about how Sun just might have got frozen and dead out there in the glen. I don't know, but something about it struck him deep. He just got sadder and sadder. And maybe that's why I'm on this bus.

My whole time that week without Sun was maybe the strangest of all. Well, I know that now, but I sure couldn't see it then. All at once I was just so *active*. Running like crazy from one dumb thing to another and never getting all of it done. I never reminded myself that I didn't have any more to do that week than I ever had. Except to take care of Jeremiah, too, as well as my own Running Moon. It's like I got so *involved* with everything. I got really deep into school, couldn't get enough of it. Couldn't wait for it to start every day and I felt sick at heart to see it end. Study-hall time, I'd do so much math and get so full of these number base systems. I wrote this story, too, about a world called Evif where everything in numbers was done with base five. Like 0, 1, 2, 3, 4 and, next, 10 through 14 and 20 through 24. On and on. It took 2400 years for the Evifgnis to discover that the name of their world was Five spelled backward. It was the woman Eno-A who found it out.

The ride is long. The ride is long. That goes through my mind until I can't stand it.

But that next Saturday I got so busy doing my homework and some beginning algebra. Mr. Wiggins told me, "Arilla, you sure are leaping ahead on your math." Truth. All week long I'd been taking the facts test for fractions and decimals. I passed them and some for percentages and dividing. I passed them all and no more than three mistakes on each one. I even stunned myself. Now I'm beginning some algebra, ahead of most of the kids.

On Sunday I knew my brother would be coming home from the hospital, but I just got so busy. I had to go out to see to Running Moon and Jeremiah. Clear out to the Trebiens' and the road not even sanded. I didn't much mind it — old Jeremiah sees me and breaks away from the other horses. He was looking for Sun, I guess. So I sat on the fence and talked to him for a long time, telling him how Sun wouldn't be coming for a good while, that he was going to have to let me ride him or let somebody else do it. I know the Trebiens will get some student helpers to take care of him in handling. But they'll never be as good and expert as Sun is.

I take Running Moon for a short ride, which doesn't make sense, getting all the leathers on her and then taking them off again. I just did it from habit and not for much pleasure. Rubbing her down, picking her hooves, brushing her. And come home late from sitting on the fence by Jeremiah. I've got used to the dark, walking so fast all the long way back. It's like I know there are no phantasmagorias for real like there used to be. Just little small ones way back in my head. I'm home and it's like I'm all pure physical, with no mind for thinking through the dark like that. The sound of the Skateland meets me halfway and it won't make a register going bing-a-ling like it used to. I leave it waiting in the road.

My head knocks against the bus window. I startle up in my seat. Buses with their gentle roll and sighing air brakes never let you know if you are sleeping. Just some dozing, I guess, for we have come off the divided highway. I'm sure glad of that. Mom told me that toward the end I will see little towns where you wonder why anyone ud want to live, they are so washed up and no people showing.

This guy sitting next to me all the way is dressed like some trainman and with a black lunchbox on the floor, crowding my feet. This guy twitches a lot in his sleep, so I'll stay clear over by the window because it's weird to see someone twitching like that. Probably some nightmares. But pretty soon he gets off at a place called Aurora. A lot of people get off.

I settle back and stare out. We follow a narrow road, like going off and being lost in a country of white with snow fields going on forever. I do feel safer on it, since the bus can't go so fast and because there doesn't look to be any patches of ice. Just thick snow already plowed and packed down hard. It's not snowing here, either. The sky is this mass of gray high up, with a white sun looking for a world like a moon. Peeking through and racing along with us every now and then. Wonder if it knows it's me. Girl, don't be silly. But who's to say if it does or not? You never can tell.

Folding my hands together over my shoulder bag and feeling the trembling in them. Up to the edge of my nerve, for sure. But no matter how hard I try to be calm, there is still that feel of nerves in my fingers or in my stomach. It'd be awful to get bus-sick way out here and have to stop the bus and puke on that white snow. Just settle back and close your eyes. You know it's been this way since Sun was hurt and the whole week after clear up to now. Maybe it all really is too much for someone as young as me. Don't think that. Because I have to do it. Because Sun is laid up and can't do it like he always has.

This shoulder bag is like all the girls in school have. They are made up in the same quilted material, but they can be of different shapes and colors. Mine is a blue print; real nice, with an over-flap and a big brown square button to hold the flap in place. And shaped almost round with gold stitching up and down the wide shoulder strap. Everything I need is in this bag and never will I take my hands off it. Oh, I'm so glad Mom let me wear my leather jacket and corduroys with just a wool sweater underneath, and my boots. I always do get overheated.

But my life depends on my shoulder bag. There's my wallet in it, my comb and brush and some make-up I sneaked out and which I never use hardly at all. Just some powder and a little lipstick to give me some color. There's a pack of tissues and a card with the address. And more than enough money in the wallet to buy my ticket home if I have to.

Now that brings me some panic again, having the money to return. I force myself calm by holding my bag as tight as I can for a minute. Asking Mom why the need for the money, I remember, and she said, "Just in case you need it."

And I said, "Do you think Dad won't want to come home?" She looked at me like nobody ever said that out loud before.

Mom said, "Arilla, someone has to go, to show our great concern."

And I said, "But do you think he wouldn't come back on his own?"

And she said, "I won't think that far. I can't."

The mystery of grown-ups, I tell you. All of it, everything, leaves me with my nerve up to the edge. And even worse since that Sunday they brought Sun home, and the way I forgot all about how he was going to be there. No, I didn't forget;

I knew he would be there, but I was being so *active*. Just not thinking and come bounding into the house. Glad to be out of the dark outside, even when I wasn't too scared of it anymore. I came in, not aching tired at all; at least, I wasn't thinking about tiredness. Wasn't thinking at all. I was in a movement of hurrying and no mind to work anything out right.

I bounded up the stairs. And with no thought, only moving and going. I couldn't wait to see my brother. Knew without knowing he'd be there. Knew, and being mindless with knowing, that he'd be ready with the fast word and the put-down. Just a complete picture of the way it'd always been, with no words to go with it. No thought. Every morning Sun is up before me. And always at night he goes to bed after I'm asleep. So seeing him all at once that Sunday was the worst shock anybody named Arilla ever had.

Mom was sitting there by his bed. Sun was lying down and I don't think I'd ever seen him when he wasn't sitting or standing. Him, forced to lie down by the worst-looking bandages, and a cast to lie just so still. There was an inch-wide band around his head, the awfulest, whitest headband he ever wore. He had this white cast clear across his shoulder and down his arm, with this tongue-like part coming out under his hand, like to rest his hand on it. And this real inflated wrap of plastic all around his knee for to cushion it, I guess.

I came in there with this fluorescent light by the bed for him to read by, shining down on him. Such a white light, it made that cast and bandages become the same as the white sheet. It made it look like half of some kid was lying there. When I adjusted to it, I could see it was a whole person there, but not one that was my brother at all. Some teenage kid looking pitiful and weak, with a big bruise across one cheek, and a lot of skin scrapes looking red and bloody all over his lips and on his chin, which was a little swollen.

So stunned, the kid lying there couldn't've been my big brother. Couldn't and never was. Only, the next second I knew it was and always had been. And he didn't have a smart thing ready for me. Not a "Hello, Moon, what's up?" Or "Hey, Ms. Moon Maid, get me some coffee, can't cha see I'm injured worse than a Comanche?" He was looking right at me but with no kind of force of command. Oh, his eyes! They just had all kinds of pain in them, pain like I couldn't figure. And oh, so slowly, he turned his face into the light and let his eyes close shut.

Inside me that day, it wasn't just that the Sun had fallen. For sure and for real, down and out. But that he could never rise again the same. Never as bright, never as fierce and powerful for me again. Which left me with nothing for-sure certain.

And the first time in that long period of Sun being hurt and me going for help . . . The first time in that long week of me being so all-fired up and active . . . Standing there, with Mom looking worried from me to Sun, I covered my face with my hands and cried in the worst sobbing I'd ever done. Until Mom come to her senses and got me on out of there.

Why I had to bawl like that, I'll never know completely. It sure wasn't all crying for my brother. It was some for me, too. Because I'll never quit seeing the sight of him just ordinary, like any other hurt kid. And some relief, I guess, that it wasn't me lying there. And sorry, awful sorry that it had to've been him and not me. Somehow, someone like Jack Sun Run should never have to find himself down. Because of what it must feel like, picking yourself up.

Even later on, when he called for me to come back in there, it wasn't the same old Sun. I'd just been lying there in my room, so real ashamed for crying and tired out but still full of a lot of nervousness. I went on in there kind of hangdog, afraid he might laugh. And he's still lying there. I say to him, "What do you want, Jack?"

And he says, "I thought I wanted something to drink, but I changed my mind."

So I ask him, "Can you get on up?"

And he says, "Not without hurting a whole helluva lot."

I ask him, "Does it hurt you all the time?"

And he says, "Moon, it don't hurt unless I try to move around. Then my knee about kills me.

But it's nothing like laying out there and coming to a second."

"I can go to town. I can get you some stuff, magazines," I tell him.

"In the dark?" he says.

I didn't much want to go in the dark, but I would have.

"No," he says, "Angel is bringing me some things when she comes over later."

She did, too. Brought him magazines and a book and three apples. I expect Angel will be coming to sit with him as long as he's laid up.

But right then, when we were there talking by ourselves, Jack had to go say how I'd saved his life. Made me real uncomfortable and embarrassed.

"I have to thank you for keeping your cool and not going into a screaming fit," he says. "I can recall hearing you scream like an ole twelve-year-old, which you are. And somewhere in there I said to myself, 'Oh, well, that tears it, brother, you have had it.' But you went on and did it right — how'd you ever catch the horses?"

"Well," I say, just looking around the room for to not have to look straight in his eyes. His room had a handsome Indian blanket on one wall. And some colorful drawings of people on horseback and some old photographs of them around their teepees with some soldiers who were white.

"I clapped my hands as hard as I could," I tell him. "I thought I wasn't never going to stop, either. But then Running Moon comes to me and Jeremiah just follows."

"And you make it on back," Jack says.

"I made it back to the Skateland." I all at once notice the rink noise. Jack does, too. We listen a minute, but neither of us say a thing about it.

"How you were able to do that," he says, serious. "How you got those animals going on the ice and everything. You've come to be a horse-woman and you kept your cool."

"Cut it out," I tell him. Feeling real pleased and embarrassed at once.

When he says, "So what do we call you?"

"What?"

"What name do you want?" he says. "Now that you've gone and done this great thing, you can't go on being Moon."

I had to laugh, and feeling good, because he's like his old self. Only, I see he isn't laughing at all. Maybe a new kind of kidding, but I can't tell for sure.

"See, you counted coup," he says. "That's the Amerind way of the old times for doing something spectacular. Say there are a hundred of the enemy have you surrounded and only twenty of you fighting them. And you ride out like crazy and tap one of the enemy on the shoulder. And get out of there in one piece while bullets fly all around you."

"Really?"

"You know it," Jack says. "That's counting

coup." All at once, he acted like he knew something which I didn't, and grinned kind of like he was ashamed.

"We really aren't enemies," he says. Then, real quick: "But you did something more or less remarkable. So what'll we call you — Girl Who Saves The Sun? or Rides The Horse Fast? What name do you want?"

I'm sitting there with my mouth open. And knowing the name but I don't want to say it.

How he can look so weak and thin but older at the same time!

"So. You already have one," he says. "So what is it? Come on, you can tell me."

"If I did, you'd just have to laugh," I say.

"I won't laugh, promise," he says. "Because this is very important stuff." And not a hint of teasing. "You know it," he says. "This is no joke."

Arilla Sun Down. But I won't say it.

"I'll say it when for sure I have it right," I tell him, looking at my hands so as not to see his eyes.

I don't move. I can feel him staring so hard at me.

When he says, "It has the sun in it, doesn't it?"

Just a mind reader! It shocks me so! "Jack . . . Jack . . ."

"It's okay," he says. "It won't make me any less."

I don't believe him. "Jack, you got it all wrong," I tell him.

"A name with the sun in it will make you a lot more than you were," he says. "I bet it's got the sun in the center, the way it should."

"Jack, I am just not ready to tell my name," I say.

Arilla Sun Down. Crackling in my mind.

It means *I* brought him down. Which isn't the truth, I didn't have a thing to do with his accident. Still, it's a name for all that happened out there that day. But it isn't enough. There's more somewhere. Like I am much more of something than Sun Down way deep inside.

"I'll probably just go on and call you Arilla, or Moon," he says, "until you get up the nerve to tell me." Just smirking.

"You can," I tell him. "I don't have it ready, is all."

And to get off the subject, I ask him, "Jack, you still thinking about leaving? Like you were talking about the day of the accident?"

Turning away. At last he says, "May take me a little longer now."

"So you're still planning on getting out of here."

"I guess," he says.

"Don't you know?"

"Moon, I don't feel like talking about it no more. So why don't you skip on out of here and find yourself some jacks to play with?" Just cold.

"Well, I see that fall didn't knock out some of your mean streak," I tell him.

But I wasn't mad. I walked on out of there, and glad to go, too. I could tell he was thinking about leaving; but, for sure, he didn't want to go.

Back in my room again, all of the crying had gone out of me. I guess growing up is just awful when it first hits you you have to do something for your life. Glad to have a brother to do it before me, too. And maybe from him I could get an idea how to do it when it came to be my turn.

Should've been grateful that Jack was still alive and getting well. Oh, but I'll never forget how grand he could be! A-galloping away on Jeremiah. And bareback — just golden! Of The People.

Now his power is gone for us both forever. And that sure is some kind of sad.

12

Terrified, I jump up like an idiot and knock myself practically senseless on the overhead rack — *boiiiing!* sounding in my head.

"Ouch! Oooh!"

I'm surprised there's a dude sitting next to me. Must've got on back a ways and I never even noticed. Dozing, he comes to and throws up his hands like I'm a robber or something.

"I'm sorry." I don't know why I say it to him. Just so embarrassed, I guess.

I was thinking so hard when the driver announced the town. Then it dawned on me I was about to miss my stop. Now I'll have a headache the rest of my life from terrifying myself.

I make a move and step over the dude; my head is killing me so with this burning white pain where I banged it. Oooh! Practically takes my breath away. But I get into the aisle and reach for my case on the rack. It's not there! Yes, 'course it is, but I have to stretch real hard to get it. My hurting head is leveling out into this itching sting.

Someone helps me get the case. "Thanks." Don't look around to even see who it is. The whole bus must've heard me knock myself practically senseless. I get on out of there quick as I can. In a minute I'm off that bus I hope forever.

Don't look around and you won't see folks staring and wondering. Wondering if you are too young to be traveling by yourself. Right then I remember my shoulder bag. Oh, no! But I have it — what a fool I am! I'm holding on to it for dear life and didn't even know it.

Why am I just forever being so self-conscious! And I try to calm down. I go straight inside the bus building and set my suitcase down by my feet. Open up my shoulder bag and get the address out. Just calming down and reading it over. Mom wrote it down: You go straight out the front of the station and turn left. It's two blocks up the left side of Third Street. You come to the sign and you go in and ask for the lady.

So I pick up my suitcase, put the address back in my bag and not look around at anyone. I get on out of there to what looks like the front part. Then I'm on the street and back home.

It's so funny. This was my hometown, I guess you would call it, but there never was a bus station. It's just a dinky town with only a main street. I don't believe I was much fond of it. How you forget! Or want to, when you don't care for something. But I do know this street, which is not the main one but the one after the main one. It has a small supermarket place called Cantrell's and, across the way and up, a new-looking kind of coffee shop. The movie house is on the main street.

We never lived in town but near some low hills next to it. I look on over that way, but two- and three-story buildings block the view. I hurry on up the street, with dirty snow piled up and down each side. The streetway is mostly clear and shining black. Not far. One block, then two — I can see the sign. And then I'm there, with the red neon saying MONTANA INN — ROOMS — VACANCY.

I go up the steps and inside. There is this small entry room with a desk along the right wall. There is a lady at the desk, marking on a list of some kind and using an adding machine. Behind her is this big plaque full of keys and little boxes on the wall. The lady looks up as I come in. Gives me a once-over real slow, which scares the daylights out of me. Does she think I'm running away and wanting a room for myself? My stomach turns over and I realize I'm standing there like a fool. I come forward, put my case down next to the desk. She is working the adding machine all of the time and doesn't give me another glance. Knowing I'm there, too, and acting like that.

So I hold my breath and say, "I'm looking for Mrs. Luze Montana." Almost in a whisper, I'm so flat-out scared.

The lady never looks at me. Fingers never stopping their move over some numbers on the machine. She just starts yelling her head off. "Luze! Luze, someone for ye!" Like that. Just awful.

Some folks are just unfriendly. Even when I know it, it still hurts for somebody to treat you like nothing.

Pretty soon another woman comes out from a door I never noticed on down from the desk. She sees me, but doesn't smile, either. Man, this is some place. She comes on to the desk. With a name like Luze Montana, you'd think she'd look different. Guess I expected her to look much more Amerind. But you have to look real hard to see it, and if I hadn't been told, I'd a missed it altogether.

Not too tall. Thin as a rail and long, reddish hair. Her eyes are dark and so nice-looking; all at once I know that not smiling doesn't mean she isn't going to be friendly. Maybe this isn't even Luze Montana.

"You looking for somebody, honey?" she says, in a real husky way.

"Looking for my dad, but are you Luze Montana?"

"I'm Luze Montana." She says it like she's getting tired of saying it. "Now, what's your dad's name?"

"My dad is Sun Adams," I tell her.

"Oh, sure," she says. Gives me a watchful

smile, I guess you'd call it. "Okay," she says, and sort of laughs.

So Dad is here. I didn't dare think it, but in my mind I was afraid he wasn't here and never had been. I pick up my suitcase. "Can I see my dad?" I ask her.

"I think he's out," she says, "but I'll show you to his room." She takes a key with this tag on it off the wall plaque.

I get the feeling she is used to showing kids to rooms of their fathers. Or even wives.

"You come by bus?" she asks as we climb some stairs. She's a step on ahead of me, looking down sideways at me.

I just nod and smile.

"A lot of people come by bus now that we have a stop here," she says. "Where is the boy that usually comes for your dad?"

"What?"

"The boy," she says. "The other Sun usually comes to fetch your dad." She is making it all seem lighthearted. I feel better all of a sudden.

"He had an accident, so I had to come."

"Oh, does your father know? Wasn't too bad, I hope."

"Oh, sure, Dad knows," I tell her. And realize it must sound strange to her that Dad went off with his boy in an accident. "My brother is much better now."

We climb another set of stairs and then go

265

down this hall with a green runner. We stop at a door with a yellow number 18. Luze Montana takes the key and opens the door.

"Go on in," she tells me. "Take the key, case you get bored and want to go out. There's a shop up the street on the other side — a food shop. They have hamburgers."

"Thank you, Mrs. Montana." Taking the key.

Luze Montana pauses like she will ask me some more questions. "I'd find someone to get your dad if I knew for sure where he was." An opening for me to say things, but you don't want to open up with strangers, Mom says.

"I'll just be glad to wait," I tell her.

"Well. I'm positive he'll be back by dark. I've known your dad a long time." She really smiles. Wonder if there's any meaning in that other than the words, but I guess not.

"He's as steady as they come," she says.

So why does he go off like this? is what I'm thinking, and maybe she thinks I will say it. I won't. I stand there looking at her for as long as she can stand looking at me.

She closes the door. Man. Some strange people and places in this land, for sure. I breathe a sigh of relief and fall on the bed. Kick off my boots and hold my head for a minute. Let the little tremors of nerves all over me find their way on out of my senses. Close my eyes and breathe just as regular as I can. What a long way! I turn over.

Just a room. But it's sure good not having some people looking you over. So strange! I ease the shoulder bag off and think I am sitting on my own dad's bed. Awful strange, in a room that's your father's and you never knew it existed until a few days ago.

Mom coming to me the other day and saying, "Arilla, your father is missing."

I said, "What?"

Then she told me how Dad had skipped again, driving the college jeep he always uses. It's a crime I never noticed he was gone. But Dad is back and forth so much in between the college dining hours. And me being so busy with Sun hurt and all. I just simply did not at all realize he was gone, which is pretty awful of me, I guess.

"You're going to have to go get him," Mom said to me.

And I said the first thing comes in my head, "You are kidding me!"

"Sun can't go," she says. "Someone has to. I have to take care of Sun and keep things going. You will have to take the bus and get him."

"Mom, I've never been on a bus in my life," is what I told her.

"You follow my directions and you'll be fine." That's what she tells me.

I went running to Jack Sun. And tell him, "Mom says I have to go get Dad!"

And he says, "Wow, Moon, here's your chance to count coup again."

"Forget it! I'm not going," is what I say right back.

He looked so solemn, but before he could say another thing I told him, "I don't get it why Dad goes and why someone has to go find him. What's wrong with him — why does he *do* it?"

"You do what you're told," he says.

And then I told him I'd never understand him or any of the rest of it. "This is the queerest, dumbest family that ever there was." I remember saying that.

"Maybe so," he said, "but it's what you've got."

So here I am. I sit up on the bed.

I made it this far. It wasn't so bad, except for practically busting my head wide open. So this is what I've got, too. A disappearing dad. A dancing mother. And a half-killed, crazy brother. That's it. So here I am.

And look around at the room. Just a small room. There's like a foot-locker kind of trunk at the foot of the bed. Latches up, like it's been opened. I notice other things. Little things. A long pipe on a little table. Moccasins in a plastic wrap, opened, like they'd been maybe in the trunk and taken out and handled.

Looking at the trunk, will it matter if I open it up again? So I do.

Well, it is crammed full. Things wrapped in paper or cloth; some plastic-wrapped things opened a little and left that way on top. Some really old things, I can tell. Each has a tag stapled

268

on. I pick up a thing wrapped in blue material. I get on my knees and unwrap it. It's a silver bridle, so beautiful, with a tag saying, *From James*. Another wrapping has this stone going through a handle of wood, like a stone hammer. It has a tag, says, *From Small Dog*. There are whole hides like paintings of scenes. Leggings and belts with beadwork and turquoise. And a whole pack of moccasins, some not even finished.

Wonder why all this stuff is kept here. Dad must always have this room with the trunk. Or moves the trunk to whatever room she gives him when he comes back here?

I put the things where they belong and close the trunk. Sitting on the bed again, I can hear the street out the window and some music coming from some rooms. There's a table with a lamp, by the bed. I reach and turn on some light. A little lamplight is warming; makes the night come quicker.

I am three parts hungry and ninety-seven parts awful nervous.

Is this what you're supposed to do, sit and wait for him? Mom didn't tell me he might be out. If he was here, it never entered my mind he might not be in the room. I'm still some scared inside. It takes a while to get along with the new, I guess.

There's a pair of shoes by what you'd call a standing closet. The shoes are marked up along the sides with this salt line, drying. I get up to look closer and see they are Dad's shoes for work.

And sitting back down on the bed again.

He's not wearing his shoes, so what's he wearing? I look around the room again. Window with curtains and bringing in a little light. There are no pictures on the walls. There's something hanging from a hook like a woven leather belt. There are two nails about six inches apart on one wall. And lines darkening the wall, coming down on either side of the nails. Two lines, about a foot apart and three or four feet long, like something had hung there and had marked up the wall.

I get up again and go to the closet. Open it to find a suit of Dad's hanging there. A blue suit but no white shirt to go with it. There's another hanger with a work shirt but no work clothes to go with it. I stand there looking. Some underwear and stuff, socks on an upper shelf.

Dad probably is wearing the white shirt because it's dirty, anyway. And he's got on the work clothes. I bet he had on his warm leather jacket and his hat because they aren't in the closet or anywhere else in the room. I close up the closet and go back to the bed.

So. It'll be dark soon. I could go on off to sleep and wait for him like that. I look again at those two nails with the lines coming down. No matter where I look, and there's not a whole lot of places to look in a small room, I come back to the nails and those lines. Staring at them for a long time.

And it dawns. Slowly, but it dawns. Runners! I am so stupid.

"So that's where." Even saying it out loud — nobody can hear me. Makes me feel so much better to talk out loud. "Why didn't Mom mention it? Maybe she didn't think of it."

I grab my overnight case and get out my wool gloves and scarf. Have them on in a second. I never did take off my jacket and all of a sudden I'm burning overheated. "Get out of here and on over there before it's dark."

Do you know the way? Maybe. Sure. I'll find it.

I leave the room not much different than when I found it.

I leave and go down the two flights of stairs. At the desk I give the key to Luze Montana. The other woman is nowhere to be seen; neither is her adding machine.

"Hi there," Luze says, still lighthearted.

I have to smile. "I know where my dad is — do they still whomp on down the hill?"

"Sure. Everybody," she says. "Guess that's where he's at, but I didn't see him leave."

" 'S okay," I tell her, and I'm gone.

Outside, it's snowing again. Just those big old snowflakes that make you think you're hearing sleighbells. Just a snow shower that won't last long. I cut across Third Street and through some side streets. It sure is a town like any other little dinky place. But I know this one. I know how to go. So to follow this street, which is called McCowles, until it is just a rural route out of

271

town. Pull this scarf I wear up over my mouth.

You get out a ways — still in town, though, and some people pass me, and kids with sleds. Littler Amerind kids. How can you tell? You just know. Then there's the last intersection where all these men line the buildings. It's not even lunchtime. Oh. They don't work, and nothing to do.

With the town behind me, I'm out in what is like country, skirting some hills where there are ramshackle houses along the creases. The hills are some smaller than I recall them. Along the road that loses its tar mix and becomes just a flat, gravelly roadbed with snow making it smooth and easy to walk. Out where the light is dim — it gets dark so early. But snow is bright; the air is, too, and nothing can scare me along this road.

And on out until houses along the creases are to the side of me, and only one house is ahead of me. I slow down. Coming on the house by the road as quiet as I can. I stop a minute, since it was my house.

It is sure something to come back and see things. I guess we are pretty strange people, Mom and me, never to've come back. Maybe Dad and Sun are the normal ones, and me and Mom are different. Because I lived in that house and it wasn't so bad, as I remember. Oh, you wouldn't want to have your Birthday in it, I guess. Because it's so small, with just a front room and a kitchen as you come in the door, and two bedrooms.

The house is painted the nicest brown — who ever thought it would look good that color? There is a new, small garage with this Volkswagen car in it. The field is still fenced in. But there's a chicken coop, which we never had, and some banty chickens. A new little shed and a cow, looking brown-velvety and old. But something is more different than even that. It takes a minute to discover it. They had to cut down a tree in front to make a driveway up to the garage. That's it. There used to be a tree where they always told me I would swing when I was real little. I don't remember swinging, but I sure do recall a tree there when we moved out.

I go on and it's not far now where the road is about to end. And it's the oddest feeling to go by a house that was yours once and have it not bother you particularly. And you would think I'd at least long to see that little old room I had. I was just so jealous of Sun about that. I remember, before we left I'd get so angry because he had the whole front room and the studio couch to sleep on while I had that awful small room. I was dumb, for sure. Because it had to be awful for him to sleep like that, without a door you could shut if you wanted to.

It's a queer feeling for certain as I leave the house behind. Like I'm holding things back, whatever it is I could feel if I just wanted to. But it's gone, isn't it, whatever it is, so why feel it?

The road ends in a bank of trees, pretty tall.

There are all these footprints in the snow, going and coming. It is really so still out here in nowhere. Guess all the kids have made it on home with their sleds, to get warm out of freezing and to take some soup or something. I would love some soup right now, better even than a hamburger. Wonder if Dad will think to take me for some food?

And on through the trees, following the sled lines as kids pull them and following footprints. I feel I am speeding up inside. Whether it's because of Dad, I don't know. But I get so excited walking in all this country white. The trees full of new snow I wish would look like that for eternity. I know they won't, but it's so nice to think that every winter they will. Somehow it makes me sad the way new snow will melt and things will have to get brown and muddy before they can bloom into beauty. Makes me real thoughtful about growing and dying. And on to the next thought, which is that everything is in a big circle. Wouldn't know where I got that, but I've always been able to think about it. That I'll grow up and die, just like Mom and Dad will. But it's okay because each of us in our turn, including my brother, will grow again and make even trees with snow and even the mud some richer. It's sad, though. Awful sad, sometimes.

You break out of the trees right . . . now. For sure! You walk some six or seven yards straight up the side of what looks like an ordinary rise of land. And you are right . . . here!

Was there ever a hill so *grand!* Other hills may look smaller to me, but this one has got to be the best ever and just the way I remember it. And so hidden the way it is because, by the time you leave the road, you are climbing on a rise you can't even notice. And keep climbing to stand here at last.

To look down there and going down in your mind on the most wonderful ride you could ever want. I see the fence at the bottom; and beyond, where there is heavy mist today. I don't have the time to think what's out there. For the sled is resting on the fence. With his back to me, looking a way out there, is Dad. Knew he would be, too. Man, it's so great to be here.

"Hey, Dad!" And slipping and sliding, half killing myself down the hill. Laughing, screaming, "Dad, it's me! I made it all by myself! Hi!"

"Arilla? Well, for — I don't believe it!"

"Truth! It's me!" I come busting into that fence hard enough to shake it. Laughing. And look on out there. "Ooooh!" Mist rising from it and looking down into the deep gorge below. But only a minute. Dad grabs me and hugs me.

"I'm so sorry I wasn't in my room! How'd you find me?"

"I remembered. And I saw the sled marks on the wall!"

He had to laugh at that. "You don't miss a thing! Did you meet my friend Luze?"

"Sure. She was nice to me."

"Luze is nice to everybody like that. And you come all this way."

"On the bus," I tell him. "It was fun, too."

Then I don't know what to say. I know what I should say, but I'd better wait awhile. I brush some dirt off the sled. My eyes meet Dad's.

He has to smile. "You want to?"

"Huh?"

"To take a ride, to sled on down?"

"To whomp on down? Yeah!"

"Then let's go!"

And laughing from pure happiness. Slipping and sliding to reach that dirty path over to the side, where kids have worn it into a trail going up and down. Dad just holds me up, using the sled to support himself.

"I think I'm going to be scared," I tell him. "Never have sledded in a long time. What ever did happen to my sled?"

"Oh, we must've given it away before we left. You had outgrown it."

"Shoot." Giving him a kidding glance, "I see you never did give away yours."

And he has to laugh. "You want to be in front?" he asks me.

"Ummm. No, I'll stick to the back so's I can jump off if it gets real terrible."

"You jump off with my weight making us fly, and you'll hurt yourself."

"Well, I'll get on in back, anyway. I don't want to see!"

"Scaredy cat!"

We get situated. I feel kind of silly. Guess maybe Dad does, too. He is grinning like an idiot. Shoot, it's fun, why not?

"Get ready. Are you ready?" he says.

"Ready!" I get my arms around his back and hold tight on to his coat.

And, man, we are gone! We move, we are flying. We sail on down — fan-tastic!

"Whoopee!" Dad lets out a whoop that echoes all over the place.

"It's so fast, oh, my goodness! I peek and see snow streaking by. And see the fence just when Dad turns the sled sideways. We hit the fence on the side hard enough to make it sound, *whoooeeem*. We let that old sled slip out from under.

We sprawl against the fence. "That is really something," I tell him. "Remember how I would come out here after school and whomp on down till dark? Used to take a running leap and belly-flop on the sled. Wonder if I can still do it."

"Try it," Dad says. He leans against the fence, just sitting quiet and looking up at the hill.

"You think I'm scared."

"For sure," he says. "I bet you are."

"Watch me, then. Here I go up." I climb the trail, which is harder the second time because you've had some exertion. I try using the sled for support and that's a big help. I get all the way up and stand there, trying to figure how to belly-whomp without hurting myself. "I'm not as small as I used to be!" I yell down.

"Truth!" he calls. "Figure it out."

So I figure how I'm going to get my whole self flat-out on the sled. See, you hold the sled in your hands and run forward. Then fall on it with some kind of wallop. Only, I will sure bust open my stomach if I try that. So I get on my knees and ease down on the sled. Taking hold of the rope, twisting it around my hands, and then grab the steering.

"That's the easy way!" Dad calls.

"You better believe it!" I push off. Oh, wow. "Oooooh!"

Down and down. Faster than a speeding bullet. Fantastic! For what seems the brightest blue snowlight flashing by, and the grandest feeling of half-scared and a sure kind of wonderful.

Whooeeem. Hitting the fence, and letting that sled slide out from under. I lie on my side, taking the rope from around my hands. And lie flat on my back to make a poor-looking angel in the hard-packed snow. Look up at the sky and feel snow drop in my face. Didn't know it was falling again. And breathing hard. Peace. Sledding is, and so being thankful.

"You remember how we used to sled?" Dad says, so real gentle.

278

"I'd come on out practically every day in the winter," I tell him.

"No. I mean when you were real little," he says. "When you'd sneak away and come sledding with me in the nighttime."

I lift my head up. I scoot on over next to him, with my back to the fence.

"Truth," Dad says. "You were no bigger than a minute. And you would find your coat and boots and walk from the house clear in the dark to here. Where you'd make me take you for a sled ride."

"You are kidding me! For real?"

"As sure as I sit here. I couldn't get away from you for nothing."

"You mean I'd walk out here . . . in the dark? And sled? Well, how old was I?"

"Maybe from the time you were five and a half or so. Until we started locking your door."

"And I liked to sled even way back then? How'd I know you were out here?"

"You'd hear me going 'Whoopee,' I guess," Dad says. "There's something about sledding in the moontime. Makes you want to holler out."

"That's really something."

"There wasn't a fence here then, either," Dad says.

"You are kidding me!" I get up to look down. We both stand to look over into the terrifying gorge.

Dad says, "Everybody would slide down here without a fence to stop us. Just craziness. Your mother never would allow you or Sun to come here in daylight."

"Were there any accidents?"

"Oh, maybe a few. Seems I remember a child and an older man. And once you and I almost went over."

Now, that stunned me. Dad is looking way out, into the mist. The night is gathering there in the wide angle of space above the gorge, as if to hide it.

"How do you mean, we almost went over!"

"You talked me into sledding on sheer ice, you wanted to sled so bad. So I went along and couldn't stop the sled."

"So what happened?"

"Sun," he says. "Your brother always did wake up before I'd finished out here. I guess that time he saw you were gone. He got his horse he used to have and his lasso. Your brother could use a rope almost by the time he could run good. He could ride like an expert from the time he was six. He got out here just in time. Threw the lasso and caught us."

"Man! Sun did that?"

"Truth, I swear. But he couldn't bring us back up the hill. It was too steep, or he didn't know how to work the horse, something. So he starts yelling, screaming his head off.

"Pretty soon," Dad says, "a lot of men were

out there helping. And old James, too. He'd always be riding around half the night. Death was on his mind so much and I think he'd go looking for it. But you almost got frozen bad."

"That's something. I don't remember it at all."

"How could you? You were so little."

"But you would think I'd — " I couldn't finish it. It was all so stunning.

"Think what?" Dad says.

That I nearly died and never knew it. That my own brother saved me. My own brother who I thought for sure wanted me dead. Maybe . . . maybe he wanted to save his dad and I was just along for the ride. Stop it, that's awful.

"It's not fair," I finally say, "not to remember things when you're little."

"I don't think anybody would remember things that far back," he says. And hugs me. I lean close, feeling so nice here with him, even if my hands are getting cold.

"Maybe that's how we save ourselves from the bad memories," Dad says. "You were frozen pretty good that night and you wouldn't want to remember that."

"Maybe that's why my hands always get cold so quick," I tell him.

"Do they? Are they cold now?"

"They sure are."

"Then we'd better be going. But first — "

He did something I'd never seen or heard him do before. Or maybe I had and didn't remember it. There sure is a lot I have no way of knowing or recalling.

Because what he did right then seemed right and not nearly so unusual or unfamiliar as you might think.

The sun was down. But we never saw it going beyond the gorge because of the clouds and all. The dark was already thick at the cliff end beyond the fence. Dad turned around, looking behind us. And I was startled to see it was for-real dark. All was darkness of trees and huge black lumps of small hills. There the moon was coming up over, so big and bright, like a giant marble in a gorgeous spotlight. The clouds were all above us and the moon was way out of them. You could see it just as clear. And snow falling on us — there was nothing falling in the area of the moon. Just snow showers over us; but to the east a clear path for that brilliant marble to rise.

Dad pointed at it. All of a sudden his hand looked like it was lit. He turned back to the fence and pointed at the vastness out there. And threw back his head. Threw it back in a kind of heave.

And howled.

The sound of a great wolf circling out far into the night. With yip-yips of little cubs. And sounds of gentle wolves and fierce half-grown wolves, so eager. All to end with the call of the great father wolf, who had the deepest chest. Who was most alone and stalking. And was Dad.

The sound colliding with echoes of itself all

around; then vanishing on the moonlight of the night. Again and again. Howling.

I knew better than to say a word. It was a sound so deep of my dad, it was like being sacred. And me given a privilege to hear. I knew to keep my mouth closed.

For a long time we stood at the fence. I was freezing now, but I waited. Looking out into darkness you couldn't see through. Looking, not a word, until Dad took hold of the sled and started up the trail.

Somewhere in that moonlit walk through trees of eternity and along the road we said a few things to each other. Me trudging sometimes behind Dad; able, almost, to feel all over my skin and in my bones when the temperature started dropping.

With him saying, telling, "Long ago it must've been given to me, although I have no sure memory: a boy goes alone to a high place, a cliff. He stays there alone, looking for a spirit guardian. For the spirit that will protect him the rest of his life."

Walking past the little house that was ours. Windows lighted, making yellow patches on snow, mixing with moonglow.

Dad saying, "Back there, howling the wolf because I know the wolf is mine. No matter that I may not want it — I am not a believer — it is still mine."

Walking the road side by side. The sled roped

out to glide along in a steady scud. Feeling my legs move, but my feet are nearly numb.

Dad saying, "The spirit wolf never comes. Maybe it knows. Whether or not, that isn't why I come."

"Why *do* you come, Dad?"

"Oh, people do what they will," he says. "Some will go bowling — you think that's so different? It's a way of releasing themselves. Or skiing. Or hunting far out in the woods to wait for animals to kill. I come here, to release myself."

I know what to ask him, but I want to see his face when I do. I must know for sure. There are some things said that have to be the truth. I know to wait, but I am bursting with it. Knowing better, I just burst out with it. Ashamed to have to say what no one has ever asked him.

"Dad. Would you ever come back home if and ever one of us didn't come here to get you?" For fear it is the worst thing to ask him.

But from asking, the air so close around us seems to clear. Dad lets out a jagged sigh. Puts his arm around my shoulder again. Walking that way, and a long silence as we pass light sprinklings in creases of hills. Now onto a road surface that is no longer snow-iced over gravel. He clutches my shoulder and is silent. I know he is never going to tell me. He tells me.

"How can I put it," he says, "when I don't know the answer myself?"

"It must be either yes or no," I say, so full of

fear. Never have talked to my dad like this. It makes me feel older.

"It's a circle," he says.

That slows me in my tracks, staring at him. Wasn't I thinking it just a while ago that life was a circle?

"I go and come here," he says. "Someone goes and comes here after me. I go back and they go back with me. You do not break the circle," he says.

"You allow it," I say.

"Truth," he says. "You accept it."

There is no yes or no. Only what goes and comes back.

We go through icy streets, narrow and poor. Men stand in the cold in front of neon signs. They blow on their hands and lean from one boot to the other.

"Why do they hang around and freeze themselves?" I ask Dad.

"Why not?" he says.

Soon we are on Third Street and almost to Luze Montana's. Dad says, "When Sun Run comes here, we go where you saw the men and we play pool."

"Sun knows how to play pool?"

"And very good, too."

"I wouldn't like it, around so many poor men," I tell Dad.

"I wouldn't take you there," Dad says, "but not because they are poor. Are you hungry?"

285

"Starving!"

We cross the street and walk up to the hamburger place.

"You want to eat inside or take it out?" Dad says.

"Take it out, if it's all right." Inside, it is so bright.

"We'll eat at Luze's, in the room."

We go in and we order food to carry out. It's a place where Amerinds come and order food to carry out. I see none of them sitting down to eat the food. We order big cheeseburgers and chocolate malts, and four packages of french fries. I'm going to die, waiting to feast on all that wonderful food. The smell of cooking is making my stomach turn over. No bowl of soup now. I want a feast.

It seems to take them a whole month! Finally we get the feast and hurry it through the cold to the Montana Inn. Looking like an oasis in some painted desert. Red neon in the almost empty street. Small towns seem to empty when night falls. Except for towns with Amerinds. Amerinds are walking around. Walking themselves forever in circles. Two of them come walking out from Luze Montana's as we walk in. Holding the door, they don't look directly at us. It's not polite to look or to smile foolishly.

You have to allow knowing and never knowing how you know.

In Dad's room we have the feast. Little talking while we eat, and that's fine with me. Dad wants only half of his cheeseburger and that makes more for me. I get so stuffed, my stomach aches. But I sip and sip until the malt container has only a little foam. Dad and me sitting cross-legged on the floor facing one another. We get to giggling at the fun of it. I bet Sun and him never sat and ate like this.

Later I ask Dad is there a bathroom. He shows me where out in the hall. I go and come back, and take a seat in the one chair in the room. Taking off my boots to let my feet slide on the carpet, warming them good.

"So Sun saved my life when I was little," all at once I say.

Dad nods, sitting there with his arms folded across his chest.

"So I saved his life, too, when he got hurt in the glen."

"You did well," Dad says.

"Sun thanked me for it."

"We all thank you," Dad says.

Looking around. Dad has wiped off the sled runners and has hung the sled back on the wall. The dirty cleaning cloth is tied to one runner.

Seeing the leather belt hanging on its hook.

"I looked in your trunk," I tell him. "Those are some beautiful things — hope you don't mind that I looked."

He laughs. "Arilla, you are so polite."

Then he says, "Things I have collected over the years. From people who I knew well and who have died. The old way was to bury the things with the body. You still might bury a few things, but most are given away these days. Most given to friends to be used. I keep them here."

"And only to see them when you come here?" I ask him. "I bet Sun Run would sure like to take a look at that silver bridle."

Dad puts his hands palm-flat on the floor. Watches his hands, then eases them back under his folded arms.

"I thought to hide these things," he says, "away from your mother. Away from our life."

"But why? They're so beautiful."

"Well, a man can learn something, too. I've learned, I guess. You can't cut yourself away from things. The blood is still there behind my eyes."

I caught his meaning, I sure did. "Is it . . . is it behind my eyes, too?"

"That will be up to you," he tells me.

"Like it is with Sun."

"Your brother has been playing around with it. Sun Run making a game with it, for years."

"He's a phony, you mean?"

His hands again palm-flat on the floor. He watches them and doesn't take them away. "I think your brother hides a lot of hurt," Dad says. "He boasts with games to protect himself."

"From what?"

"From whatever it is that scares him to death."

"Oh." I know about being so scared, but I never figured that was what is eating my brother. Anyway, I'm getting tired. The whole thing is too much of a great mystery for me to even think about.

"Where will I sleep?" I ask Dad.

Finally he says, "We could go on back tonight. We could start out — might as well — and be home in the wee hours."

"Really? Aren't you worn out?"

He smiles. He still has his hat on and his hair is straggly around his face. "You have to understand about coming and going," he says. "After I come here, I have the need to leave, too. It's the nomad in us — do you know, there are kids, when listing their occupation or somewhat, will write 'nomad'? And they mean it. They mean that's what they do, going from one place to another. I don't like it better here than at home. I like it best to be moving."

"But don't you worry about your job?" I sure worry about it. "About you might get yourself fired?"

"It's a way of thinking," he says. "What you have to do comes first. You need to remember that, Arilla. Believe it."

"Okay, I will," I tell him. But I'm getting awful tired out.

And then he says something I don't really understand.

"Your mind may forget the past. But it always remains inside. You can find it out, Arilla, in your heart. Remember that."

"I will," I tell him. "But can we go now?"

"For sure, we can go right now."

"Then let's go."

"I'll go see Luze to account," he says.

When Dad comes back, I'm ready for him. Have already locked my suitcase, and grab my shoulder bag. "Can we take the sled?" But he sees through that. Knows I am trying to get everything that belongs to him out of here. I still have to. "There's the hill of the standpipe in Spangler Park."

"There are no hills like the one here," he says.

"Well." Figuring some more and getting nervous, but having to ask anyway. "Sun would dearly love to see the contents of your trunk."

Dad throws back his head and laughs.

"You know he would," I tell him, "you know it!"

"For sure," Dad says. "All the time he's come here, he never once looked into my trunk. You guessed it. And never once took it on himself to go through my things. You're the character, the one with the gift of curiosity."

"Can we, Dad? Take it on home?"

"Your mother . . ."

"But it's yours. You said, 'What you have to do must come first.' Didn't you say that?"

"You'll have to help get it down, then."

"Man! Sure!"

So we take hold, but then Dad remembers he's left some clothes. He gets what's left out of the closet, throws it on top of the stuff in the trunk. I carry his work shoes. We take hold of it again. It's some heavy but not too bad if we drag it. A man we run into coming up helps us back down the stairs. We make a lot of noise; and by the first landing, just above the lobby, Mrs. Montana comes to take a look at what is going on.

"Well!" she says and gives me that kind look she has. She knows not to question. Just looking and standing out of the way as we come on down.

"So," she says. "I'll be seeing you." To me, in that husky voice.

No time to think about it. I only smile because I want to get the trunk on in the jeep before Dad maybe changes his mind.

Dad thanks the man helping and stands at attention a minute before Luze.

"Luze, thanks again," he tells her.

"Never you mind," she says, kidding. I can tell she's a great kidder. I can tell something else, too. Mom says there are some grown women who think Dad is romantic-looking. Luze Montana is sure one of them, I can tell. But I don't mind. I know Dad is ours.

"You take care, you hear?" Dad says to her. "And keep up the good work."

"Oh, I got to," Luze says. "Go easy now."

Outside, I stand with the trunk at my feet while Dad goes off to get the jeep down the way. He soon comes back and double-parks it in front of me out in the street.

We hassle the trunk on in the back seat. I throw his shoes on top. Then we sit there in the car to warm it up.

"How long will it take?" I ask him.

"Depends. See how the roads are," he says.

"Let's don't take any back roads. I can't stand those curving back roads. Makes me kind of ill."

"I wouldn't," he says. "We are superhighway drivers."

"For sure."

And we take off. Me in the front seat right next to him. Smelling the way cold cars and upholstery smell. Once we get out of town, the only lights are from the dash and the headlights. I watch the headlights cut on through the dark. Nice. I sit just so still and shivering a little, and full of excitement. Man!

Once we are on the road going east, making for the I-75 North, Dad turns up his beams. We can see more of fields and hills. Snow-covered. Ice patches. We skid over them and on through fast. I'm not scared with Dad driving. I sink on back, feeling the heater turning the car warm. Feeling myself deep tired and almost all through exhausted. My eyes are wavering.

"Will you fall asleep?" I ask him.

Turning to me. "You mean, if you close your

eyes?" And back to the road. "I never have yet. Go on to sleep. We got a ride ahead."

"I want to see the highway first."

So I wait. A half-hour later, about, we come to the on-ramp approach and soon stream into traffic of headlights.

"This late," I say, "cars and trucks still going."

"Just like I told you. The nomad," Dad says.

There's nothing like gliding down a super-road. The motor roaring and wind whooshing by — or you cut through it, I don't know which. Finding a lane where you can travel without changing speed. And getting in ahead of trucks when you can.

"Rolling warehouses," Dad says as we pass three of them in a row, hugging the outside lane.

"They don't worry a thing about speed limits," I tell him. Dad doesn't, either. Getting on ahead so he has the empty road. Dad is driving like he's late for life.

"Slow down."

"There's not a soul on up there," he says.

"Just some ice waiting for us, if we're unlucky."

"Okay." And slows it close to seventy. Free on up our lane. Rolling. And how much skating is like this.

"Dad."

"Yeah?"

"Do you ever wonder what I need for the no-mad in me, too?"

A long piece of land going by, lit up first and

next vanishing behind before he says a word. Don't say you're sorry, you haven't had the time to think about me.

"So tell me," he says.

Okay. "Roller-skating is what I love to death, I really do," I tell him.

"You know how to roller-skate?"

No need to tell him. He figures it out. Sun going out and probably that I go with Sun and Angel, too.

"So you have kept up your night wandering. Wait till I get your brother!" he says.

"Don't blame it on Sun. But I need to roller-skate in the daylight. Like every Saturday, when Mom is at the studio. I don't have to stay so shut up in the house. What's gonna get me? I need to skate and I don't need so much horseback riding. Just skating once on the weekend and maybe once in the week. Like maybe on a Wednesday from six to eight until you get home. We can eat together."

"So," he says.

After a minute I tell him, "I'm not really asking."

"I gather that," he says.

"Will you tell Mom?"

"Can't *you* tell her?"

"I have to tell her about the trunk."

He lets out a soft howl. "Thanks for sharing the dirty work." And laughs.

294

That's it. It's what I've been getting up the nerve for, more than anything else. Now I can rest, watching us eat up the highway. Glance at the speedometer. How I love cars!

And wondering, do I write this trip for my autobiography? You could change it and make some stories out of it. Say that I had to go to my first hometown to pick up some stuff we left there. Say it, write it, after how Sun got himself hurt. But change his name to this boy I know who gets hurt and I have to go on a bus ride. Maybe that is writing, changing things around and disguising the for-real. They say dreams you have are some disguising of what happens to you and what worries you. Or what you wish for.

"Dad."

"Yeah?"

"Why don't you ride with me some, now that Sun Run can't? Jeremiah needs some exercising and you could see how good I'm getting. Will you?"

"Maybe if you take me skating."

"Really? Mom'll *kill* us!"

"We'll take her skating, too," he says.

I just fall over, cover my face, and laughing. "But don't tell her all at once."

"I won't," he says.

"Maybe a little bit at a time over a couple of weeks."

"So she won't notice it," he says.

"Yeah!" And laughing my head off. Just a picture of Mom at the rink on a pair of skates is enough to split my sides.

"And maybe teach her to ride, too," Dad says.

"Oh! Oh, my goodness, you'll never get a dancer on a horse!"

"You wanna bet?"

And laughing myself silly. Even a worse picture of her, riding backward, facing the tail end. Or slipping to the side, staring at her other foot up in the air. Like saying, What is it doing up *there!* Oh, Mom, I love you, don't get mad.

Well, I could write Mom on a horse just like I could write her as a dancer, or even on skates. I could have a name for myself more than Sun Down. It'd be what I gave myself for what I do that's all my own. I sure will have to think about it.

"Dad."

"What?"

"Slow down."

"You want to get home, don't you?"

"But not as a ghost."

He howls a comic wolf for a second. "Spoken true," he says.

And we fly on down the road.